ROSE
from the
GRAVE

To Edna,
With sincere gratitude;
Love,
Candace

Candace Murrow

Singing Tree
PUBLISHING

ISBN 978-0-9827881-5-8

Library of Congress Control Number: 2011914092

Singing Tree Publishing
www.candacemurrow.com

Printed in the United States of America
Book design by Kathryn E. Campbell
Gorham Printing, Centralia, Washington

For Gary, as always

ACKNOWLEDGMENTS

Sincere appreciation to the people who helped make this book possible: My readers, Sue Atwood, Victoria Tennant, and Kathy Peterson, for their time, effort, and excellent feedback. My editor, Barbara Fandrich, whose expert editing made the book shine. Realtor extraordinaire, Nancy Conner, for being a sounding board for anything pertaining to the real estate business. Lena Karunamaya, my friend and coach, whose guidance encouraged me. My mother, Frances Clogston, my sister, JoAnn Ableman, and my husband, Gary, for their loving support. As always, to the Creative Spirit within.

ROSE
from the
GRAVE

PROLOGUE

He thought he'd stuffed these tendencies, kept them hidden in the shadows since that fateful day he made a mistake and hurt that poor girl. He was much younger then, teased and jabbed, full of resentments. But he'd put his youthful past behind him, moved on, and made a respectable life for himself. All those disobedient thoughts were put in their place. Everything was under control until that woman came along and messed up his life.

He could still remember her bony neck, delicate as a sparrow's, cupped tightly in his hand, her body's contours soft against him, and the sweat trickling down her chest, acrid with fear.

It wasn't supposed to end that way. She'd struggled, yes, but too soon her body went limp.

One would think this unfortunate event would scare the tendencies into submission, but no. It only set them free to desire another outlet. And now he had no choice but to find relief again.

CHAPTER 1

The door burst open with such force it banged against the doorstop. Kat slid a grocery sack on the counter and grabbed the receiver, breathless. "Hello?"

Dead silence.

"Hello? Is anybody there?" She heard the aggravating click.

She'd raced inside after a wrong number, and now she stood in the middle of her refurbished oak floor in her wet boots and dripping raincoat. This was all she needed after spending the better part of the morning with her number one difficult client, a man who'd been searching for the perfect house for the last five years and had changed his mind endless times, today included. One more year in the real estate business and Kat definitely needed a change.

She fled to the mud room and deposited her coat on the washing machine, unzipped and stepped out of her boots, then grabbed the nearest dishtowel. Just as she finished sopping up the puddles on her lovely kitchen floor, the phone rang again. She tossed the towel in the sink, snatched the receiver, and barked, "What!"

A pause ensued, long enough for her to consider hanging up, until a man whispered in guttural sounds she could barely make out, "Pussssycat."

She dropped the receiver as if it were charged with electricity and shook her head in disgust. Those odd, disturbing calls couldn't be happening again. Just as her mind began to touch on the dreaded weeks following her sister's death, the rain pelted the windows, scattering the memories.

To compose herself, she took a long, even breath and ran her fingers through her hair, letting the auburn strands cascade over her shoulders. For added distraction, she tuned the radio to News 1000 and focused on the weather report. The forecast called for showers, typical for a dreary Seattle October.

Three years ago in October, during her last official vacation, she'd lounged the week away in a rented Mexican villa. Picturing the glistening sands and shimmering sea, she wished she were there now, minus the man she'd walked away from—Jeff, the attorney, a nice enough guy but boring.

She preferred her men with an edge, men who could spark the edge in her, but the men she opened her heart to were the dangerous kind, and it never, ever worked out. For the umpteenth time she vowed never to tread those waters again.

A persistent knocking drew her to the front of the house. Considering the call she'd just received, she stayed behind the closed door and asked the visitor's identity.

"It's me, Maggie. Open up before this wretched wind blows me off the porch."

"What are you doing out in this miserable weather?" Kat asked as Maggie Loggins, owner of the real estate company Kat worked for, blustered in. "I just got home. You almost missed me."

Maggie, Kat's friend and mentor, was in her sixties, her hair highlighted and styled in a handsome cut, her makeup professionally applied. She always wore designer suits and hats, her appearance reflecting her success. Today was no exception. She shed her raincoat and produced a document from her briefcase. "I need you to sign this."

"What is it, and why did you make a special trip to bring it over when I could deal with it in the morning?"

"You were in such a rush to get to your appointment today I didn't have time to talk to you."

"About what, and how does it warrant a trip out in this driving rain? Couldn't it wait?"

"Kat, dear, why don't we sit down?"

Maggie's quiet tone jarred Kat into realizing her own words were coarse and abrupt. She paused to soften her reply. "It's been a rough day. Would you like coffee or to stay for dinner? I could make a salad, or we could order in."

"I can't stay, but I think we need to have a talk."

"What is it, Maggie?"

With eyes that could laser through a brick wall, Maggie gave Kat a look that made her squirm. "For starters, you look so worn out these days. You've been working longer hours than usual. You're forgetful. I've even heard you snap at your clients. And, Kat, you look like you never sleep."

"I don't, not even with the Valium."

"It's been this way ever since you buried Brianna."

Kat's eyes stung. The hurt from her sister's death was as tender as if it had happened yesterday. She clamped down on her lower lip to steady her emotions.

"Let's sit down, all right?" Maggie sat on the couch while Kat took the easy chair next to the fireplace.

"You know what bothers me the most, Maggie? I can't even fathom why she did it. She had everything to live for."

"I know, dear," Maggie replied. "You've been wrestling with this for the last six months. You're weary and distraught. Why don't you consider taking some time off? Jim can cover for you, and you can pick up when you get back."

Kat cradled her arms. "That's what Dr. Rosen recommended when I saw him this afternoon. He suggested I take a leave of absence."

"See? Great minds think alike." Maggie smiled. "Seriously, Kat, I'm worried about you. After what happened, you started getting those awful crank calls. That would have been enough to drive anyone over the edge. Thank goodness they've stopped."

Kat glanced away for a moment, offering no response.

"They did, didn't they?"

"Yes . . . maybe. I did get some weird calls tonight when I got home. I thought the first one was a wrong number, but when he called the second time—"

"He called more than once?"

"Yes, and he made a connection to my name, odd as it was, or if he didn't, he was damn lucky."

"Did you call the police?"

"What would I say? I have no clue who it might be."

"I told you to get caller ID."

"I rarely use my landline, and besides, the calls stopped for a while. Now, I just don't know."

"Then unplug it or get rid of that outdated piece of junk."

Kat shrugged. "I guess I should."

"Why don't you get out of town for a while and get some perspective? Come back when you're stronger and better able to cope with things."

Kat wandered into the kitchen, leaving Maggie in the living room. She pulled a carton of yogurt from her grocery sack, intending to place it in the fridge, but paused, leaned into the counter, and peered off into the distance.

Maggie stood in the doorway, observing. "What's on your mind, Kat?"

She looked at Maggie with lifeless eyes. "I haven't taken care of Brianna's personal belongings. I haven't been in her house since that one time. It's been unoccupied for six months, and I need to put it on the market. I haven't wanted to deal with it until now."

"There you go," Maggie said. "Not that going to Rosswood would be the best vacation I could dream up for you. I mean, a cruise to the Islands would be a whole lot better, but maybe taking care of Brianna's affairs is something you have to do. For closure. And maybe you can find the answers you're looking for as to why she killed herself. Maybe that's just what you need to do to get through this."

Kat nodded, her mind already projecting to the house on the dead-end street. She stared into her friend's eyes. "I've never told you this, Maggie, but I've had visions of Brianna. I keep seeing her face, mostly in dreams."

"No wonder you can't sleep."

"Her face is horribly distorted," Kat said, "as if I'm seeing her at the moment of death. Could carbon monoxide poisoning cause a person to die with fear in their eyes? She has this bloodcurdling fear in her eyes. She must have panicked at the last minute, as though she wished she hadn't done it, but it was too late."

Maggie drifted to the counter where Kat was standing and touched her shoulder, causing Kat to jerk. "See there? Your nerves are raw." She rubbed her palm up and down Kat's back. "Listen, dear, as of tonight you are officially off the job. I want you to pack your bags and get out of this house first thing in the morning. And no arguments. A change of scenery will do you good, even if it is only Rosswood. Maybe facing Brianna's death head-on will clear things up."

Maggie wandered into the living room, trailed by Kat, and picked up the document she'd brought. "Sign and date this so I can go. It's the commission split you and Jim agreed on the last time you were out of town. Jim's onboard with this. Between him and me we'll handle things." She waited while Kat signed the paper, then packed it away.

Kat slipped the raincoat over Maggie's shoulders. "Thanks for listening to my problems."

"Are you going to be all right?"

"I feel better already just having a plan. Maybe someone in Rosswood can shed light on Brianna's state of mind because I just can't understand why."

On the porch Maggie said to Kat, "You don't have to stay in Brianna's house when you're there. You can always get a room in a nice bed and breakfast, or rent a place for a few weeks or months, however long it takes."

"I'll be fine."

"Don't come back until you're ready," Maggie said. "Keep in touch and let me know how you're doing."

"I will. If you need to send me anything, send it or fax it to the Rosswood post office. I'll let them know, and I'll pick it up there. And thanks."

After giving Kat a long, warm hug, Maggie hurried down the sidewalk, hunched against the rain, and drove off in her black sedan. Kat put away her groceries but skipped dinner and went straight to her room to pack.

Lately, Kat had been afraid to sleep in her own bed because the visions, which had increased in frequency, usually haunted her there. With her pillow and blanket in tow, she aimed for the sofa and thought of her sister.

The last time Kat had talked to Brianna, the day before her death, Brianna shared her hopes of breaking into the business of writing children's books, and she was enthusiastic about spending time with a neighbor.

A week before, she'd sent Kat a picture of herself smiling and sporting a spiky new hairdo. Brianna had fought depression all her life, but Kat never dreamed she would kill herself.

Kat adjusted the pillow to her satisfaction and fell asleep, but tonight she couldn't get away from the dream. Her sister's anguished face startled her awake.

A shrill ring sounded from the kitchen.

Shivering from the chill with her pulse pounding in her ears, she staggered into the kitchen. Without thinking, she picked up the receiver. "Yes?"

A long pause, a sharp breath, and the agonizing click.

CHAPTER 2

Kat veered off the interstate and came to a halt at the stop sign. Six miles to the right was the town of Benton. Anxious to get to Rosswood, she signaled left and crossed the overpass. A mile from the freeway was an older rustic motel set back against the trees.

She advanced down the two-lane road, slicing through firs and pines, the sun casting fingered shadows across her winding path. With the window opened a crack, the air inside was enlivened with a fresh pine scent, a far cry from the sooty diesel smell that hung over the city.

Fiddling with the radio, she couldn't find a decent station, not even country. The silence, except for the slap of tires on pavement, was both welcoming and irritating. She needed to escape the constant static of phone calls and clients, but she was simply not prepared for the quiet. She tried whistling, but her feeble attempt was pitiful.

Unfortunately, Rosswood was still over twenty miles away, and the four cups of coffee she'd downed earlier to combat the influence of the Valium were having an undeniable effect.

When she rounded the final curve, the trees opened up into a broad green expanse, and the tops of buildings appeared in the far distance. Soon she would be at Brianna's house. But a strange sputtering from her car's engine, a hit and miss, alerted her to a problem with her SUV.

The car was losing power. Kat swung to the roadside, turned off the engine, and cursed.

Of all the times for something to go wrong. At least it hadn't happened two hours ago when she would have been stranded up in the mountains away from civilization. Although the beginnings of the town were evident, in her high-heeled boots walking was not an option. Yet, getting to a restroom was a definite concern.

After checking for cars in her rearview mirror, she popped the hood release and scurried out. The dry air burned her nostrils. The wind coming off the surrounding mountains whipped through the valley, blowing her hair in all directions. She smoothed it down the best she could and hiked up the collar of her short leather jacket.

On both sides of the road were vast tracts of undeveloped grassland, but a good stretch of the land across the road from Kat was partially lined with a chain-link fence, laced with barbed wire. Inside, a large wooden placard read "Future Home of Wheeler Resort." The sign was riddled with bullet holes.

Kat propped up her car's hood. While she poked at the radiator hose to check for leaks, a pickup that had seen better days slowed alongside her, then swerved off the road and parked ahead of the SUV.

Ignoring the truck, she bent over to check the ground for a water spill when a wet nose butted her rear end. She whirled around, squealing. Her face flushed with shock and anger at the golden retriever who was now nosing her crotch. She lifted her arms to the heavens and backed into the front bumper. "Get away. Get away."

"Zeke, come!" A notable-looking man, tall, slender, seemingly out of character in his dusty jeans, boots, and cowboy hat, swaggered toward her, his lips barely suppressing a grin. The dog charged back and stared up at him, awaiting further command. "Sorry about that. Need any help?"

As much as she hated to depend on anyone, especially a stranger, even if he *was* catalog handsome, she had no choice. Anything mechanical was a foreign language. "If you don't mind." Her gaze shifted to the dog, who was inching forward, looking as if he were about to get curious again.

The man, attentive to her concern, sauntered back to his truck and pulled down the tailgate. "Here, boy." The dog leaped into the truck bed, and the man secured the tailgate. "Are you afraid of dogs?"

"Not well-behaved ones." Kat peered under the hood. She was in no mood to chitchat, not with a full bladder begging for relief.

He stood beside her, and despite the thickness of her jacket sleeve, she could feel his warm, muscular arm pressing against hers. To break contact, she purposely took a step to the left.

As soon as he viewed the engine, he wiggled the battery cables and checked the spark plugs. "Loose spark plug wire." He cocked his head and raised his brows as if to say any idiot could have figured it out. At least that was what Kat read in his expression. "I'll get some pliers to tighten the connector. One of your battery cables is loose, too. I'll get a wrench."

Before he even touched his toolbox, he removed his hat, ran his fingers through his thick, black hair, specked with silver, and favored his dog with a long, gentle stroke. He appeared to be around fifty, ten years older than Kat. Finally, he settled his hat in place and dug around for his tools, taking an inordinate amount of time. The dog paced the bed, whining and wagging his tail.

The man looked familiar to Kat, probably one of the many townspeople she'd seen in passing when she came here to identify Brianna's body and talk to the sheriff about her death. She'd only stayed in the town a day, long enough to arrange for the burial and to lock up her sister's house.

"Look, could you just speed it up?" Kat stuck her hands in her pockets and crossed her ankles, praying for him to hurry. While he tightened the cable, she said, "I just had the battery changed at one of those franchise places. It's hard to find good help in the city."

He stopped working the wrench. "Maybe if you didn't have this gas-guzzler, you could afford to take your car to a real mechanic."

Though he grinned with the remark, the muscles in Kat's jaw tensed. She pointed her thumb in the direction of his pickup. "And that beat-up piece of junk doesn't pollute the air?"

"Hey, now you're insulting an esteemed member of my family." He gave the wrench one last twist and tugged it off. "Why don't you give it a try?"

She stomped around him, slid into the seat of her SUV, and cranked the key. The engine roared to life.

He locked the hood in place, strolled over, and leaned down so he could look at her with the most unusual, Caribbean blue eyes she'd ever seen, almost aqua.

If he and his dog hadn't been so obnoxious, she would have been interested. No. She wasn't going down that path. Good thing the dog wasn't the only obnoxious one. She rolled down her window to see what he wanted.

"Can I help you with anything else? Are you going to be in Rosswood a while, or just passing through? You're Brianna's sister, aren't you? I'm Chance Eliason."

She didn't have time for this. "Thanks for your help, but I don't need anything else from you."

"You sure?" He winked and made a clucking sound with his tongue.

With only a curt smile, she hoped to render her disgust for his hackneyed male response. He wasn't budging and seemed to want to pass the time, time her bladder wouldn't permit. "I really have to go, but thanks again for your help." To give him a strong hint, she edged the car forward. When he pitched backward out of the way, she stepped on the gas. Now to a restroom.

She checked the rearview mirror and noticed he was standing right where she'd left him, watching her drive off. An appealing man, but she had no real interest. The quicker she disposed of Brianna's property, the sooner she could get back to Seattle to tend to her future: fixing up her house to sell and accumulating enough money to retire in Hawaii. What was *not* on the horizon was getting involved with any man, especially a two-bit cowboy.

CHAPTER 3

Chance stared at the SUV speeding away from him and shook his head in amazement. Kat Summers had come to town. The woman was definitely uptight and feisty. When Brianna had showed him Kat's picture, she'd warned him.

He gave Zeke a pat, but before he got into the cab, he inspected the land across the road and the brand new barbed wire fence. Anger rose in him like a choking weed. A man like Wheeler, who would erect a daunting fence like that, was one more reason to keep the resort out of Rosswood.

Chance drove a short distance and turned right onto the dirt road that led to his ranch house. His forty acres provided an adequate sanctuary for his newfound family: twenty-five rescued burros. As his truck neared the house, the braying started up, sounding like a symphony of incompatible trumpets. He swerved right and pulled up to the barn.

A short, weathered man with a round face and straw-like hair set a bucket by the fence and strolled up to Chance. "You look like you got tangled up with a mountain lion."

Chance did his best to soften his expression. "Rusty, you're not that far off. Brianna's sister's in town."

"She a looker, like Brianna?"

"Yeah, she's a looker all right. She's as pretty as a cactus in springtime, complete with spines."

"That bad, huh?"

"Let's just say I'd rather wrestle a mountain lion."

Zeke paced the truck bed, whining, until Chance unhooked the tailgate. The dog flew off the truck, circled Chance's hired hand, and went in search of a post to pee on.

Several burros in various shades of brown, gray, and black crowded the wooden fence to get close to Chance. The wind picked up strength, and he grasped the top of his hat. He nodded toward a lone white burro lingering by a scrub oak, well away from the herd. "How's Banjo doing? Is she letting you anywhere near her?"

"I think it'll be a while before that old girl gets over the miserable treatment she suffered," Rusty said. "It's a downright shame what some of those animals went through."

"We might have to meet her halfway. If that's the best we can do, so be it. At least she can live out the rest of her life in peace." Chance gave the closest burro a friendly pat. "I've got a quick call to make, and then I'm heading into town to pick up a few things. I might stop off at Bertie's. I won't be gone too long."

"Sure thing, boss."

Chance started off toward the house with Zeke galloping after him. Kat slipped into his thoughts again, and he wondered how she and good-natured Brianna could have come from the same stock. If he ever ran into Kat again, he'd dare himself to ask.

CHAPTER 4

In the last six months, Rosswood hadn't changed. It probably hadn't changed in a hundred years. Kat slowed through the sleepy little town that looked as if its wooden sidewalks and fake storefronts had been lifted out of the Old West and set down in the foothills of the Cascade Mountains. She could almost picture a gunslinger riding his horse through the center of town, which, she gauged, couldn't have been more than four blocks long, if that.

Nowadays Rosswood was nothing more than a backdrop for summer campers and tourists and in the autumn months hunters hoping to nail a deer.

Small town cops were notorious for nabbing out-of-towners. Even though it was painful for Kat, she kept her car at a reasonable speed.

Hunger had driven her to town before going to Brianna's house. She could find a restroom there. On the left side of the street, she noticed a café, a market, and a beauty shop, and on the opposite side an office, a movie theater, and Bertie's Grill. No McDonalds or Starbucks in this God-forsaken place. Up ahead, separate from the tacked-on storefronts, was the post office. From her previous visit, she knew the sheriff's office and an auto repair shop were up one of the side streets.

Kat could never understand why her sister chose to live in such a backward community. City life was Kat's style. She promised herself she would tend to business as quickly as possible, and if she had the time she would fly to Maui for a short vacation before returning to the toil of work.

She nosed her SUV into an angled parking spot in front of Bertie's Grill. She locked the car doors, as she would have done in any city, never mind the fact that this town only boasted a total of 756 residents according to its "Welcome to Rosswood" sign. One could never be too safe.

She dashed into Bertie's, more than happy she'd made it in time, and scanned the back wall. The lighting was dim, but once she'd homed in on the green restroom sign, everything else in the room faded.

The place could have been empty for all she knew as she hurried around chairs and past a pool table, nearly getting poked in the arm by a backward-butting cue stick. She pushed through the restroom door.

When she emerged, relieved and relaxed, all the sights and sounds of the eating establishment flooded her senses. She'd been so focused on her way in she hadn't noticed the country sounds coming from the jukebox, the clink and clatter of plates and silverware, and the aroma of fried onions, burgers, and beer. The room itself was half-filled with customers, mostly men.

As she strode toward the bar, the noise level plunged; all chatter stopped, except for a few whispers and the jukebox's country whine. Kat ignored the stares and took a seat at the far end of the bar away from three men grouped together and looking her way.

A husky woman with short, frizzy hair and a wide smile across wrinkling cheeks set a glass in front of one of the men and strolled toward Kat. She had on a stained apron over a plaid shirt and blue jeans. With a wet cloth, she swiped the wooden surface. "What can I get you?" she asked in a whiskeyed voice.

"A deluxe burger, fries, and an Anchor Hawking." Why not indulge?

"You must be from the city. All we got here is the usual, nothing fancy."

"Well, let's see." Kat leaned sideways to view the beer on tap. "I'll just have ice water."

"You look familiar." The woman squinted, studying Kat's face. "Where have I seen you before?"

"I was here six months ago taking care of family business. My sister lived here."

"Yeah, yeah, I got it. I remember. You're Brianna's sister. Umm . . ." She brandished her index finger at Kat.

"Kat Summers."

"Yeah, that's it. I saw a photo of you. Kat, now that's an odd sort of name."

"Short for Kathleen." She swiveled to peer around the room and back to the bar. "I suppose Brianna came in here a lot."

"She sure did. She worked here part time until she, you know."

"She worked here? She never mentioned it." She hadn't mentioned it the last time they talked, but they rarely talked.

"Sure did. Great kid, too. Hard worker. Although she had her down times. That was a while back though. She'd been doing real good. By the way, my name's Bertie. I own this joint." She wiped her hand on her apron and offered it to Kat.

Kat promptly shook hands, but something confused her. No time like the present to start asking questions. "Did you say Brianna was doing better? What did you mean by that?"

"Just a sec." Bertie filled Kat's water glass and exited into the kitchen. After belting out the lunch order, she returned through the swinging doors, followed by a man about Brianna's age, thirty-five, who took her place behind the counter. Then she came around to where Kat was, plunked down on a neighboring stool, and looked Kat over. "You're one of those lucky types. Beer, fries, and a burger? If I gorged on that in one sitting, I'd balloon up like a tent, never mind having a good case of heartburn."

This woman was rough around the edges, but in a strange way she reminded Kat of Maggie. "What were you saying about Brianna?"

"Oh, yeah. Where was I?"

"You said Brianna was doing better. That was my impression."

"Like I said, she had some rough times, but the year before she died, she seemed to have her feet on the ground. She'd come in here smiling nearly every day."

"Really. What turned her around? Do you know?"

"Look, I never meddled in her personal life. She never confided in me that way. Kept those things to herself, although there were stories going around. One day she just seemed happier. Might have had something to do with Chance."

"Chance Eliason? What does he have to do with anything?"

"You know him?"

"I just met him coming into town. What did he have to do with Brianna?"

"He's a neighbor of hers, and all I know is she started working for him, helping him on that ranch of his. That's all she told me, but she seemed happy for it."

"Earlier you mentioned something about stories. What sort of stories were going around about her?"

Bertie retreated into thought for a moment and gazed at Kat with a stern look. "I don't believe in spreading rumors. You know, I hear a lot of stuff in a place like this, but most of it is just tongues wagging. I've learned to turn a deaf ear to that sort of thing. I'd rather not indulge." She slid off the stool. "I've got work to do. You staying in Rosswood for a while?"

"For a while. Is there a B&B around here, or a hotel?"

"That's like your fancy beer. Nothing like that near town. Closest motel is about thirty miles out, toward Benton, called The Sleeping Inn." She edged away from Kat. "We got a café across the street, but I hope to see you in here again." She rounded the bar past the man closest to Kat and slapped a hand on his shoulder. "Your order's coming right up."

As Bertie aimed for the kitchen, the waiter squeezed past her, set a sack in front of one of the men, and continued with Kat's order. The man with the sack left the Grill, but one of the other two men kept staring at Kat.

When the waiter set Kat's plate in front of her, she changed her mind and asked to have her lunch boxed up. Her comfort level was dropping by the second. She purchased her lunch and a bottle of spring water and walked out into the sunshine.

The light was a blinding contrast to the inside of the Grill. While turning left, but squinting in the opposite direction, she collided with a hard body, her sack tumbling to the ground. Flustered, she bent to pick it up at the same time as the man, and the rim of his hat hit her in the middle of her forehead, knocking her off balance. He grabbed her elbow to steady her. As she righted herself, she stared into the eyes of Chance Eliason.

"You." Faced with his sultry smile, she instantly knew how Brianna could have been taken in by him. She yanked her arm free.

Still smiling, he handed her the sack. "Maybe you ought to pay more attention to where you're going."

"Maybe I could say the same to you. If you'll excuse me, my lunch is getting cold." She walked off in a huff and unlocked the car door.

"Can I buy you a beer or a cup of coffee?"

"No, thanks."

He stood in front of Bertie's, watching her drive away, a stunning picture of a man who seemed way out of place in this Podunk town. She placed him in the love-'em-and-leave-'em category, wondering if he was the cause of her sister's problems, wondering if Bertie was alluding to Brianna having an affair with him.

Kat pulled up to the post office, a tiny brick building with an American flag fluttering in the breeze. While she ate her lunch in the SUV, her mind wandered. If Chance and Brianna *were* having an affair, maybe she fell for him like she was prone to do. And maybe he was all wrong for her, like most of the men she dated. Maybe she fell hard, and he promised to marry her, but instead he dumped her, and that was why she'd committed suicide. That could account for the abrupt turnaround for an unstable person like Brianna—happy one day, the next day feeling horribly depressed.

The more Kat thought about it, the more her theory seemed real to her. Before leaving Rosswood, she'd have it out with this Chance Eliason.

Finishing up, she nibbled on the remaining fries and tossed the rest in the lunch sack. She got out and locked her car, hurried up the post office steps, and entered the cramped one-room structure. The air was thick with musty paper smells, along with a strong hint of body odor.

A woman with her back to Kat twisted enough for a passing glance and went back to talking to the clerk behind the counter. Kat recognized him as the man with the unruly red hair seated closest to her at Bertie's.

A real charmer, he complimented the woman on her appearance. Yet, the woman was clearly overweight, her hair stringy, her clothes baggy and unflattering. He went on to ask her about her husband's gout. She leaned toward him, purposely excluding Kat, and didn't seem to be in a hurry.

To pass the time, Kat turned her attention to the wall across from the postal boxes to the left of the counter. On a bulletin board were ads for a stationary bicycle, for babysitting at reasonable rates, for free kittens, and one for selling a used pickup.

The last ad gave Kat an idea. She had to get rid of Brianna's car. Although it was an old beater with a sordid past, maybe someone would buy it for parts.

She dug through her purse for a notepad and wrote up a quickie ad: Old Car. Will sell for parts. U-haul. She added her cell phone number underneath and tacked up the ad with a stray pushpin. The thought occurred to her that displaying ads on federal property was probably illegal. But then this was out-of-the-way Rosswood.

After the woman left, Kat took her place at the counter, hoping to state her needs and get out. "My name is Kat Summers."

The man set an envelope aside. "I know who you are. I saw you at Bertie's. You're Brianna's sister." His voice was soft and syrupy. "I saw you when you came through town before. I never got to say how sorry I was about Brianna." For a moment his eyes rolled toward the ceiling as if he were capturing an old memory. "That girl lit up this town. We all miss her."

"Thanks for sharing that." In reality Kat wished this meddlesome man would can the sentimentality. She wanted to stay in control; no more tears, especially now. "I'm going to be here a while and wanted to notify you in case anything comes for me. I have business in Seattle, and whatever is mailed or faxed here might be important."

"I'll sure do that, Ms. Summers."

"Kat."

"Kaaat," he said, lengthening the vowel sound. "What a delightful name." He tittered. "Meow."

Kat smiled, indulgently waiting for him to stop giggling. "When I was here last, I stopped in and talked to a woman about sending me Brianna's mail. Was there anything that didn't get sent that I could pick up now?"

At the table behind him, he thumbed through a stack of folders and found one, likely with Brianna's name on it. "Nothing here but the usual junk mail. Do you want it, Kaaat?" When she shook her head, he came up front.

"You know," he continued, "she used to come in here almost every day. She'd get a lot of magazines. She told me someday she'd be a famous author, and I'd want her autograph. We used to laugh about that. She'd come in with the manila envelopes to be mailed to editors and the like, and she'd make jokes about sending out another story, so she could add to her pile of rejection letters." He made a tsking sound. "She used to get quite a bit of mail from publishers, but after a while she stopped sending so many out."

Kat wished to end the conversation, but obviously the man liked to talk. "Well, if anything important does come for her, will you put it with my mail?"

"Oh yes, I'll gladly put it with yours."

"Fine."

"I make deliveries late in the afternoon or whenever it's convenient. My wife, the woman you talked to last time, minds the shop, so to speak. If you get any mail, I can deliver it."

"I don't know where I'm staying right now. I'll just pick it up here."

"Whatever you like, Kaaat."

Kat was relieved to get out into the fresh air again. When she'd decided to come to Rosswood, she hadn't taken into account how difficult it would be to speak to strangers about Brianna. Those painful feelings were surfacing again, along with second thoughts about coming here. Kat wanted to bolt. But she couldn't. She had business to do, Brianna's business.

CHAPTER 5

Backtracking through town, Kat passed Chance Eliason's truck parked at Bertie's. Soon she would confront him and summon the truth about his relationship with her sister. But not now.

She passed Hank's General Store and considered picking up a few staples, but if she stayed at a motel, she wouldn't need them. Besides, she would rather have a tooth pulled than converse any longer with the locals about Brianna. She'd had plenty for one day.

She drove away from the center of town for about a mile on Randall Road, the same road she'd come in on, and turned left down North Maple Lane. Several small homes in various stages of disrepair were grouped together close to the main road. A little farther on, on the opposite side, was the sparkling white Rosswood Community Church, the size of a one-room schoolhouse. After that were a few empty lots, overgrown with grass and littered with papers strewn from the wind.

The street curved slightly, and on the right amid gnarly old maple trees was an isolated cottage, painted a dirty brown. Not a great choice. But at the time Brianna had begged for the down payment, not many habitable homes were on the market.

When Kat spotted Brianna's car in the open one-car garage, her insides grew rigid as steel. The rusted-out Ford brought up anger so intense she had to take a deep breath just to stay in control. She slammed her palm on the steering wheel. "Damn it, Brianna! Why'd you do this to yourself? Why didn't you tell me you were in such deep despair?"

She turned the anger inward and scolded herself for being too self-involved, practically turning her back on her sister, the only family she had, or ever would have. She wiped the tears from the corner of her eyes and sat motionless for a full five minutes. Strangely, after this eruption of rage, she felt her muscles ease from the tension, giving her temporary relief.

Before going inside, she peered at the wooded property across the street, taking note of the dirt road weaving through it. The road was overgrown with grass, and the woods were too dense with overhanging limbs to see where it led.

Brianna loved her sanctuary. When she told Kat about the house she wanted to purchase, she raved about the quiet, even though the house was so close to town. In the back the property bordered a pasture, its fence stretching all the way to Randall Road.

Meandering toward the door, Kat was careful not to trip over the lumps and bumps of the old cement walkway, bulged and cracked from winter thaws. The wiry grass in the front yard was on the tall side and browned in patches from lack of summer watering.

The tree limbs created a barrier to the sun, and the house had been closed up over the long stretch of summer. The interior was cold and dank. The chill seeped through to her bones.

The living and dining rooms were combined with an open kitchen to the left. Across the main room through a doorway was the only bedroom.

To save on the oil bill, Brianna had bought portable electric heaters. Kat plugged one in between the kitchen and the bedroom and edged toward the warmth.

Kat had left everything in the house as it was the day Brianna died.

The burnt orange afghan was draped over the back of the saggy sofa. Brianna's rubber boots were next to the front door, one upright and one on its side, a detail Kat had overlooked when she first entered the house. On the kitchen windowsill were two of Brianna's rings, a gold band with an onyx setting and a gold pinkie ring, presents given to her by her ex-husband. It gave Kat a shiver of unease to see these, but she refused to spiral into sadness.

Kat opened the refrigerator door and nearly gagged. Inside were jars of mayo and mustard, a half loaf of bread, a chunk of cheddar bluish with mold, and an opened carton of milk. She shut the door and backed away from the putrid smell.

In the bedroom the down comforter Kat had purchased for Brianna as a housewarming gift lay across the bed. The covering was a rich dark brown.

Kat opened all the curtains, returned to the warmth of the heater, and marshaled her thoughts. Before she listed the house, it would need a thorough cleaning, and she would have to sift through Brianna's clothes and personal items to see what to keep and what to dispose of.

Surprisingly, being here didn't feel as disturbing as she thought it would. If they had found Brianna's body in the house, instead of the detached garage, it would be different. After disposing of Brianna's car and closing the garage door, Kat could dissociate completely from the means of her sister's death. Getting rid of the car would be her first priority.

Considering the work she had to do, she hated the thought of driving to and from a motel thirty miles away, at least forty-five minutes on these winding roads. Staying in Brianna's house seemed like the practical thing to do.

As much as she despised trucking into town again, she needed food, and as long as she'd be here a while, she might as well get cozy with the locals. Who knew when or if she might need help?

She turned off the heater and checked under the kitchen sink for scouring powder and detergent and in the bathroom for soap and toilet paper, all of which were on hand.

In town she parked in front of Hank's General Store, a picture from the past. The white paint was chipped in places, revealing the weathered wood underneath, and the windows, holding old ads for cigarettes and pop, were wavy with age. Inside, the black-speckled linoleum was scuffed and worn, and fluorescent bulbs hung over cramped aisles stocked to overflowing with every grocery item imaginable.

She smiled at the balding, middle-aged man minding the cash register, grabbed a basket, and continued down aisle after aisle, picking out bread, cereal, milk, peanut butter, bananas, a couple of frozen dinners, a bag of chips, and a bottle of Chablis, enough for a start. She threw in a bottle of Windex and a Hershey bar.

The bell on the door jingled, and the clerk exchanged greetings with a man he addressed as Doc, but Kat was too far in the back to see the man. By the time she worked her way to the front of the store, he'd disappeared down the far aisle.

The clerk slowly and methodically rang up each item from Kat's basket. Gritting her teeth, she had to remind herself to be patient and go with the easy flow of Rosswood.

He paused, leaving the last item on the counter, and said to Kat, "Nice day, all right. But a little chilly."

"Uh-huh." She glanced out the window just to seem interested.

"Think winter's coming early this year. I can feel it in my knees."

"Hmm . . ."

"You're the Summers woman, aren't you?"

News traveled fast around here. "That's right. I'm Brianna's sister, but you probably already knew that."

A crash and the clatter of rolling cans caused Hank to look toward the rear of the store. "Need some help back there, Doc?"

"I can manage," the man said, disgruntled, "but you might consider stacking these soup cans away from the corner here."

"Sure, well, just holler if you need help." Hank leaned closer to Kat and said in confidence, "I call him 'Doc Butter Fingers.' He's the clumsiest fellow I've ever come across."

Kat felt sorry for the man and hoped he hadn't heard Hank's remark. She couldn't see the doctor, but it gave her the idea to look him up after she got settled in. Who would better understand Brianna's emotional state than her doctor?

Hank glanced toward the rear of the store again, then gave Kat his full attention. "I hear you're going to be in town a while."

"That's right."

"Well, then, I wanted to let you know we have a delivery service if you happen to be staying in the local area, say within a ten-mile radius. Just call in your order, and we'll put it on your tab. You can pay up the end of the month."

"I'll be within your delivery area, but I don't plan to be here that long."

"You can pay by the week, whatever's convenient. We have a trustworthy young man who delivers for us. Nothing to worry about."

"Thanks, but I can come to town to get my groceries. I'm only a mile out."

"Brianna's place, huh? Sorry about Brianna."

"Thanks, Mister . . ."

"Hank. You can call me Hank."

"Okay, Hank." She looked at the bag of chips on the counter, and he finally placed them in the grocery sack. Halfway to the door, she stopped and asked about the property with the barbed wire fence on the edge of town. "What's with the sign?"

"Oh, that." Hank laid his arms on the counter and clasped his hands. "We got us an all-out war in this town."

"What kind of war?"

"A big-shot real estate developer named Wheeler wants to build a flashy resort with a golf course and spas for all those rich city folk. Some of the townspeople are dazzled by all the money that'll come into this community, but the rest of us don't like the idea of changing this town. We like it the way it is."

"Most people don't like change."

"You got that right," he said. "And I'm one of them. So was Brianna. She'd been fighting like mad to keep old Wheeler out. It's a wonder he didn't shoot her on the spot when she stood up to him at one of our town meetings. She was a tiger, that girl."

Kat felt the blood draining. "Excuse me, but I really do need to go." She hurried from the store and sank into the driver's seat of her SUV. She wondered if Hank realized how insensitive his remark was, but considering his rude comment about the doctor, she didn't think Hank was the type to screen anything that might come out of his mouth.

When Kat returned to the house, she hauled her groceries inside and went back for her suitcases. A short while ago she was resolved to stay the night in her sister's house, but as the afternoon faded into evening, she wasn't so sure.

CHAPTER 6

If Kat had any doubts about camping out at Brianna's, the strain she felt after talking to the locals convinced her otherwise. She was downright fatigued and couldn't face searching for a motel.

In Kat's line of work, conversing with strangers was a necessity, and it came easy to her. She stayed conveniently detached from her clients' emotional issues, a detachment she'd learned from growing up in a dysfunctional family. Without much effort, she'd learned how to erect protective walls around herself. Today she'd let her guard down, and nothing had been as emotionally draining as the conversations she'd had concerning Brianna.

While her dinner cooked in the microwave, she rummaged through a kitchen drawer in search of a corkscrew, confident she'd find one since she and Brianna both enjoyed the taste of wine, another habit they'd picked up from home sweet home.

She set the steaming dinner on the table and rounded up the bag of chips and the glass of wine. The smell of turkey and dressing, as artificial as it was, couldn't mask the musty odor of the house. Tomorrow she'd give it a full airing.

After eating the meat and picking at the dressing, she munched on chips and sipped wine until the glass was empty.

She left the mess on the table to deal with in the morning and wandered into the bedroom to see what state Brianna's bed was in. When she tossed back the comforter, she was shocked.

Brianna had a penchant for neatness, and Kat expected the sheets to be pulled taut and folded back and the pillow straight and aligned. Instead, the mashed-in pillow was askew and the top sheet was in a rumpled mass, the ends pulled out from the corners.

On her breeze through the house, after her sister's death, Kat had also neglected to see the bedside lamp that was knocked to the floor. She returned the lamp to its rightful place.

It wasn't like Brianna to leave her room in such disarray. As a child, her side of the room was always perfect, unlike Kat's. Their mother loved telling the story of finding banana peels under Kat's bed. Kat shrugged acceptance. Making a neat bed that harrowing day was probably the farthest thing from Brianna's mind.

That angry feeling broadsided Kat again. She stared at the bed and bellowed, "You didn't even leave a suicide note to tell me what *was* on your mind." She stomped out of the room, furious, wondering when, if ever, this insufferable anger would burn itself out.

Sleeping in Brianna's bed wouldn't happen tonight. The sheets needed changing, and that would have to wait till morning. Once she was snuggled in her pajamas on the couch under the warmth of the comforter she'd dragged in from the bedroom, she tossed and turned, trying to get comfortable, and fell into the dream that had been tormenting her ever since Brianna had died.

The vision of Brianna's twisted and distorted face was so vivid Kat wasn't sure at all if she was dreaming because when she woke, panting for breath, the vision was still with her. It slowly faded away.

"What do you want, Brianna? Why are you haunting me?" She glanced toward the bedroom, half expecting Brianna's ghost to appear.

Outside, the wind howled.

When would these visions leave her alone? This was the worst one yet. She'd heard stories about troubled, earthbound souls, but she only wanted to believe Brianna was dead and gone.

Kat nestled her hip into the sagging cushion. The comforter warmed her back to sleep until a shrill noise entered her consciousness, a relentless ringing that wouldn't let up. From a lack of resolve on her part to settle Brianna's affairs, Kat had continued to pay Brianna's household bills—her mortgage, utilities, and regrettably her phone bill.

She stumbled into the kitchen and grasped the receiver. "Hello."

The answer came as a scratchy static noise, followed by a long pause, a heavy sigh, and the click.

She held the receiver at bay. "Okay, Kat, get a grip. This had to be a wrong number." She hung up, but she wasn't convinced.

First the visions and now the aggravating phone calls. Why were they following her wherever she went? This line of thinking actually frightened her. The call *had* to be a wrong number. Still, to feel secure she lifted the receiver off the hook and let it dangle. After a minute the sharp warning beep finally died down.

Rattled and totally awake now, she riffled through her purse for the Valium. She swallowed a pill and set the bottle on the end table. For peace of mind she left the light on. She tugged the comforter over her head and let the Valium lure her into a hazy sleep.

≈

Chance stared out his bedroom window at the north side of his property, which would soon lie dormant through winter. Yellowed grass was tinged with green. The morning reached out to him like a beckoning Siren, a perfect time to run.

Completing his running attire, he slipped on a faded blue T-shirt with the words "Topping Ventures" inscribed in small black letters. This was the shirt's last wearing because he intended to retire it to the ragbag, shredding the final tie to his former life. His years in Boston seemed light years away from his life in Rosswood.

His bedroom was plainly furnished: queen bed, a dresser, and night-stands, all in a dark stained oak. He was getting used to living simply, living the single life, though he preferred living with a woman.

He'd dated one woman in Rosswood, but it hadn't worked out. He thought they might remain friends, but she'd chosen to move away. He pictured her in his bed: her dark curls and olive skin framed by the white sheets, her soft curves yielding into his angular body. She'd satisfied his needs. What he didn't miss was her meek personality, and he'd let their relationship wither from neglect.

He preferred his women bold and feisty, like the Summers woman. No, not like her. Definitely not like her. She was over-the-top feisty.

He did miss the sex. That was where running fit in. It helped release the tension. It kept his mind clear and focused on other things, if only temporarily.

The air outside was fresh and crisp. The sun in the eastern sky peeked over the pine trees. Zeke rushed up to him, wagging his tail, in anticipation of the run.

"Are you ready to go?"

Zeke let out a long, low bark.

Chance exchanged waves with Rusty as Rusty headed for the barn to feed the burros. With Zeke keeping pace, Chance jogged the length of the long, narrow driveway and veered toward town. About a mile down Randall Road, he turned right onto North Maple Lane with the intention of checking his property line.

At the third house in, an old man swept his porch, whistling, as Chance ran by. He stopped and waved, and his mongrel dog raced out to greet Zeke. Zeke paused for the sniffing ritual, then bounded after Chance.

He approached Brianna's house and slowed to a halt, breathing hard, catching his breath. Kat Summers's SUV was parked in the driveway. Bertie had told him she was sticking around, but he never pictured her as a rundown-cottage type, not a high-maintenance city girl like Kat.

Noticing a light on inside, he thought it best to make direct contact with her to let her know he was going around back to check his fence. He didn't want to be mistaken for an intruder. If the woman owned a gun, he had no doubt she would use it.

Zeke pawed the door. Chance knocked, checked his watch to make sure it wasn't too early, and was about to turn away when a cranky voice from inside asked who he was.

"It's your backyard neighbor, Chance Eliason."

The door swung open. Zeke barged in and nosed Kat into the back of the couch. She raised her hands toward the ceiling and yelled, "Get him away from me."

"Zeke, out!" The dog twirled around and rushed headlong into the front yard, and Chance secured the door.

Kat's glare was icy. "You and your odious dog. What are you doing here?" Though her eyes were flashing mad, she was sizing him up from head to toe. "Out for a morning run, and you thought you'd stop by to give me a thrill?" She dismissed a response with a flick of a hand. "What time is it?"

Her comforter was half on the floor, and she stood in bare feet with her hair matted on one side and sticking up on the other. Her chocolaty eyes were red-rimmed and puffy. She had on silk pajamas the color of midnight blue. The top hung cockeyed, half off her shoulder, allowing him a glimpse of a heart-shaped tattoo with the words "Wild Child" inscribed in red ink. The material couldn't hide the shape of her breasts and taut nipples underneath. If it weren't for her disagreeable temperament, she would be the most intriguing woman he'd ever seen.

"Well? What are you staring at?"

"Is this how you wake up in the morning, all blustery? If it is, I pity your poor husband, if you have one."

"I don't, thank you very much." She lifted the comforter off the floor and set it on the couch.

He wiped the sweat from his brow. He was hot from running, and she was only making matters worse. "I saw the light in the window, and I thought you were up. I wanted to let you know I'd be in the backyard looking over my fence. I didn't want you to think I was a prowler."

"Is that your property back there? Why can't you check the fence from your own side, or was this a big excuse to see what I was doing here?"

"See what you were doing? First of all, I was jogging past Maple Lane, and it was an impulsive idea, automatic even. I used to look in on Brianna, and I thought I would check on her house. I didn't know you were here. And secondly, you're not that interesting."

"Fine." Kat fisted her hips, putting tension on her pajama top. The middle button unfastened, creating a wide gap that exposed her flesh. She quickly hunched inward and crossed her arms, her face registering a brilliant pink.

Chance tried, unsuccessfully, to choke down a chuckle.

She reached for the comforter and pressed it to her chest. "Okay, that's it. Go see to your precious fence."

Shaking his head, he reached for the doorknob and muttered under his breath, "Nope. Nothing like Brianna."

"What did you say?"

"I said . . ." He faced her, ready to spit out an insult, but he looked into her eyes and read the pain behind the anger. His growing contempt melted away. "Look," he said, softening the pitch of his voice, "why don't we call a truce."

"What for?"

Because of the snappish way she'd answered him, it was all he could do to stand still, instead of taking this petulant woman across his knee or better yet into his arms. She was so feisty, but she was also so sexy and irresistible in her slinky little pajama set. Her large features, spread evenly across her face, reminded him of the beautiful Julia Roberts.

He took a step back. He couldn't believe he had thoughts like this, especially about Kat Summers. He glanced at the ceiling in a heaven-help-me prayer and blew out an exasperated breath. "Don't you agree we've been at each other's throats ever since you rolled into this town? Brianna was a friend of mine, and I really don't want to fight with her sister. I don't think she would have liked that."

Kat traced the floor with her gaze and seemed deep in thought, making him feel as if he were on trial by the toughest judge. "I do have some questions for you." Her voice had lost its edge.

"Fire away."

"At least let me put on some clothes before we talk." She draped herself with the comforter and sauntered off, the material trailing her like a wedding veil.

Chance couldn't believe he was actually making progress with the woman.

He spread the curtains a tad to check on Zeke and found the dog lying in the grass under a low-hanging maple branch, his eager eyes fixed on the door.

Now that Brianna was gone, Chance found it somewhat difficult to be in her house. He glanced around, looking for any evidence of her, first in the kitchen where he noticed the phone off the hook. Across the room he observed what was left of Kat's dinner—remnants of a frozen meal, an empty wineglass, and a bag of chips—not Brianna's style, not even the wine.

Closer to him on the end table was an opened prescription bottle. He couldn't resist picking it up.

As he was examining the label, Kat appeared in the doorway in jeans and a long-sleeved maroon sweatshirt with "Loggins Realty" inscribed in white letters above her left breast. Her hair was swept back in a ponytail away from a face with no trace of makeup. In one day she'd transformed herself from a hot-shot city woman to a country girl. He liked what he saw.

She walked toward him in purposeful strides. In one fluid motion she snatched the bottle out of his hands.

"You know, alcohol and pills don't mix."

"It's none of your business."

He nodded toward the phone. "Is there someone you'd rather not talk to? An old flame or a man you've got on the string?"

She hung up the receiver and marched back to Chance. "That, too, is none of your business. I thought we were having a truce."

He flipped his palms in the air and leaned back. "Guilty as charged." He expected her to throw him out, but instead she asked him to sit down.

He moved to one end of the couch, assuming she would sit next to him in a friendly gesture, but she dragged a wooden chair from the table and sat opposite him with the round braided rug between them, a hostile position in his view, her arms high across her chest.

"What did you want to ask me?" His eyes were drawn to her bare feet with toenails lightly polished in pink, but her exaggerated cough snapped his attention upward.

He'd barely sat down when she blurted, "You were sleeping with her, weren't you."

Her accusation was a slap in the face. "Where did that come from?"

"Just answer me."

"Not until you tell me where you got that idea."

"From Bertie."

"Bertie? What exactly did she say to you?"

"She said Brianna was spending time with you at your ranch."

"And you naturally assumed I was sleeping with her."

"Well, were you?"

Her belligerent tone irked him. He hated being grilled. It reminded him of his past, and he reacted to it with a stone-cold stare. "Brianna and I were friends, and I take offense at your implication." He stood and walked toward the door.

She sprang from her chair. "Sorry if I offended you."

He looked at her straight on. "Are you?"

"I'm just looking for answers," Kat said. "I don't know why Brianna took her life. Yes, she had problems, tons of them. Considering her roots, she had a right to every one of them. But I can't believe she would do such a thing unless something happened that knocked her for a loop. She was always very fragile. My theory is she was involved with someone she really cared about. Maybe she'd even fallen in love with him. He strung her along, and then he dumped her. To me that would explain why she was so distraught."

"And you thought that someone was me."

"You're the last man she spent time with."

"Then you're not a very good judge of character, and did you ever stop to think she might have had other male friends?" With a hand on the doorknob, he said, "You can rest assured, Ms. Summers. I wasn't sleeping with your sister." On his way out he slammed the door.

CHAPTER 7

Kat couldn't decide whether the chill in the house stemmed from lack of heat or from Chance Eliason's ice-cold presence. Whatever the cause the house needed a good warming. She switched on the heater.

She went into the bedroom and peeled back the curtain, just wide enough to see Chance raking his hair and stalking the fence line like a bull wanting to bust out of a corral. His face was hidden from her, but she suspected he was cursing.

She left him wiggling one of the fence posts and went into the kitchen to make peanut butter toast for breakfast. In the cupboard she searched for a jar of instant coffee but found only boxes of herbal tea. There were jars of dried herbs, vitamin bottles, and a container of protein powder. This amazed her. Brianna had never delved into health foods. As far as Kat could remember, Brianna had always had dreadful eating habits, same as Kat.

While standing in the kitchen and eating her toast, she could feel the tension from outside seeping through the walls. She couldn't relax until she heard Chance whistle for Zeke and saw him jog away from the house.

She didn't care if Chance was upset with her for questioning him. She had a right to ask about the relationship he had with Brianna, had a right to make sense of Brianna's death. Couldn't he understand her motivation? With no suicide note to go by, Kat was determined to find someone in this town who could provide her with answers.

When Chance was inside the house with her, she'd had a difficult time focusing. In such a small space the man's presence was powerful, almost suffocating. Projecting herself with force, bordering on anger, had been the only way she felt she could match his power.

His power was intoxicating indeed, and regrettably she was attracted to it. His looks didn't help matters either. His features weren't symmetrical; his nose angled to the right, one side of his mouth tipped upward, but in total he was very attractive. Dark hair on his arms and legs dusted Mediterranean skin. His sweat-soaked shirt had clung to a broad chest. He wasn't overly muscled, but his hard, powerful thighs hadn't escaped her attention. But neither had the ease with which his demeanor changed from warmth to ice.

From her experience in the business world, men like Chance wouldn't gravitate to a place like Rosswood. That in itself made her wonder what his background was and what he was really doing here.

Brianna's phone startled her out of her thoughts. Considering the strange call she'd had in the middle of the night, she hesitated before picking up. A man introduced himself as Tim Holmes of Holmes Auto Repair. Lenny Faulkes, the postman, had told him about Kat's ad, and he wanted to come by to look at Brianna's car.

"How did you know I was here?"

"Everyone in town knows you're at Brianna's house."

Small town gossip. Kat arranged to see him in an hour, giving her enough time to clean up.

The one-person bathroom was just large enough for her to circle around in. The portable heater took up half the space. It took Kat a full minute to regulate the water temperature. She slipped out of her clothes and squeezed into the metal shower stall. The hot water trickled over her body, providing her with more warmth than she'd experienced since her arrival in Rosswood. By the time she'd washed and conditioned her hair with Brianna's coconut-scented hair products, the water was lukewarm. She rinsed as quickly as possible before she was totally immersed in the cold.

She dried herself with a clean towel she'd found under the sink, dressed in a hurry, and blow-dried her hair. Out of habit she applied makeup, although she wondered why she even bothered to look good in a place like Rosswood.

Five minutes before the hour was up, there was a knock on the door. A sandy-haired man with sideburns, about her age, no taller than her five foot ten, gave her a nod. When he smiled, the cleft in his chin rose, and his eyes drooped downward. He wiped his palm on his greasy coveralls and extended it to Kat. "I called about the car."

She shook his trembling hand, but he snatched it away with an apologetic smile. "Nervous condition. Worse in the morning." With a curious look he stepped to the side and peered into the house.

"You said your name's Holmes. Are you related to the sheriff?"

"He's my dad. Best damn law enforcement officer in the county."

"I talked to him when I was here before. He helped me with the arrangements for my sister."

"I sure was sorry to hear about what happened to her."

Kat preferred to move the conversation along. "Why don't we look at the car?" She grabbed her jacket, and he made way for her to walk ahead of him. "You can go in and check it out if you want. I'd rather not go inside. I assume you know the history of it."

"Everyone in town knows about it, but I really don't need to check it over. I just want it for the parts. That's what your ad said, didn't it? I can buy it for the parts? I've got my tow truck here with me."

They both glanced at the truck with the black cab and "Holmes Towing" painted on the side in bold white script.

"I can haul it right away once we settle on a price. How much are you asking?"

Surprised anyone would call this quickly, Kat hadn't even thought that far ahead. "Gosh, I don't know. It's not much of a car. I don't even know if it runs." Wishing it out of her sight once and for all, her sales acumen disappeared like smoke. "You name a price."

"You don't have anything in mind?"

"Not really," she said. "What do you think it's worth?"

The way he stared at the car, not moving an inch to examine it, Kat figured he was more spooked by its history than he let on. Afraid she wouldn't be able to unload it, she said, "I'll give it to you free and clear. I just want it gone."

He raised his brows but didn't seem overly thrilled or surprised. "Okay, then. I'll have to ask you to move your car."

"Of course." She wrestled her keys from her jacket pocket, backed the SUV out, and parked in front of the house.

He maneuvered his truck into place, and she stood on the grass and watched him hook up the old Ford. When Kat came to Rosswood to see about Brianna, the sheriff had given her its contents: her keys, papers in the glove compartment, mittens, a stuffed dog she had in the back window, and other miscellaneous items. Kat worked the car keys off the ring that had a metal medallion engraved with the letter B.

He yanked the driver's door open and fished around inside. He brought Kat a red wool stocking cap, and his hand shook worse than before. "I found this in the back seat."

Kat clutched the hat to her body. "You should see about that."

"See about what?"

"The shaking."

"It's nothing." He slowly backed away from her and got in the cab of his truck.

"What about the title?"

"You can bring it around when you want," he shouted to her as he revved up the engine. As he inched down the driveway, Brianna's car, in protest, creaked and groaned like a beleaguered cow.

"Wait." Kat caught up with him before he made the turn onto the road. "Did you know Brianna? You didn't call my cell phone. You called Brianna's number."

"Sure, lady, I knew Brianna. Everyone knew Brianna." He stepped on the gas and sped up without so much as a wave or a thank-you.

Kat was too thrilled to be rid of the car to dwell on Tim Holmes's rude departure. The best thing about a small town like Rosswood was that word traveled fast, and the ad at the post office had paid off. One burden was lifted.

As to the dirty, musty garage, apart from burning it to the ground, she could do nothing about it except close the door and hide the hollow shell. She yanked on the rope to drag the door downward, but it caught at the halfway point. She yanked it again. It wouldn't budge. The metal arm was warped, and there was no way anyone could force the door to the ground short of hammering the arm straight. She tried tugging again, but the door snagged in the same old spot. Odd.

Everything about Brianna's death was odd. One day she was happy. The next day she killed herself in a garage with a door that wouldn't even close.

Kat shook her head in frustration. Enough of this. She came to Rosswood to take care of loose ends and get out, and that was exactly what she intended to do.

Inside the bedroom she opened the door to the closet and wasn't prepared for the wrench in her gut at the sight of Brianna's clothes: jeans, flannel shirts, some dress slacks, a blouse or two, and other odds and ends. Clothes were never as important to Brianna as they were to Kat. A small chest of drawers, snug in the corner, held Brianna's lighter garments. Kat scanned the top shelf of the closet for clean sheets but found only an extra blanket draped over a cardboard box. A laptop lay next to it. She'd examine that later.

She gathered the dirty sheets. A portable washer/dryer was wedged into the kitchen corner originally intended for a table. She hooked the appliance up to the sink and stuffed it full with one sheet.

About a year after Brianna had moved into the cottage, she'd complained to Kat about how much she despised using the Laundromat. Although Kat had balked at the idea, she'd purchased the appliance and at great expense had it delivered to Rosswood. She was glad to have it now.

After she'd given Brianna a hefty down payment for the house and sprung for the washer/dryer, Kat had refused to offer any more monetary help. When Brianna died, she was a month behind on her mortgage. Could money issues have contributed to her downward spiral? Kat wished she knew.

She slipped on one of Brianna's flannel shirts, opened the windows that weren't stuck shut, and dumped the spoiled food from the refrigerator into the garbage can by the garage. After the fridge was scrubbed clean, she stood back and admired her work. Not bad for a person who hated to scrub anything beyond her toes. The house certainly smelled fresher.

She made up the bed with the newly cleaned sheets, knowing later her back would be grateful for it. She sat on the comforter to calculate how much more had to be done before she could leave Rosswood. The rest of the house needed cleaning. A fresh coat of paint would brighten the interior. Painting the exterior would definitely raise the value. She'd have to hire someone to do the work, but that could be done before she left, and she wouldn't have to be present.

And then there was the chore of going through Brianna's clothes and personal items, deciding what to keep and what to give to the thrift shop. However unpleasant a task that might be, she could possibly be out of Rosswood within a week. But for one day, she'd done enough. She longed for some fresh air.

On the closet floor she found a pair of sturdy walking shoes. It gave her a squeamish feeling wearing Brianna's shirt and shoes, but she hadn't packed well for a week in the country, not with her high-heeled boots and her flimsy leather jacket. She searched everywhere but couldn't locate a parka or other warm coat. The flannel shirt would have to do.

Outside, a light, crisp breeze fluttered the leaves that remained on the maple limbs. A robin flew up to one of the branches. Beyond the tree's reach, the sun warmed Kat's face.

She walked at a brisk pace down Maple Lane past the church parking lot. As she approached the main road, a gray-haired lady eyed Kat from her front porch with neither a nod nor a wave. At the junction a Jeep drove by Kat, and the driver did a double take. Along Randall Road a truck slowed, and a bearded man in a ball cap offered her a ride, which she politely refused.

The walk into town was only a mile long, but by the time she hit Central Street, her feet hurt in the shoes that were a size too small and narrower than her own. She spotted the beauty shop with an interest in getting a foot soak and a pedicure. But this was Rosswood, not Seattle. Still, she might get lucky.

As she stopped to cross the street, an older couple stared at her, and she recalled what Tim Holmes had said: everybody in town knew Brianna. They probably recognized Brianna's clothes. Passing the general store, she saw Hank craning his neck to get a better look at her. She quickly ducked into the Honey Comb Beauty Salon.

CHAPTER 8

Yellow wallpaper, patterned with black combs with a bee perched on top, covered the salon's walls. A ceramic beehive sat on a narrow oak-veneered desk. The odor of permanent wave solution mingled with a honey scent from a diffuser near a table stacked with magazines. The space held an odd assortment of chairs. Beyond the desk, well into another area, were two work stations opposite two shampoo sinks.

A heavy-set woman with recently permed hair drew a quick breath when she saw Kat. She excused herself and squeezed through the doorway, leaving behind a whiff of the pungent aroma.

Behind the desk a hazel-eyed woman with thin lips, a prominent nose, and teased blond hair was counting a stack of bills. Despite the work she did, her pink blouse and white polyester slacks were bright and clean.

She scooped the money into a pouch and stuck it in a drawer, then smiled a look of recognition. "What can I do for you? Looks like you might need a color again in a couple of weeks or so."

Kat instinctively touched her hair.

"Roots. I can spot 'em a mile away. Bet your hair is as dark as Brianna's."

"As a matter of fact it is." Not only did this large-boned woman resemble Bertie in size, but she also talked in broad, blunt strokes, just like Bertie. "I'm Kat Summers. How did you know I was Brianna's sister?"

"The shirt and the shoes, plus you resemble her."

"I don't think we look that much alike."

"I guess not," the woman said. "Her features were more delicate than yours, little button-nose features. But, hell, she showed me your picture. I did that cute haircut of hers. Made her look like a pixie."

"I liked that style on her very much," Kat said. "I'm staying for a while to take care of Brianna's things. I was wondering if you did pedicures."

"Normally we do, but the gal I hired took off with her boyfriend and left me high and dry," she said with more than a little sarcasm. "Anything else I can do for you? Need a trim?"

"No, not today."

She stole a quick glance at the desk clock. "That being said, I have about forty-five minutes until my next appointment. I'm heading to the café for a bite to eat. Would you like to join me? We could chat over lunch. I could use the company."

Kat thought for a moment about whether or not to take the time. "A cup of coffee sounds good, and my feet need a rest. These shoes are a little snug."

"Great, and by the way, my name is Wilma Combs." She tossed a glance at the wallpaper. "Get it?"

Before Kat could comment, Chance Eliason stepped into the salon, carrying a handful of papers. Kat had to move aside to let him through.

He offered a quick smile. "Ms. Summers."

"Mr. Eliason."

Under Kat's blank, steady stare, he focused back on Wilma. "Here are the flyers for the town meeting on Saturday."

"Oh, goodie." Wilma made room for them on the desk. "Is Wheeler going to be there?"

"That's the plan."

"We'll see if the little weasel shows up. I hope he's up for more of our hometown abuse."

"We'll see, won't we? I better finish delivering these." He tipped his hat to Kat. "Good day, Ms. Summers."

"Mr. Eliason."

When the door closed, Wilma arched her penciled-in eyebrows. "It couldn't have been any colder in here if somebody filled this place with an iceberg. What's up with you two?"

"Oh, nothing. At least nothing to waste your time with. Shall we go?"

The Rosswood Café was by far older than Bertie's, although the checkered linoleum looked as if it had been recently scoured and buffed. The smells were more varied in the café; fried odors mixed with the aroma of soup, pancakes, and coffee. Straight back, a lunch counter with padded stools fronted the open kitchen. Formica tables were snug against windows and scattered in the center of the room.

The café, busy but not filled up, hummed with chatter and clanking dishes. Wilma led Kat to a window table halfway to the kitchen.

A woman with deep wrinkles on her forehead, dressed in dark slacks and a white blouse, swung by with water and menus. She left and returned with a coffeepot and addressed Wilma. "The usual?"

Wilma replied with a nod. "And coffee."

"What about you, miss?" she asked Kat. "Need more time?"

Kat felt the rush in her tone. "What's your soup today?"

"Vegetable beef. Homemade."

"I'll have a cup of soup and coffee, black."

The waitress righted the heavy, cream-colored mugs and filled them to the brim. "One grilled cheese and one cup of soup coming up." She was gone in a flash.

"Bev's a hard worker. Her husband had a heart attack two years ago, and she can barely support both of them." Wilma surveyed the room. "Sheriff's at the counter having his usual ham on rye. See that young gal with the frizzy hair and faded blue jacket at the far end, next to the wall? That's Tilly, short for Matilda. She's our resident cuckoo. Comes into the shop once in a while to stare at my customers. I have to shoo her out. She's a little touched is all, doesn't talk much. She lives with her grandmother on Maple."

"Near Brianna's house?"

"Yeah, but closer to Randall Road," Wilma said. "Whenever Brianna came to town, Tilly would follow her around. Brianna was kind to her. I guess Brianna defended her when some of the local boys teased her pretty bad."

"That sounds like Brianna," Kat said. "When we were growing up, she was always taking in stray pets and kids."

"See that emaciated-looking man with the thinning hair, sitting in the corner? That's Pastor Fletcher. I'm sure he'll be around to see you one day soon. He visits every new person in town, some more than others."

Kat couldn't interpret the smirk on Wilma's face. "I don't think I'll be here that long to warrant a visit. Tell me, Wilma, were you and Brianna friends?"

She returned her gaze to Kat. "Not the chummy variety. Other than coming in for haircuts, she'd stop by to say hi once in a while."

"Did she have any girlfriends in town, ones you would consider close?"

"Nah. You know how some women take to men better? That was Brianna."

Kat knew that about her sister more than anyone, though she'd hoped Brianna had changed.

"I'd go over to my cousin Bertie's for a beer after work, and Brianna would be flirting up a storm. Used to see her playing pool with the guys."

Kat's attention was drawn away from Wilma's chatter to the sheriff, who was walking toward them. His hair was a deep brown, silvery in places. He had a full mustache under a broad nose laced with spider veins. His high cheekbones gave him a youthful appearance. The cleft in his chin was the only feature he shared with his son. He held the top of his hat with one hand and the brim with the other. "Afternoon, Wilma."

"How're you doing, Gordon?"

"Nice to see you again, Ms. Summers," he said. "Word has it you're staying in town a while."

"Just long enough to gather Brianna's things and get her house in order, ready to sell. Not too long."

"What? A month or so?"

"Good heavens, no. Hopefully, a week, two at the most."

"If you need anything while you're here, I hope you'll give a holler."

"I might need someone to paint the exterior of the house if the weather cooperates. Of course, that might be next spring."

"I'm sure we can find you someone to do the work," he said. "Just let me know when you need them. In fact, you wouldn't need to be here. I could personally oversee the job. You and I could stay in touch by phone, so you wouldn't have to waste any more of your valuable time sticking around here."

"That's very kind of you, Sheriff," Kat said. "I'll give that some thought. And thank you."

"No problem at all." He seated his hat on his head. "Excuse me, ladies."

"Oh, by the way," Kat said, stopping him, "would you thank your son for hauling off Brianna's car? That was a weight off my shoulders. I really appreciated it."

"Sure enough." He continued out the door.

Wilma kept her eye on the door until it swung shut. "Did you know

Brianna had a thing going with the sheriff's *married* son?"

Kat wondered if this was one of those stories Bertie had warned her about. "Do you mean Tim Holmes? Do you know that for a fact?"

"Everyone knew it." Wilma's face beamed with confidence. "Several times when I was at Bertie's, Tim would come in and sit in a booth alone, without his wife, mind you. Pretty soon Brianna would take her break and sit with him. They'd be holding hands."

Kat felt her defenses rise. "Bertie told me there were rumors floating around. Maybe that was one of them. Maybe you were mistaken."

"I saw it with my own eyes," Wilma said. "As far as Bertie goes, she and I don't see eye to eye on a lot of things. Take the resort project. She wants it and I don't. And with Brianna, Bertie acted like a mother hen with her, all protective. Bertie saw what she wanted to see." She swiveled from her chair. "Will you excuse me a minute? Nature calls." She trotted off to the back of the café.

While Wilma was gone, Kat sipped her coffee, reflecting. Deep within, she knew Wilma had seen exactly what she'd seen. Kat knew Brianna's ways. Still, she didn't want to believe it.

On her way back to the table, Wilma stopped to speak to an elderly couple. Kat overheard them ask about her, which made her feel even more uncomfortable about being in Rosswood.

When Wilma was seated again, Kat's curiosity about Tim Holmes and Brianna kicked in. "What do you mean, they had kind of a thing going? What kind of a thing did they have? A flirtation?"

"A full-blown affair in full view of this town," Wilma was more than willing to offer. "You ask anyone. And I know it for a fact because his wife, June, is one of my customers. She's a timid thing with three snotty little kids at home. She came in crying about it one day. It seems he hadn't been home for several nights. Don't get me wrong. I liked Brianna, but she didn't seem to make very good choices in men. Always gravitated toward the married ones."

Since their order arrived, Kat hadn't eaten a spoonful of soup; she had no appetite for it. All that trickled down was the coffee, leaving a bitter trail. "You said 'ones,' plural. There were others?"

"I'm afraid so, but maybe this is enough to lay on you for one day."

"No, I want to know it all," Kat said. "It seems I had a different view of my sister's life in Rosswood these last five years. Please tell me, so I don't get broadsided by an angry spouse while I'm here."

Wilma looked up and gave the middle-aged pastor a thin smile as he scooted by their table. When he'd left the café, she nodded his way.

Kat reared back. "You're not insinuating . . ."

"The truth of the matter came right out of the horse's mouth." Wilma's eyes sparkled with delight at spreading the news to Kat. "His wife, Patsy, comes in to have her hair dyed every other month, though she needs it more than that. Now, she didn't tell me right out, but her best friend spilled the beans when I was shampooing her hair. Next time Patsy comes around, I pry a little, and she has to say something. She denied it, but not very convincingly. She finally spilled the story, but she asked me not to repeat one word of what I heard. And I swear, as much as I wanted to, I kept my mouth shut about it."

Kat could hardly believe that.

Wilma continued, undeterred. "I was a little intimidated by him being a pastor and whatnot. Lightning can strike those who sin, so I'm told. I'm only telling you because Brianna's gone, and being her sister, you have a right to know."

Kat felt as if a dam had broken, and all of Brianna's sins were pouring over her, but she might as well know the details. "Was it a one-night stand? Did it last long? How in the world did it happen?"

"Hell, I shouldn't talk about it," Wilma said, "but you are her sister and have a right to know the full story. Apparently, it happened shortly after Brianna arrived in Rosswood. He went to her house to welcome her to the community, looking for converts, really. She let him in and that was that. According to Patsy, he would make excuses for going to the church every day when there wasn't a need to. Then he'd mosey on down the road to Brianna's. Mighty convenient, if you ask me."

"How did it end?"

"It had been going on about a week or two when Patsy finally got suspicious and followed him to the church one morning. Somehow she waited out of sight and saw him park and walk down the road. She waited for an hour, and when he came back to the church, she confronted him. Funny thing was, after all that *converting*, I don't think Brianna ever went to church." She sat back and heaved a huge satisfied sigh, as if she'd slipped off a twenty-pound jacket.

Surprised, but not in total shock, Kat wondered if there were any more *stories*. When the waitress refilled their cups with steaming coffee, Kat found the aroma more than comforting. She blew across the top and took a guarded sip. She braced herself for whatever else Wilma had to say.

"There were other rumors floating around, but those two affairs were the only ones I knew of for sure." Wilma paused. "She might have had something going on with Lenny over at the post office. But I'm sure that's a big fat rumor. No doubt he spread it himself."

"Why do you say that?"

"Because he likes to exaggerate everything," Wilma said. "He likes the ladies, and he was starry-eyed over Brianna. He only wished things were that way between them. He's the kind who lives through other men's escapades. Besides, his wife keeps him on a short leash. He can't breathe without her knowing about it. Clare Faulkes, now she's a piece of work."

"What do you know about Chance Eliason?"

"Chance? Not too much." Wilma thought a moment. "I do know

he had a wife who died of cancer, and he has a daughter in college. He came into this town about the same time as Brianna and bought the ranch near the Pine Road cutoff. He's made himself a respectable place in this community. Everyone seems to like him. Other than that, he's sort of a mystery." She lifted her palms in the air. "But who cares? He's so damn easy to look at."

"How did you know about his wife?"

"He dated one of my customers. She said he was pretty closed up about his past. The only other woman in town he was close to here was Brianna. She'd do anything for him. He walked on water as far as she was concerned."

"What about him and Brianna? Did they have an affair?"

"That, I'm not sure of. I think she thought of him more like a father figure or an older brother. She seemed to lap up kindness from wherever it was offered."

Kat agreed wholeheartedly with Wilma's assessment of Brianna, but she was curious about Chance. "What happened to that woman you mentioned, the woman he had a relationship with?"

"She said he just stopped calling one day, never did know why."

"That sounds typical. So, does the woman live here in town?"

"She was a schoolteacher, but she wasn't here very long," Wilma said. "Shortly after they broke up, she transferred to another community. Broken-hearted, I guess. I don't think any woman could tie that man down. He's one of those men you dream about, but you can't have, like those movie stars. Whew! If I had a chance with him, I'd have me one good ride, all night long."

Kat laughed out loud, loosening the tension that had gripped her.

"I'd love to sit here and chat all afternoon," Wilma said, "but old Mrs. Tate is coming in for a perm. If I make her wait, she'll be staring at me in the mirror with her pursed little lips for two hours straight."

Her face lit up with a sneaky grin. "Of course, I could always get back at her and give her hair the George Washington look." She took a last sip of coffee. "Sure was nice talking to you. Stop in and say hi next time you're in the neighborhood."

"I will."

"If I think of anything else about Brianna, I'll be sure to let you know."

"You've given me plenty to think about. But if there is anything, I'm staying in Brianna's house."

"Yeah, I know." Wilma paid her bill at the counter and had the waitress wrap up the sandwich she hadn't touched. Words had tumbled from her mouth, but nothing except coffee had made its way in. "Take care, honey," she said as she paused by Kat, "and stop by the shop to talk anytime."

Kat stayed to finish her coffee. She took a sip of cold soup, trying to digest everything Wilma had told her. The sheriff's son, Tim Holmes. No wonder his hands were shaky around her. The pastor. So much for piety. Lenny, the postman? If what Wilma said was true, could Kat believe anything he'd said about Brianna? Or was everything Wilma said pure gossip?

As for Chance Eliason, perhaps there was something about him and Brianna even Wilma wasn't aware of.

CHAPTER 9

Kat left the café, pleased to be outside in the unsullied air where she could clear her head, overburdened with information she would rather not have known. Despite Brianna's weakness for married men, along with the heartache it might cause everyone involved, Kat thought Brianna had moved beyond those antics. Kat distinctly remembered Brianna telling her she was enthused about her life. Bertie said Brianna was happy, especially this last year. What happened to change that?

Kat wandered toward Hank's. Too much analyzing for one morning.

Inside the store Hank was handing a carton of cigarettes to a customer, one of the three men who'd sat near her at Bertie's. She recognized him by his plaid wool jacket and the dark stubble on his face. When she walked by him, she could feel him following her with his eyes.

She grabbed a basket. Though she was halfway down the middle aisle, the man's crude comments about her upper body rang out loud and clear. Something about him gave her the creeps, and she was relieved when he left the store.

She scanned several coffee brands and chose a jar of Folgers. Without a coffeemaker, instant would have to do.

She roamed the other aisles and picked up two cans of beef stew, a bag of peanut butter cookies, and a roll of antacids. At the back of the store were tools and miscellaneous household and clothing items. Brianna had a drawer full of wool socks but no slippers, and Kat had left her slippers at home. Among the miscellaneous items, she picked out a cheap pair of slip-ons.

At the end of the aisle she noticed the girl with the blue jacket and frizzy hair staring at her. In an instant the girl was gone in a flash of blue.

Kat strode to the front of the store. The door rang shut, and all she saw was a fleeting shadow. "Was that the girl named Tilly who just left?" she asked Hank as she deposited her basket on the counter.

Hank nodded and rang up her groceries in an uncharacteristic hurry. His face was strained, and patches of pink blushed both cheeks. "I'm sorry about Doug." He kept his eyes on his task. "He can be rather coarse at times."

"No harm done," she said. "Who is he anyway?"

"Doug Jones. He works on a ranch east of here. Comes into town more than I'd like. Kind of a rough fellow."

"Remind me to stay out of his way."

Hank slowed his pace and looked at Kat. "Do you know about Tilly?"

"I just heard about her from Wilma," Kat said. "The girl seemed to be watching me when I was in the back."

"Don't pay her much heed," Hank said. "She's an odd duck. She doesn't talk much, but she seems to have eyes in the back of her head. She turns up in the strangest places, and when she does speak, she comes up with the darnedest things." He shook his head and pushed the grocery sack across the counter.

Kat paid the bill and swept the sack into the crook of her arm. "Thanks, Hank."

"You getting along all right out at Brianna's house?"

"Everything's fine."

"I don't mean anything by this," he said, "but for the life of me, I don't know why you'd want to stay there in the first place after all that happened."

"I have work to do," Kat said. "Anyway, I don't intend to be there more than a week."

"You staying there nights all by yourself?"

"No reason not to."

"You're a brave one. I'm not one to be superstitious, but . . ."

"It really isn't that bad." Kat wondered how she could gracefully make her exit since he seemed to want to talk.

The bell jingled again. Two women entered and stared at Kat as if they'd never seen a stranger before. When Hank greeted them, Kat slipped outside. Saved by the bell.

She dug through the sack for the antacids and popped one in her mouth. Questions concerning Brianna were gnawing at her. Maybe it was time to pay the doctor a visit to see if he could add anything that might help her understand her sister's plight.

Except for a few teenaged boys lingering in front of the movie theater next to Bertie's, the town was deserted. Either people had left or they were inside the shops and restaurants.

She crossed the street and aimed for the building with two curtained windows. Written in red script, the sign on the door read "Doctor Steven Conklin."

No one was entering or leaving, but the door was unlocked. Kat slipped inside and was a little taken aback at how stark the room was: a tall ceiling; scuffed, beige-patterned linoleum; hard-backed chairs lining one wall; a metal desk facing the entrance. No receptionist was seated behind the desk to greet her, nor were there any patients sitting in any of the chairs. No pictures hung on the walls. The only sign of life was a vase of purplish-blue flowers on the edge of the desk, if dried flowers could be placed in that category.

She was about to leave when a stocky man in his forties, a little on the paunchy side, dressed in jeans and a wool shirt, with dull brown hair tamed to the side, came out from a back hallway. He had a large forehead and a squat nose set between the most piercing slate blue eyes she'd ever seen, like two BBs staring back at her. Kat recognized him from Bertie's as one of the three men sitting at the bar.

"May I help you?"

"Are you the doctor?"

"I am." His warm, welcoming smile showcased large, impeccable teeth. "But I'm not taking appointments today."

"I don't need an appointment," she said. "I wanted to talk to you about Brianna Whitley. I'm assuming you were her doctor."

His face lost its glimmer. "Yes, I was. There was a doctor in Benton, but she chose me. So, what is it you want to know?"

"I'm not sure, really." Kat realized she was twisting her ponytail in nervous spirals, a habit she'd acquired in childhood. She wasn't impressed with his brusque manner, odd for a person in his position. "Brianna had a history of depression, and I wondered if she ever came to you with her problems."

"Why do you want to know now?" he said, almost challenging her.

"It's the first chance I've had to slow down and think about it," Kat said. "I've been wondering about her mental condition. From what other people in town have told me, she seemed happy. I'm having a hard time believing she'd do what she did."

"I'm not sure you'll ever know why, Miss . . ."

"Summers, Kat Summers. I'm Brianna's sister."

"Yes. Forgive me." As his smile returned, the lines in his face faded. "I'm so sorry. I get so absorbed in my paperwork. I overheard you talking to Hank." He gestured to shake hands, so she shifted the grocery sack. He grasped her shoulder, as a politician would do, then slid a hand down her arm and embraced her hand with his. The warmth of his hands offset the intensity of his eyes. "I do apologize. I'm so deeply sorry about Brianna."

"No need to apologize." Kat slid her hand from his grip. "May I ask you a few more questions?"

"Whatever you need to know."

"I wondered if you saw her afterward."

"I'm afraid I didn't."

"Weren't you called in?"

"No, I wasn't," he said. "The sheriff couldn't locate me. He said she was deceased when he found her, so he called the coroner in Benton."

"Oh, I see."

"Come sit and we'll talk." He guided her by the elbow to one of the chairs against the wall, and she deposited her sack on the floor. When she turned back, he was staring at her shirt. "This is Brianna's, isn't it?"

"I needed something warm to wear."

"I'm sure she wouldn't have minded. She was like that," he said. "Now, where was I? Oh, yes. She used to come to me for the usual problems, colds, checkups. She seemed troubled at times, but as much as I tried to draw her out, she would never open up to me. I tried and I tried with her. It seemed to me she had a lot of pain inside."

"If you knew the half of it."

"Is that right?" He patted Kat's hand with his hot, moist palm, waiting for her to elaborate.

She reached for a strand of hair to twirl but caught herself. She also caught herself before she revealed too many secrets about Brianna to a stranger, at least a stranger to Kat. "Let's just say she had a rough childhood and leave it at that. When was the last time you spoke to her?"

"Oh, let's see now. It couldn't have been more than a day before she died."

"How did she seem to you? Was she depressed or upset?"

"Oh, no," he said. "In fact, I remember her being happy. I saw her in Bertie's at lunchtime, and she was flitting around that place making all the men feel welcome. Flirting, actually. She had a way with the men, you know. I tried to warn her about that, but she wouldn't listen to me. Just told me I was an old fogey."

"That sounds like Brianna."

"I tried and tried," he said, shaking his head. "She wasn't an easy girl to get close to. But to me there was no indication she would leave us that way."

"I'd like to believe that's true, but I'm just not sure."

"Of course one never knows what goes on inside the minds of others." He patted her hand one last time. "I have to get back to my paperwork now."

Kat gathered up her groceries. "Thanks for your time, Doctor."

He opened the door and placed his hand on her shoulder. "I hope you find some peace of mind about your sister, and please stop by for a chat anytime. Or let me know if I can help in any other way. I'm at your service." He squeezed her shoulder before closing the door behind her.

So far, no one in this town, not even the touchy-feely doctor, had given her an adequate answer. Kat was determined to discover why Brianna took her life. Until then, there could be no peace of mind for Kat.

The sun had dipped into the western sky, and the shadows were lengthening across the center of town. The air was cooling fast. Kat took off for home.

At the edge of town, where Center Street curved into Randall Road, a vehicle's horn sounded, and Chance Eliason's truck made the turn in front of her. He slowed to a stop and rolled down his window. "Can I give you a lift home?"

"I can manage." Except for one thing: her bladder was ready to burst.

When the truck inched forward, she yelled after him, "Wait. I changed my mind. I'll take that ride." She climbed into the cab and set her grocery sack between them. "After the last time I saw you, I didn't think you'd give me the time of day."

He stepped on the gas, jerking the truck forward. "Maybe I'm trying to make amends."

She narrowed her brows. "That would be quite a miracle. So why the change of heart?"

He gave a shrug. Speeding up, he bypassed Maple Lane.

She looked to the left, toward Brianna's. "Hey, where are you going? You missed my street."

"I'm taking you to my place. I want to show you something."

Not again. Her bladder ached. Why did she have to pee every time she was around this man? "Listen. I just had two cups of coffee and bouncing around in this truck isn't helping matters."

"You can use my bathroom."

"How far do we have to go?"

He swung left onto a dirt road. "We're just about there."

She clenched her teeth and gripped the edge of the seat to cushion the bumps. When he pulled up to a sprawling brick rambler and cut the engine, she stayed put until he told her Zeke was out in the field with his hired hand. She bolted out of the truck to a chorus of braying burros. "Are those yours?"

"All twenty-five of them," he said. "We can talk after you've done whatever you have to do in there."

She glared at him. "Pee. I have to pee. And can we hurry?"

He unlocked the door and gave her directions to the bathroom. "I'll wait for you outside."

She rocketed through the great room and took a left down the hallway. While in the bathroom, she looked it over. The colors were muted, and nothing unusual stood out. It was a typical guest bathroom, clean and surprisingly neat.

Afterward, to satisfy her curiosity she traipsed down the hall to the master bedroom in search of something that would attest to his character, or reveal a secret, but the room was uninspired, typically male with masculine colors, beige and brown comforter and pillow shams, the bed neatly made.

She went into the guest bedroom, but again, nothing exciting, save for a little more color, a green bedspread with yellow accents. Both rooms were sterile, no pictures or knickknacks, nothing that would give her a clue about him.

She continued into the third bedroom, which he'd made into a study. A cherry wood desk took center stage. A bookcase covered one wall, and she perused the books to garner an idea of his reading tastes. Most were history and political books, but a few were thrillers and mysteries. On one of the shelves was a framed photo of a woman and a young girl, both with straight, mid-length blond hair and both attractive, his wife and daughter no doubt.

Kat held the picture a moment before wandering to the desk. His laptop was closed, but to one side was a stack of papers. Typed on the top page were the words "Black Cash." Whatever the hell that was. Thumbing through, she realized she was looking at a manuscript of some sort, perhaps a novel.

The front door opened and closed, and Kat swiftly set the papers in order and rushed from the room. At the end of the hall, she collided with Chance.

"We seem to be making a habit of this," he said.

"Oh, sorry." She took a healthy step back.

"I thought maybe you got lost."

"No, I was just . . ." She glanced past him, looking for an excuse to guide the conversation away from herself. Her gaze settled on the furniture. "You know, I love your modular furniture." She strode to the sofa and ran her palm over the cushions. "I like this combination of leather and fabric. What's the color? It's unusual."

"It's called thyme."

"Thyme. It's delicious."

He folded his arms and stared at her with his intense, perceptive eyes, which told her he knew exactly what she'd been up to, making her squirm a little.

She would put him on the defensive. She marched up to him and looked him in the eye. "So, why am I here? This is kidnapping, you know."

He laughed, cocking his head backward. "You're something else, Kat Summers. I offer you the use of my bathroom, and you accuse me of kidnapping."

"I never asked to come here in the first place," she countered.

"Do you ever back down?" His eyes lost their fire. He seemed suddenly weary.

"I'm sorry, really, but I'm not used to being taken somewhere against my will."

"All I wanted to do was show you how Brianna spent her time here. The other night you pushed a button, and I overreacted. I'd like to apologize."

"Why didn't you just ask me to come here?"

"Because I knew you'd refuse."

"So, you coerced me instead."

He tossed up a hand. "Yes, I admit it, but now that you're here, can we go outside? I'd like to show you what made Brianna happy." He paused. "Please, Kat."

Kat studied him for a moment. His plea seemed honest, even

emotional. Maybe she'd read him wrong. Maybe Wilma was right about Chance Eliason being a stabilizing force in Brianna's life.

Kat followed him outside to the corral where the noisy burros greeted him. Several of the animals crowded each other at the fence line, just to get near him, trying to nuzzle his arm.

"Come here." He held out his hand to Kat. "They won't hurt you." But Kat hung back, wary. "You and Brianna aren't anything alike, are you? She loved these animals. She took to them right away."

Kat inched closer but not close enough to touch them. "She always brought home strays."

"How come that quality never rubbed off on you?"

Kat shrugged. "Bad experience, I guess. I got bit by a dog when I was five. A bad tear on the arm. Something like that stays with a person."

"That explains a lot," he said. "No wonder you're afraid of Zeke. I'm sorry if I was insensitive to that."

"You didn't know," she said. "You've sure been apologizing all over the place."

"If it's warranted." He rested a foot on the lower rung of the fence, but he had to move away because one of the burros kept nosing his shoulder. "That's Mojo. He's one of the oldest jacks."

"Did you name them all?"

"Brianna did. Like I said, she loved being here."

"How did she come to work here?"

He shoved his hands in the pockets of his jeans. "I used to see her around town. One day I was sitting at the bar at Bertie's and she came in crying to Bertie about something, which I couldn't hear because of the music, but she was pretty upset. Afterward, she sat next to me, and Bertie brought her a hamburger. At the time she didn't tell me why she was crying, but she did say she wished she could earn some extra money."

Mojo tapped him in the back, and he moved farther away. "I offered

Brianna a job on Saturday and Sunday mornings, and she jumped at the chance. She'd come out here to feed and water the animals, clean the barn. She fell in love with it. She liked being in the outdoors. She was a natural on the ranch. It lifted her spirits."

Kat, though still curious about the personal relationship he'd had with her sister, didn't feel it was the right time to ask.

"What are you doing for dinner?"

"Dinner?" Did she want to spend that much time with him?

"Do you have other plans?"

She pictured herself curled up in her pajamas, holding a plate of warmed up canned stew. "Well, yes, no, not really."

He broke into a smile. "I happened to notice the contents of your grocery sack."

"You looked in my bag?" While she was snooping in his house, he was pawing through her groceries. *Touché.*

"Were you planning on having cookies and beef stew for supper?"

"Maybe I was and maybe I wasn't." Who was she kidding?

"I also noticed the frozen dinner and chips on your table last night. I don't know how you stay so trim and healthy eating like that."

"It's an art form I've perfected."

"I think you could use a lesson in nutrition," he said. "It must run in the family. I had to teach Brianna a thing or two. She used to come out here half-starved."

"That explains the vitamins and protein powder in her cupboard."

"And I got her to quit drinking so much alcohol."

"What else did you teach her?" she tossed at him. When he narrowed his eyes, giving her a cold warning stare, she knew she'd better back off. "So, are you inviting me to dinner?"

"I was, but if you're not comfortable here . . ."

"It beats spending another evening alone in that house."

"That makes me feel better."

Kat winced. "Why is it that I always put my foot in my mouth when I'm around you?"

"I must bring out the best in you." He walked past her toward the house.

He'd just delivered an insult, and Kat honestly wondered if they could spend a whole evening together without inflicting any pain.

CHAPTER 10

Chance Eliason's kitchen was bright and cheery, owing to the two sky-lights he'd added. Kat sat on a stool at the breakfast counter and watched him thin-slice a chicken breast and afterward chop and slice an array of colorful vegetables.

"This is how you should eat most every day," he said, though by his amused expression she was sure he didn't believe his advice would sink into her hard head.

She grinned at him without saying a word. On her empty stomach the wine was shooting upward, a direct route from mouth to brain.

Once he'd placed the chicken and vegetables in separate skillets, the sizzling odors blended into a tantalizing aroma. Her mouth watered with anticipation.

"More wine?"

Kat held up her partially filled glass. "Nope. This is fine."

He finished sautéing and filled two plates. She insisted on eating at the counter since it seemed less formal and felt less like a date. For some reason she felt on edge, perhaps because she hadn't had a man cook her dinner in a very long time, or perhaps it was the wine.

While they ate, the conversation remained neutral. They discussed the weather, how different the climate was in Rosswood compared to

Seattle. He brought up the town's history and explained to her how mining had played an important role in its settlement.

After the meal he asked her to sit with him in the living room. With food in her stomach, the dizzying effects of the wine had diminished.

"Do you mind if I take off these shoes? I've been in them all day. They're Brianna's, and they're a little too snug."

"By all means. Make yourself at home." He picked up the bottle of wine and refilled their glasses. He sat in one of the corner units of the modular sofa while she sat in the middle with her feet propped up on the coffee table. "Comfy?"

She nodded. "Thank you for cooking me dinner. It was scrumptious."

"My pleasure."

Some time went by before Kat spoke. "May I ask you something?"

"Of course."

"What's the story with all the donkeys? I mean, you don't seem like that type of man to me."

"What type is that?"

"You don't seem like the type to live in a place like this and to live a life taking care of animals. Wilma said you'd only been here five years, about the time Brianna moved here."

"It didn't take you long to find the town gossip."

"If you don't want to tell me."

"It's no secret why I came here, if you really want to know."

"I do."

He took a deep breath in and let it out. "Long story short, I was working in Boston when Meredith and our daughter, Stella, moved to Seattle. While Meredith was there, she was diagnosed with cancer. I took a leave of absence from my job and came out here to be with her and help her through the chemo. It was an aggressive form of cancer. When she died six months later, I never went back."

"I'm sorry about your wife."

"Ex-wife. We'd been divorced several years."

"Really. Not many men, or women for that matter, would do what you did, sacrifice their time and energy for an ex-partner."

"I never fell out of love, even though she filed for the divorce. But that's another story." He broke eye contact with Kat, giving her the feeling the recollection was painful.

"Why did you decide to stay out here?"

"Taking care of someone dying of cancer changes your outlook on life, what's important and what isn't," he said. "I couldn't stomach the job anymore, and I had Stella to think about. I scouted the area, found this ranch, and turned in my resignation. Shortly after that I got interested in saving the wild burros in the Southwest from being shot or sold to pet food companies. I had all this land to put to use, and for once in my life I wanted to do something meaningful."

"You sound somewhat bitter about your job," Kat said. "What was it that you did for a living?"

In an instant the compassion in his eyes melted away. "That, I don't want to talk about." He smiled at her again. "What I do want to talk about is you, and if everything Brianna said about you is true."

Kat hugged her glass and drew her knees to her chest, wondering just what secrets Brianna had revealed. "And what exactly did she tell you?"

"Nothing bad, I can assure you. In fact she raved about how smart you are and what a successful realtor you turned out to be, considering your background."

"What did she say about my background?" That information was sacred, not to be bandied about.

"Nothing specific, only that you pulled yourself out of a messy situation and made something of yourself. I'm curious about what you went through."

"Like you, I don't care to discuss my past." Aware of the intensity in his eyes, she lowered her gaze and stared into her wineglass.

A dog's barking cut into the moment. Chance excused himself and opened the front door a crack. After conversing with someone named Rusty, he brought Zeke inside by the collar and walked him toward the kitchen. Zeke wiggled and whined, trying to jerk free to get to Kat. But Chance held tight and guided him all the way through without letting go. Kat heard the inside door leading to the garage open and close. Chance came back and took his seat.

"Because of me, poor Zeke has to stay out in a cold garage."

"It's not going to hurt him." Chance picked up the bottle of wine and offered her more, but she refused. He poured more for himself.

He'd had at least two full glasses of wine and didn't show it in the least; he neither slurred his words nor raised his voice as people tended to do when they drank too much.

Kat was beginning to feel lightheaded again and therefore brave enough to ask a question that might launch her into the same dangerous territory as the night before. "May I ask you something?" So much for control.

"Anything within reason."

Within reason? Inhibitions, be damned. She set her glass on the table. "I want to know more about your relationship with Brianna, everything." But the warmth in his eyes cooled, just like it had the previous night. "I didn't mean it that way. Honestly. Just let me explain."

"How *did* you mean it?"

She suddenly wished she hadn't pursued this line of questioning. "I know Brianna worked here, and you spent time with her for a year."

"Your point is?"

"You're a very attractive man," she said. "Why didn't you and Brianna become more than friends? It only seems natural."

"Haven't you ever been friends with a man?"

"Sure. Well, maybe, the ones I've worked with anyway."

"I'm not attracted to every woman I meet," he said, raising his voice a notch. "Brianna was beautiful, yes, and under different circumstances I might have pressed for more than friendship, but your sister was very vulnerable, Kat, and I don't go after women who are that vulnerable. Brianna needed support, not another relationship. Does that answer your question?"

"Yes, and you can pull in your fangs. I wasn't accusing you of anything."

He draped his arm over the cushion and relaxed back. "I've done it again, haven't I?"

"If you mean jumped down my throat for no good reason, I'd have to say yes, but I won't hold that against you." She drew her knees closer to her chest and began to rub the tops of her feet.

"Cold?"

"No matter how much wine I drink, or how high the heat is, my feet are always cold."

He scooted toward her. "Here, let me help." He laid her feet in his lap and ran his large, warm hands over the tops and under the arches, massaging again and again.

"This is heaven," she purred, her eyes drifting shut. When she opened them again, he was smiling that sultry smile of his. She worked at ignoring the tingles shimmering up her legs. Get back in control, Kat. Ask anything. "Can you tell me about Brianna's relationship with Tim Holmes? Wilma told me a few things."

"I'll tell you what I know," he said. "After Brianna was working here a while, she began to trust me more, and that was when she started opening up about her personal life. She told me the reason she was upset the night I saw her at Bertie's was because she'd just broken it off with him.

Did you know he was married?"

"Wilma told me."

"Brianna wanted him to get a divorce, and he refused, so she cut him off."

"Did she tell you how he reacted?"

"She said he was furious, and soon after that he came out here to the ranch, and they argued. I had to run him off."

"Poor Brianna," she said. "I bet everyone in town hated her."

"Something like that happens, and people take sides."

"So, did he eventually leave her alone?"

"He never came back out here, and she never mentioned him again."

Kat's feet were toasty warm because of Chance's huge, hot hands, and she was swept into that dreamy, tingly feeling again. She fought for control. "I'm really grateful to you for helping Brianna when she needed it and helping turn her life around."

"I can't take credit for that," he said. "She worked hard that year to straighten herself out."

"But you offered her the opportunity to do something productive."

"Well, yes, but she was also beginning to sell her stories, and that raised her spirits, too."

"I just don't understand it," Kat said. "If she was doing so well, why would she kill herself? Everyone in this town has been telling me how well she was doing."

"I never understood that either," he said. "I was out of town the week it happened. I was shocked when I came back and heard the news."

"Did you ever read any of her stories?"

"When I asked her to bring them over, she told me they were children's stories and said I'd be bored. I never pressed the subject."

"You know, it's odd. The postman told me she was still sending them out, although not so often, but he never mentioned anything about her selling them."

"Maybe she didn't tell him."

"He seemed to know everything about the subject." Kat glided into thought. When she focused again, she was sure Chance had moved closer. Panicked he might do something rash, like try to kiss her, she swung her feet to the floor and grabbed her shoes.

"What's the hurry?"

Her current picture of Chance was that of a very admirable man, and she wanted to keep it that way. In all honesty though, she didn't trust herself. One more flutter of those dark eyelashes was all it would take to push her over the edge into a place she unquestionably didn't want to go. When she'd finished tying her shoes, she looked up and saw Chance at the door, keys in hand.

All the way back to Brianna's house, he talked about his trips to Nevada to rescue wild burros and how he stayed home now and took in abused animals from the surrounding area. He talked as if nothing out of the ordinary had passed between them. Perhaps the chemistry was a figment of her imagination. Perhaps he hadn't inched closer to her at all. Perhaps he wasn't going to kiss her. She felt like a fool for even having these thoughts and for ending the evening as abruptly as she had. It had to be the wine.

When they finally arrived at Brianna's house, Kat was relieved to be on her own turf again. But something was wrong. The light was on inside, and she had no recollection of leaving it on.

Keeping her thoughts to herself, she exited the truck. Like a gentleman, he escorted her into the house and set her grocery bag on the end table.

"Thank you for dinner," she said. "After tonight, it's going to be hard to want to eat the beef stew I bought today."

"You're welcome to come back tomorrow night," he said. "I have a whole collection of recipes."

"It's tempting, but I have to concentrate on getting this place in order."

"Why don't you take down my phone number in case you change your mind?"

After he wrote his number on the pad she'd given him, she reached for the doorknob, expecting him to take the hint, but he stood firm. She waited for him to say whatever he had to say, but instead of talking, he raised her chin and brushed her lips with a soft, subtle kiss, a kiss that left her wanting more.

"Goodnight, Kat Summers."

She stood in the doorway, watching him stroll to his truck, her heart swaying with his every step, but the phone's shrill ring jarred her out of her fantasy mood. "Damn that phone." Without thinking it through, she clamped onto the receiver and barked a hello.

A short pause, followed by rapid breathing, and then a click.

She left the receiver off the hook and waited for the bothersome warning beep to end. The call was pure coincidence. But was the light on a coincidence? She couldn't remember leaving the lamp on.

The house was cold and drafty. The bedroom curtains were rippling in the breeze. She slammed the window shut and locked it in place. She could have sworn she closed the windows before she left the house, but had she locked them? She needed more sleep. That was a fact.

She quickly dressed in her pajamas and wedged a chair under the doorknob, just to be safe. To keep her mind off her unfounded fears, she climbed into bed and thought of Chance and the kiss, the unexpected yet thoroughly satisfying kiss. She melted into sleep, into what felt like a dream.

A sharp, squealing sound, like a siren, whistled in her ear, but no visual accompanied it, no ambulance or police car. She grasped for the meaning but tumbled into consciousness. She forced her eyes open.

At the foot of the bed was a filmy likeness of Brianna. Kat sat up to get a better look, but the image was sucked into the shadows. The house creaked twice, then grew deathly still.

Kat refused to give credence to what had just happened. She took solace in the fact that soon she'd be finished in Rosswood, finished with Brianna's affairs, and hopefully with closure there would be an end to these tormenting visions.

She checked the stability of the chair guarding the door, went in search of the Valium, her body quivering from the inside out. For the next several hours, she wanted her senses dulled.

≈

Chance couldn't sleep. His covers hung half on the floor. Too much wine. Too much conversation. Too much of Kat Summers, or not enough. He'd had a taste of her. He swept his fingers across his lips, the lips that had kissed hers. She tasted as sweet as a summer's breeze.

At times the woman was a pain in the rear. Speaking of rears, he pictured her shapely backside. He lost himself in the memory of the day she'd first come to town, the day he'd helped her with her car. The recollection was as clear as if she were standing in the room now.

As he recalled, she'd been leaning over the opened hood, her jacket hiked above her waist, and those tight, tight jeans squeezing that beautiful rear end. He could have embraced her on the spot.

But why torture himself? In time Kat Summers would be out of his life forever.

For a diversion he wandered into the study to go over his notes for Saturday's meeting. If he handled it right, he hoped to convince the townsfolk to run the likes of Wheeler out of Rosswood once and for all.

Looking across the room, he noticed the frame housing the photo of Meredith and Stella wasn't lined up quite right. On further inspection, the dust around the edges had been disturbed.

Even his manuscript wasn't perfectly stacked the way he'd left it. A few inside papers were askew.

The only other person in the house had been Kat Summers. She came in to use the bathroom and if he remembered right, she'd taken more time than she needed to.

Had she discovered his novel, which happened to be based on his life? If so, how much had the woman read, and how much of his past had she uncovered?

He felt a rise of indignation. His life's story would be revealed to the world in his time and his time alone. He relaxed with a breath. But how could he fault Kat for wanting to know more about him when he was determined to learn everything about her?

CHAPTER 11

The Rosswood Community Church, nearly as old as the town itself, had been updated over the years, re-roofed and repainted inside and out a number of times, but its basic timbered structure remained sound and sturdy. It provided space, both religious and secular, for church services, baptisms, weddings, town meetings, and potlucks. Its pastor offered comfort and counseling to everyone in the town, parishioners and non-parishioners alike, holding a wealth of secrets, including his own.

Word made it back to Chance that Pastor Fletcher did confess a personal transgression in front of the congregation, giving no detail, admitting only that he'd lost his way. He offered to step down as the town's pastor, but not knowing the specific nature of the sin, the church folk gave him a vote of confidence, and he remained in his post.

Because of the proximity of the church to Brianna's house, with no other houses in between, no one in town saw him take his morning detours, nobody knew for sure where he'd gone or what he'd done. There was only speculation. By the time his wife told everything she suspected to Wilma, the congregation had already rallied around him.

Today Chance hoped the people would rally around the idea of booting Nate Wheeler and his planned development project out of Rosswood. The weather was dreary, the sky overcast, and the wind had revved up again, not a particularly good omen; the people of Rosswood thrived on sunshine.

As he approached the church, he was heartened to see the parking lot nearly full and cars lined along the street. Some of the residents were making their way on foot, even Mrs. Frazier, the old woman who lived in the corner house. He tipped his hat to her.

He found an empty space next to the sheriff's cruiser. Sheriff Holmes had backed in and was leaning against the hood with his heel on the bumper, gnawing on a piece of straw and surveying the crowd. Chance emerged from his truck with a notebook in hand.

"Looks like a good turnout," Holmes said.

"Are you joining us?"

"Yeah, but since Brianna, your little attack dog, isn't at this meeting, I don't anticipate any trouble."

The reference to Brianna irritated Chance, but he had more important things to do than debate with the sheriff. He took notice of the people entering the church. Wilma supported the arm of Mrs. Frazier as they walked up the final steps. They were followed by two older gentlemen.

"I don't think you'll have any problems today," Chance said.

"Let's keep it that way."

"Is that a threat, Sheriff?"

Holmes shrugged. "Just doing my civic duty."

Inside, the sheriff broke to the right, and Chance walked down the left outside aisle and sat in the front row next to Hank.

The interior of the church had recently been painted stark white with paint Hank had acquired at a discount store in Benton. When the women of the congregation objected, Pastor Fletcher said the color would help raise spirits during the dark grays of winter. With that everyone agreed.

The pews were filling up with no elbow room to spare, and by the time the pastor closed the door, people were lined against the walls. He strode down the center aisle and stationed himself behind the lectern. The low-level chatter trickled to silence.

"You all know why we're here today, so I'd like to ask Chance to come forward and proceed with the meeting." He exchanged places with Chance.

Chance peered at the faces staring back at him, mostly middle-aged and older with a spattering of youth. Skimming the crowd, he zeroed in on Wilma Combs, Lenny and Clare Faulkes, Bertie sitting next to Tim Holmes and his wife, June, and Patsy Fletcher next to her husband. Doug Jones leaned against the back wall to the right. The doctor came in late and edged to the left.

Chance could already discern those folks, unlike him, who favored the development project, simply by observing their body language: slumping bodies with arms crossed and a ready-to-fight look in their eyes. He'd been in situations like this many times before, and he welcomed the challenge of bringing those individuals around to his way of thinking, although the longer he lived here, the more he realized the people of Rosswood, his adopted family, were a particularly stubborn lot.

To help ease the tension in the room, he relaxed into a smile. "Good afternoon, everyone. Thank you for coming today. We'll try to keep this short. Nate Wheeler was invited to attend, but—"

The door creaked open and all heads swiveled toward the back of the church. Kat had entered. The doctor made room for her against the back wall. Chance acknowledged her with a nod, and she returned his nod with a slight smile.

"As I was saying," Chance continued, punctuating his words, "Nate Wheeler was invited to attend. That's why I scheduled the meeting so late, to give him time to get here, but I haven't heard back, so I'm assuming he isn't showing up."

Whispers were exchanged, along with a few groans and hisses. Then a young man in the back row shouted, "Brianna whaled on him so bad, he ain't never coming back."

A collective intake of breath followed. The woman sitting next to the young man who'd blurted out the tactless remark elbowed him in the ribs. Heads turned toward Kat, who raised a hand and shook her head as if to assure everyone what was said wasn't a problem. Even from a distance, Chance could see her face pale.

He pounded the lectern with his fist three times to draw attention away from Kat and raised his voice. "I say we proceed without Nate Wheeler. We've heard his side, how he wants to bring this expansive development to Rosswood. Now it's time to voice our opinions, so we can bring our concerns to the county commissioners."

"What's the point, Eliason," Tim Holmes argued. "This town will never agree on this thing."

Holmes's comment rankled Chance, but he stayed calm. "All opinions count, no matter what they are, and we need to hear from everyone before this development gets off the ground."

He cleared his throat. "As a review for those of you who weren't at the last meeting, Nate Wheeler and Associates have already purchased acreage off Randall Road and are in the planning stage of building a resort, which includes a one-hundred-room hotel and lodge, two eating establishments, and an eighteen-hole golf course. In order to accommodate this project, a massive amount of trees will have to be sacrificed, thus destroying natural wildlife habitats."

"How can they get away with that?" yelled a man from the left side of the room. "What about the environmental laws?"

"That's a big issue," Chance replied. "From what I understand, Wheeler is in the process of acquiring the necessary building permits.

But considering the current political climate, leaning toward business, plus the desire to increase tourism in the state, I'd say he won't have a problem."

"They could drive out the deer," an older man grumbled. "Come hunting season, there'd not be a damn thing to hunt."

A low mumbling spread through the room.

"There's also the possibility that once they finish this project, they won't stop," Chance reminded them. "They'll want to build homes to go with their resort, and more people will flood into this area, people who don't have a healthy respect for the land."

"They'll take our water," spouted a bearded man close to Kat. "And pretty soon they'll need roads and such. Along with the land values, our taxes will go up."

Bertie stood and waited for the roar of disapproval to subside. "Have you ever thought you might be blowing this out of proportion? Let's think positive for a minute. Think of the business that size project could pull in and the money that comes along with it."

Lenny's wife, Clare, cranked her head in Bertie's direction. "Hey, Bertie, they'll have their own restaurants. You could go out of business yourself."

Bertie shook her head. "I don't think so. People have to eat. They'll trickle into town just for something different. It will increase my business."

"Phooey," hooted a woman's voice.

Bertie glared across the aisle at her cousin Wilma. "You got something to say?"

"Yeah, I got something to say." Wilma stretched tall. "That resort will have its own beauty salon, and that can't be good for my business."

"If you were any good," Bertie taunted, "you wouldn't have to worry about it."

Wilma and Bertie glowered at each other like two boxers ready to fight. Everyone else snickered.

"Ladies," Chance said, and they both sat down. "Let's not get personal. Would anyone else like to comment?"

Tim Holmes rose, and a man named Earl, standing against the wall along the side aisle, raised a fist to him. Everyone knew the bad blood between Tim and Earl, stemming from high school when Tim stole June from under Earl's nose, so no one in the room took offense when Earl's middle finger inched up. Tim clenched his own fist and eyeballed Earl.

"Tim," Chance said, "did you have something to say?"

Tim scowled at Earl one last time. "What I was going to say was, people have cars and cars break down. I could use the extra business. What about you, Hank?"

Hank glanced back at Tim and snarled, "What about me?"

"Your business would get a boost," Tim said. "People need to buy food and beer. And what about the souvenirs? You stand to make a real profit."

"I like things the way they are." Hank turned back around and crossed his arms, frowning.

"What about you, Lenny?" Tim said.

Lenny's face flushed the color of his hair. With his green shirt and khaki-colored pants, he looked like an upside down beet. "I've got enough mail to take care of. I'm overworked as it is." Clare pinched his arm, and he added, "I mean *we're* overworked." Chuckles erupted all around him, and his face contorted into misery.

Looking toward the back of the room, Chance noticed the doctor cozy up to Kat and whisper in her ear. "May I say something?" she said to the crowd, and everyone twisted around and stared.

Chance was relieved to direct the discussion again. "If you have something to contribute, please do, Ms. Summers."

"I know I'm not part of this community," she said, glancing at the inquisitive faces around her, "but I am a real estate agent, and I can give you my perspective. You see, I've had a lot of experience observing how communities like yours adjust to these types of projects. Most times there are the usual objections that you've all voiced here, but generally these are based on fear—fear of the unknown. Afterward, people adjust fine, and the influx of tourists and money generated from said development usually compensates for any negative consequences that come with it. And also, think about the increase in jobs. Your kids won't have to leave this community to find work."

The crowd faced forward and waited for Chance to make a comment, but a woman in the back shouted, "I agree with her. I don't want my boy to leave town."

A man said, "Yeah, and what about building the resort? We could make damn good money."

"That's a crock, Carl," Hank said. "That weasel Wheeler will bring in his own crew from outside, and as far as 'afterward' goes, how would you like working as a maid?"

Someone launched a wolf whistle. The room rocked with laughter.

"It's better than what I do now," shouted a young woman who worked for Bertie.

"Well, if you don't like it, Sue Ann—"

"Bertie, please," Chance said while pounding the lectern. When he glanced toward the back of the room, Kat had disappeared.

"What about the noise," someone yelled. "It just won't be the same."

Others chimed in, and the meeting continued for another half hour. Finally, Chance weighed in. "Listen, everyone. I've heard a lot of arguments today, pro and con, but no matter how you feel about it, can we at least agree there needs to be an in-depth study of the effects this proposed development will have on our community?"

Some people nodded, some didn't.

"To address our concerns over water and wildlife issues, I think we should demand that the county ask for an Environmental Impact Statement. Can we agree on that? Raise your hands."

Chance scanned the crowd as hands rose. His gaze fell to the middle of the room. "Bertie, can we agree this development needs more scrutiny?"

She nodded and reluctantly raised a hand.

"How about you, Tim?"

Tim shrugged. "Whatever."

"All right then." Chance opened his notebook and held up a piece of paper. "I've written up our concerns in this petition, which I will take to the county. I ask that you sign it before you leave here. Are there any questions?"

Sue Ann raised a hand. "If I sign this, does it mean I'm against Wheeler's idea?"

"Let me assure you," Chance replied, "all of you, this is not a vote against the development. It merely asks the county to force Wheeler to study the project more thoroughly before he proceeds. Are there any other questions?"

Everyone looked side to side at their neighbors, but no one spoke up.

Chance set a pen and the petition on a chair near the lectern. "Don't forget to sign before you leave. This meeting is adjourned." While people lined up and down the center aisle, he called the pastor over.

"Good meeting, Chance. A lot accomplished today," the pastor said.

Recalling Kat's unwelcome remarks, Chance thought otherwise. "I have an urgent errand to run, Pastor. Would you mind collecting the petition after everyone signs it? I'll pick it up later this week."

"Anything to help."

Chance wove past people in line, stopping now and then to shake hands and to listen to comments. Tim Holmes and his wife hadn't lined up like the others and left the church in front of Chance. To soothe his nerves, Chance let the cool air ripple over him, but nothing would ease the tension he felt.

The sheriff stood next to the cruiser with the door opened and waited for Chance to walk by. "Relatively calm in there. Not like the last time, but you're beating a dead horse. You'll never stop Wheeler."

"I would think you'd want him stopped, Sheriff. More people, more headaches for you, more ugly business thrown your way."

"I could use the business." He slid into the front seat and throttled the engine.

Tim Holmes's truck followed the cruiser out of the parking lot. Chance watched father and son drive away. Wheeler wasn't the only person he wished would leave the community.

Chance climbed into his pickup. Now to the real business at hand: a talk with Kat Summers.

CHAPTER 12

Kat was totally exhausted. The Valium she'd taken the night before had made her loopy, and all morning she'd roamed the house in a fog, but it was better than allowing her rational mind to ponder last night's shocking image of Brianna's ghost.

The best thing to do, she'd decided, was to perform physical tasks, work her muscles to the bone, or go for a jog. She opted for cleaning the house, one room at a time, as if by nightfall all this effort would sweep the images out of the house, out of her mind.

By afternoon the kitchen had been the only room scrubbed. After a refreshing shower she'd wandered outside to take in the fresh air. On her walk she noticed the cars at the church and remembered the town meeting from the flyer Chance had brought into the beauty salon. Curious, she'd gone inside.

She hadn't planned to say anything, but the doctor had voiced his view to her about the possibilities of new blood coming into this community, and she'd spoken up. The harsh and unforgiving look on Chance's face was enough to drive her from the church. The man had a side to him that gave her a chill.

She scraped the last of the beef stew into a pan and placed it on the stove. It looked and smelled like dog food, the gravy variety.

One look at the phone reminded her she'd forgotten to have it disconnected. Come Monday, she'd take care of it for sure. She toyed with the idea of placing the receiver in its cradle, but the thought of another idiot phone call persuaded her to leave the receiver dangling.

A pounding on the door rattled her already frayed nerves. She answered it tired, hungry, and in an irascible frame of mind. Chance stared back at her with the same nasty look she'd received at the church.

"What do you want?" she asked him curtly, but she'd already guessed why he was here.

"I have something to say to you, Ms. Summers."

"Ooh, Ms. Summers. Am I supposed to be scared?"

"Maybe."

His flippant tone aggravated her, and if he wanted a fight, she intended to give him one. "I'm not sure I should let you in with this cantankerous attitude of yours, but I'm curious." She moved aside, watching him set his hat on the end table. "So, you plan to stay a while."

Glaring, he grabbed the hat and stuck it on his head.

"Honestly." She rolled her eyes in disgust.

He marched to the phone and slammed the receiver in place. "Don't you ever hang it up?"

"Aren't we considerate."

"That's more than I can say for you."

"Would you like to explain that comment, along with your hostile behavior?"

He faced her with a fierce stare. "Next time you barge into a meeting where you don't belong, mind your own business."

"Are you referring to the contribution I made? If I remember right, you were happy to have an informed contribution."

"Informed, my ass. You don't know anything about this community."

She dug her fists into her hips. "I'm a real estate professional, Mr.

Eliason, and everything I said in that meeting was the truth."

"Ooh, a real estate professional," he said, mocking her.

She felt all the energy in her body swarm to her head in a feverish flush. When she finally found her voice, all she could say was, "You don't know a damn thing."

"I know one thing," he said. "You real estate people are all alike. You and the developers would bulldoze the life out of a community for the almighty dollar."

The veins in Kat's head throbbed. "That's not fair."

"And another thing, Ms. Summers, you're nothing like your sister. She knew what was important and what wasn't. She hated the idea of the resort."

"Aha!" Kat walked up to him, aiming her index finger, and jabbed him in the chest. "This isn't about the development. This is about how you like your women."

"What?"

She kept jabbing, emphasizing every other word. "You want the women around you to follow along with your ideas and not have an opinion of their own. Is that why you couldn't stay married?"

One more jab, and he grabbed her by the wrist. "Don't drag my marriage into this conversation. You know nothing about it."

The phone rang. Kat's shoulders hunched with tension. Her head jerked toward the sound. Chance let go of her arm, but she wouldn't move.

"Aren't you going to answer it?"

She ignored him.

"What's the matter?" He stepped in the direction of the phone.

"No. Don't."

He disregarded her warning. After a few seconds on the line, he slammed down the receiver and looked at Kat, concerned. "Have you been getting strange calls while you've been here? Is that why you leave the phone off the hook?"

"Something like that."

Chance grabbed the receiver and let it fall. The warning signal stopped beeping just as the cord twisted and grew still. "I suggest you have it disconnected."

"I'm planning to."

He grasped her elbow to nudge her toward the sofa. "You better sit down. I forgot to tell you something about Brianna when you were at the ranch."

"Why? Is it that bad that I should sit? I prefer to stand."

"Fine." He let go of her arm. "After Brianna broke up with Tim Holmes, she started getting calls."

"What, like the man hung up when she answered?"

"That, and sometimes he would say things or just breathe into the phone. She could never figure out who it was because the voice was always disguised or muffled in some way."

Kat shivered at the thought that both she and Brianna were victims of these phone calls. It seemed too much of a coincidence.

"Are you all right?"

"Sure, why not?"

"Your hands are shaking." He wrapped his hands around hers. "What is it, Kat?"

"This is so weird, Chance, but shortly after Brianna died, I started getting those same kinds of calls at my home in Seattle."

"And now here. Do you have any idea who it might be? Can you think of anyone who knows both of you?"

"It's highly unlikely. We ran in different circles. But whoever it is probably thinks Brianna is still alive. Why else would he keep calling here?"

"Unless . . ."

"Unless, what?"

"What if he *is* the same man who's been calling you in Seattle and he *does* know Brianna is dead? If he's calling you here now, then he knows you're in town. I don't like the feel of this. I think you should stay at the ranch. I have a perfectly good guest room."

"That's impossible," she said. "I have work to do here. When I get home, if the jerk keeps calling me, I'll notify the police. It's probably just a stupid prank."

"That's the best case scenario, but I don't think this is a time to be stubborn."

"I really appreciate your concern, but this is just a silly coincidence. Nothing has ever come of it, and it never will. I'm fine here alone."

Chance ran the back of his hand over her cheek. "I think you're downplaying this too much."

"I'm not."

"I think you are," he said, "but I won't argue with you. You have my number in case you change your mind. I'll check on you tomorrow."

"That's not necessary."

"I'll come by tomorrow."

A part of her wished she'd taken him up on his offer, yet she still didn't trust herself to get that close to him. She'd always condemned Brianna for her involvement with married men, but the truth was Kat had her own demons. She had a weakness for men like Chance Eliason. For her he was trouble with a capital T. She hadn't been with a man in three years, and if she fell for him she was likely to fall hard.

She went back to the kitchen to reheat the stew. Her gaze fell on the dangling phone cord. Was the man calling Brianna the same pervert calling her? Perhaps Maggie was right. She should have gone to the police.

The stew tasted bland, mushy, and totally disgusting. To mask the flavor, she munched on crumbs from the opened potato chip bag. She held up the wine bottle, checking for how much was left, and poured a half glass. If Maggie could see her now, Kat was sure this wasn't what she had in mind when she told Kat to go on a vacation. This definitely wasn't the Ritz.

Kat checked her watch. The time was after seven. Going to bed early had its benefits. She could catch up on her sleep and block out any anxieties concerning those irritating phone calls. Then again, there were the visions to consider, the visions that hadn't stopped.

A knock at the door reminded her it hadn't been locked. She parted the curtains. No cars were parked out front or in the driveway. She leaned her weight against the door, thinking how silly her fears were, and asked who it was.

"Pastor Fletcher."

The name brought to mind Wilma's story about Brianna's first conquest, and Kat stared at him in the opened doorway in a cold, inhospitable manner. "What do you want?"

Startled, he hesitated answering. He wore the same clothes from the meeting: dark slacks and a baggy black cardigan over a white shirt. The color of his nose was a deeper shade of pink than the rest of his face, his dark, bushy eyebrows wiry and untamed. "I wondered if I might have a minute of your time." He tried persuading her with a smile. For added strength, he hugged a Bible to his chest.

"Well, then, come in."

Clutching the Bible tighter, he walked cautiously to the sofa, his eyes wide and searching. "I'll only stay a minute."

She took the wine bottle to the kitchen, though she wasn't sure why she'd made the effort. She sat across from him at the table. No way would she sit next to him.

The pastor glanced into the bedroom and hastily brought his

attention back to Kat. "My wife is waiting for me at the church. She's the one who suggested I drop by tonight to invite you to attend Sunday services tomorrow. She's a very thoughtful person, my wife, always thinking of others. Patsy, her name is Patsy.

"I saw you at the meeting earlier," he continued. "I felt very badly about Bri . . . about the loss of your sister. I thought maybe a church service might offer you comfort. Are you of any particular denomination? Well, no matter, all are welcome. Did you say how long you will be in town? If you're staying a while, we would surely welcome you to our congregation."

He was getting on Kat's nerves, and she had no intention of attending church services. To put an end to the ramblings of this hypocritical man, she leaned forward and pierced him with a stare. "I know about you and my sister, Pastor."

He swallowed with great difficulty while squeezing the life out of his Bible. "Whoever told you that?"

"Then it's not true?"

"Well, now, in a sense it is true that I strayed, but only in my mind. I admit I had lustful thoughts, but I never acted on them. I mean no disrespect to the memory of your sister, but she could be very, shall we say, tempting." His eyebrows squirmed like caterpillars.

Kat wasn't about to let the blame fall on Brianna. "And you couldn't get up and walk out of this house?"

"I was weak, and she was a beautiful woman, like you."

"Why did you keep coming back?"

"Because I thought I could talk her into attending church, but . . . the flesh is weak. My thoughts would stray."

Kat stood. "I think you should go."

"You won't tell, will you? I've made peace with myself and my wife, and my congregation. If you stir this thing up again, it will only muddy

Brianna's name, and you wouldn't want to do that to poor Brianna, may she rest in peace." Kat's incensed look drove him to the door. "I'll take my leave, then, and by the way, when did you say you were leaving Rosswood?"

"Goodnight."

Grasping his Bible, he hurried down the street, muttering to himself. The man was dripping with guilt, but with Brianna gone, no one would ever know the truth. At least he wouldn't be bothering Kat again.

Kat craved a hot bath with steam rising through fragrant bubbles. A shower would have to do, anything to rinse off the energy of the day.

In bed by nine she woke later in the night from her cell phone tinkling its high-pitched melody. She rolled over on her stomach, plunged her hand into her purse, and fished for the metal object. Maggie had better have a good excuse for calling this late. "Maggie?"

Silence, a twitter of laughter, then "Pussssycat."

Kat snapped the phone shut. The call was a splash of cold water. Wide awake now, she made sure the door was locked. The night was jet black, no stars shining through the branches, only a twinkle of light coming from the direction of the church.

She lay awake in bed, her mind playing catch up with her heart. He'd called her Pussycat, same as the jerk in Seattle. And instead of calling Brianna's landline, he'd called Kat's cell phone.

She checked her cell for the last incoming call and punched in the number. It connected to voice mail.

In Seattle the man never called her cell. His calls were always on her landline; he never deviated. How did he get her cell phone number? Then it struck her. The ad at the post office. She'd written the number on the ad. Unless he'd followed her from Seattle, the man lived in Rosswood.

She let her mind meander further along that line of thinking. If the man was in Rosswood, was he the same one who'd harassed Brianna? If he was someone Brianna knew, why would he harass Kat? It didn't make sense. As she'd told Chance, she and Brianna ran in different circles. Unless the calls to Brianna and the calls to Kat were totally unrelated. But that seemed unlikely. It was too much of a coincidence. The calls to Kat had started up immediately after Brianna's death.

Whoever the prankster was, Kat wanted the calls stopped. If he lived in this small town, there was a good chance she could discover who he was and put an end to the calls once and for all.

Until now he'd been lucky since neither she nor Brianna had caller ID. By calling her cell phone, he was slipping up. The key to his identity lay in finding the owner of the phone number.

CHAPTER 13

Sunday morning came too soon for Kat. She stretched and yawned and closed her eyes again and forced herself to get up. Over jeans she wore another of Brianna's shirts, a gray-and-red plaid wool, hoping to stave off the day's chill.

She'd left Seattle for the purpose of de-stressing, but because of the strange calls and haunting visions—both of which she'd hoped would stop by now—her nerves were still on edge, and she'd lost even more sleep. Leaving Rosswood immediately seemed like the logical course of action, but she had no guarantee these disturbing occurrences wouldn't hound her when she got home.

The first thing to take care of was ripping the ad off the bulletin board. Though the damage had already been done, she still wanted her phone number erased from public view.

On her way outside, a scruffy-haired tabby, a kitten about six months old, dashed from around the corner of the garage and tried to worm its way into the house. Wrinkling her nose, Kat nudged the kitten with her foot. "Go on now." But the kitten stood its ground and wove back and forth against her legs. "I don't have time for this. Go away."

She closed the door, shutting the kitten out. She waited a minute, hoping the little nuisance would run off, but as she cracked the door open, the kitten nosed the gap and mewed pitifully.

Kat set a saucer of milk on the step. The kitten purred and lapped the milk as if it hadn't eaten in days. "I don't even like animals. You be gone before I come home."

While the kitten was occupied, Kat escaped to her car and proceeded down Maple Lane. The organ's punctuated tones, blaring beyond the church walls, reminded her of her conversation with the pastor. Whatever the truth behind his and Brianna's relationship, he certainly wanted Kat to leave Rosswood, to leave his less-than-holy past alone.

As she passed the church parking lot, which was filled to overflowing, it dawned on her it was a Sunday, and in Rosswood even the post office lobby was closed. That was what lack of sleep and a minimal amount of nourishment would do to a person. Nevertheless, she drove into town and parked in front of Bertie's.

Before getting out of the car, she noticed movement in the side mirror. The girl, Tilly, dressed in the same blue jacket and frayed pants, hovered near the rear fender. Kat rolled down the window and waited for the girl to make a move.

The girl crept alongside until she came within a foot of Kat's window. "Brianna was my friend," she said. "Tim wasn't Brianna's friend."

Kat twisted around. "What do you mean, 'Tim wasn't Brianna's friend'?"

Tilly inched backward and ran behind the car. Kat scooted out to pursue the girl and in the process received a stinging shock from the car's metal frame. She paused, cursing and shaking her hand. When she finally rounded the rear of the car, Tilly had vanished. What had she meant about Tim and Brianna? Hoping to catch up with her later, Kat let it go for now and followed the aroma of fries and bacon into the Grill.

Sunday morning at Bertie's was not what Kat expected. She figured most of the locals would be in church and only a few customers would trickle in for a cup of coffee or an early lunch. But the Grill was crowded and had the usual jukebox blare and click, clack of the pool balls. Up front near the bar she found a small booth.

In her initial sweep of the room, she didn't recognize anyone. Most of the customers were men younger than Kat. When she peered at the pool tables, her stomach hitched. Staring back at her was Doug Jones, the man who'd made the crude remark about her at the grocery store.

She thought about leaving, but Bertie came to her table with a coffeepot, blocking the view and breaking the connection. "You gave a good speech at the meeting." Bertie filled Kat's cup. "You got my vote."

"Thanks, but I think I alienated a few folks in the process."

"You mean Chance."

"Why would you single him out?"

"From where I was sitting, his was the only face I could see that lit up like Rudolph's nose. He must have turned ten shades of red."

"Yeah, well . . ."

"Don't mind him. He's got his views, and we got ours."

"I hope you serve breakfast here."

"Anything we can put in a sandwich."

Kat thought a moment. "How about a little cheese and bacon on toast."

"Coming right up."

Bertie started walking away, but Kat called her back. "Who are all these men in here?"

She hiked a thumb over her shoulder. "These guys? They work for an old rancher east of here. They come in here every Sunday morning, just like clockwork. Some of them are a little rough around the edges, but they pay their tabs."

"When you have a couple of minutes to spare, I'd like to ask you a few questions."

Bertie hesitated, a puzzled frown forming.

"It's about Brianna."

"I don't deal in gossip. No second-hand news."

"I know," Kat said. "It's nothing like that."

"I'll make time after I get a few orders out." She worked her way back to the kitchen and broadcast Kat's order.

Kat savored the steaming brew, richer than instant, but she yearned for a cup of Seattle's Best. To avoid making eye contact with anyone, especially the men, she snatched a newspaper from the table next to her.

Engrossed in the headlines, she suddenly smelled a hint of tobacco. Jeaned thighs butted against her table. When she finally glanced up, Doug Jones was chalking a cue stick and staring down at her. "Play pool?"

She returned her gaze to the newspaper.

"I saw you in Hank's the other day. You in town long?"

She ignored him, keeping her eyes on the paper.

"Thought we could play a friendly little game. Then I could get to know you just like I knew Brianna." He strutted back to his buddies who were hooting and laughing. One of them gave him a thumbs-up.

Kat surged with contempt.

Bertie slid Kat's order across the table and sat down. "What did he want?"

"What do you think he wanted?"

Bertie flicked a look his way. "He's a cocky son-of-a-gun."

"He made an ugly comment about Brianna. Did she know him?"

Bertie folded her hands on the table. "I don't know what happened after hours, but Brianna used to flirt a lot with these guys. I warned her against it, but she wouldn't listen to me. Said she was keeping them happy."

"Did she flirt with him?"

"I guess she did, for a while anyway, until he stopped coming in here."

"Why was that?"

"Not sure." Bertie squeezed her chin and narrowed her eyes in thought. "All I know is about three months before she died, maybe more, he just stopped frequenting this place. He started coming back again a week or so afterward. Don't know any more than that. Is that all you wanted to ask me?"

Kat rummaged in her purse and presented Bertie with a piece of paper. "Do you recognize this phone number?"

Bertie held the paper up to the light and handed it back to Kat. "Can't say that I do."

"Someone called me on my cell phone and didn't leave a message. I didn't recognize the number and wondered if it belonged to someone in Rosswood. It was probably a solicitor."

"Or a wrong number." Bertie moved to get up until Kat coaxed her back into her seat for one more question.

"Remember the remark that was made at the meeting, the one about Brianna arguing with the developer? Were you present when it happened?"

"I was there, all right." Bertie's eyes were suddenly more animated. "It was at the meeting when Wheeler first presented the project to the community. After he finished his presentation, she stood up and lit into him. I'm sure you know how emotional she could be about the things she cared about."

Kat nodded, though she hadn't been close enough to Brianna in recent years to know *what* she cared about.

"She accused Wheeler of being a land scalper and corporate hog. We didn't agree on this issue, but I had to admire the girl. She had the passion of a preacher. You should have seen the man's face. Redder than the devil. He looked like a rocket ready to launch." She shook her head, chuckling.

"Did he say anything to her?"

"There were words spoken, but I don't remember what," Bertie said. "By that time the whole church was rocking. It was noisier than all get out."

"Did you and Brianna ever talk about it afterward?"

"Not much, but she did say she was going to pay him a visit. I'm not sure she ever got the chance. Well, I've got work to do." Bertie rose from the table. "You take care."

"Thanks, Bertie."

Jones and his friends had already left the Grill, and Kat finished her breakfast with no other distractions. While she paid her bill at the bar, Sheriff Holmes took a stool nearby. She paused, wondering whether or not to mention the phone number since Tim Holmes was the one person in town who had both numbers. "Sheriff, may I talk to you a minute?"

"Have a seat." He turned to Sue Ann, who was wiping the surface in front of him. "I'll have the usual."

Kat perched on a stool and waited for Sue Ann to deliver the sheriff's coffee. "Sheriff, I know about your son's relationship with my sister."

Without reacting, he ripped open a sugar packet and emptied it into his cup.

"Do you know if he called Brianna frequently after it was over between them?"

The sheriff took his time, stirring his coffee. When his gaze met hers, Kat felt the heat. "What are you insinuating?"

Tread lightly here. "I'm not insinuating anything. I'm trying to find answers. It seems she received several calls before she died, and they're still coming in on her line."

"What sort of calls?"

"Whoever it is phones and never says much, maybe a word or two, if you know what I mean."

"And you immediately thought Tim would be the one harassing your sister."

"I didn't say he was harassing her."

"Listen, Ms. Summers, I don't know what you've heard," he said, "but let me set you straight. If anyone was getting harassed, it was Tim. He tried to break it off with your sister, and she wouldn't have any part of it. She pestered him to get a divorce, and when he refused, she wouldn't leave him alone. She'd show up at his place of business and pick fights with him in front of customers. If I recall, she threatened to ruin his business and his marriage." He paused. "Hypothetically speaking, if he was the one doing the calling, why would he keep it up after her death? What would be the point?"

"No point at all." Forget about the phone number. She planted her feet on the floor.

"Next time you go around accusing someone unjustly, I suggest you think it through."

Kat cringed at the lecture, but fought back a snappy retort. "Thank you for your time, Sheriff." She strode out of Bertie's, trading the heat for the much-needed cool air.

That didn't go well. She'd irritated the sheriff, not her intention, but in turn he did paint a different picture of Brianna and Tim's breakup than Chance did. Next time she saw Chance, she would confront him about it.

On Center Street the traffic was crawling along. A truck, older than Chance's, slowed down to let her cross.

After Saturday's meeting she was hesitant about frequenting the general store, considering her and Hank's opposing views on the development project. Though when she entered, they exchanged smiles, which was a good sign.

She left him waiting on a customer and combed the aisles for canned tamales and pinto beans. She found a can of spinach for her token green vegetable. At the counter she unloaded her goods and asked Hank if she could have a few empty boxes. While he rang up her groceries, she grabbed three. One fit, tipped on end, into another.

"You know," Hank said, after she'd returned to the counter, "some of us in town are dead-set against Wheeler's ideas."

Here we go. Time to placate. "I know that now, and I'm terribly sorry if I offended you."

"Uh-huh." Although he seemed satisfied she'd acknowledged his stand on the issue, his smile hadn't returned. He needed time to soften.

"By the way, Hank." She handed him a piece of paper. "Do you happen to recognize this number?"

He squinted against the light. "Can't say that I do." He handed the paper back to Kat and turned his attention to a woman who'd come to the counter with a newspaper.

Kat thought about Wilma. If anyone in town knew who that number belonged to, she would, but her shop was closed on Sundays. Even if it were open, Wilma was on Hank's side regarding the development project. Better let a little time pass before approaching her.

Kat tried gracefully backing out of the store with her groceries and boxes but got tangled up in the doorway. She tugged the box stuck in the doorjamb and whirled around, flustered. She'd run into Chance again.

He had on sweatpants and running shoes. His T-shirt was damp in places. His hair curled out from under a ball cap. He picked up one of the boxes that had toppled. "Need some help?"

"It would be appreciated."

He assisted in carrying the boxes across the street and stashed them in the back of her SUV. "Are you packing up?"

"I thought I better get started before I'm run out of this town."

He leaned against her car, close enough for her to smell the distinct masculine scent, perspiration mixed with a hint of citrus from his deodorant, the smell of a man who'd been exercising, a very appealing odor to Kat. It reminded her of a time she'd jogged with a boyfriend and afterward they'd ended up in bed, soaked in sweat.

"Did you take my advice and leave the phone off the hook?"

She pulled herself into the moment. "Yes." She didn't see the point in telling him about the cell phone call, didn't want to be shuttled off to his house because of his overblown opinion of some silly prank. She could handle this herself.

"Good. Now, could you give me a lift home?"

"Sure, if you don't have an ulterior motive."

He tweaked her nose. "Just asking."

She didn't believe him in the least. As she drove away from town, she could sense him scrutinizing her. "You'll have to tell me where to turn. I know it's before Pine Road," she said as they passed Maple Lane.

"Keep going straight."

"What for?" She knew she was supposed to turn soon.

"I want to check something out."

They traveled past his private drive and then past the Pine Road cutoff.

"Look up ahead."

Kat slowed to witness two men inside the development property near the bullet-riddled sign.

"Pull over," Chance said. "I want to have a word with him."

"Who?"

"Wheeler. The guy in the green shirt. Pull over."

"What are you going to say?" When he didn't reply, she swung onto the shoulder as far off the road as possible and cut the engine.

"I just want to talk to him."

By his growling tone, Kat had images of the men in some gunslinging standoff. She checked for passing cars and scurried after Chance.

Nate Wheeler was instructing a younger man with shoulder-length hair on replacing the sign when Chance yelled out, "Hey, Wheeler, are you packing it in?"

Wheeler was completely bald, and as he approached the fence where they were standing, Kat observed he'd shaved that way on purpose; his head was shiny with a slight shadow around the sides. His eyebrows, along with his tidy mustache and goatee, were a slick black. The man was younger than Chance, shorter, and sexier than she'd imagined. He had a beefy build and sharp features. He gave her an appraising once-over, then settled on Chance. "What do you want, Eliason?"

"I see you're in town and wondered why you couldn't make it to the meeting yesterday."

"Previous engagement."

"You could have notified me you weren't coming," Chance said. "That would have been the considerate thing to do."

"Too bad. I guess I'm not the considerate kind." He started walking away.

"Wait, mister."

At Kat's command the developer wheeled around and stared at her with a look of pure disgust. "And who are you?"

"I'm Kat Summers, and I want to ask you about my sister, Brianna Whitley."

"And I'm supposed to know who that is?"

"Don't be smug, Wheeler," Chance said.

"Look, lady, I didn't know your sister other than that little run-in at the church."

"I understand she planned on paying you a visit afterward."

He fished a cigarette and a lighter from his shirt pocket. He lit up, sucked in a breath, and blew out a stream of blue smoke. "One day she showed up at my office in Benton. So what?"

"May I ask what you talked about?"

"We exchanged a few words about the development." His lips twitched into a grin. "I bought her a cup of coffee as a peace offering and . . ." He took another drag off his cigarette.

"Was that all there was to it?"

"Give me a break, lady. I've got work to do." He strode back to his partner, clipping short the conversation.

Back in the car Kat said, "I don't buy it. I do believe she visited him in Benton, but I don't believe he sent her on her way. He was going to say something else about it. Did you notice his self-satisfied grin? That said everything."

"He was wearing a wedding band, if you're suggesting what I think you're suggesting."

"All the more."

"She despised the man."

"She took up with Tim Holmes, didn't she, and he's not a very likable man. She never did have good sense when it came to men. She married a man named John Whitley for about a year before she moved in with me. I had to help her untangle that mess. God, he was a cruel bastard."

"She never mentioned him. Until you came here, I never knew Whitley was a married name."

"She wouldn't have told anyone. That's a chapter in her life she wanted to forget. And so do I. He just about killed the both of us before I could rescue her away from him."

Kat made a U-turn, and Chance pointed the way to his secluded drive. As she pulled up to the house, Zeke met the car, whining and barking.

"Stay here and I'll put Zeke in the garage."

"Don't bother," she said. "I'm not getting out."

"I thought you might like a good home-cooked meal. I've got a roast in the Crock Pot. I can't eat it all myself."

She had to laugh at herself for falling into his trap. "I thought you had no ulterior motive, and what about last night? If I remember right, you were madder than hell at me."

"That was last night. I'm over my bullheaded rage. I figure we can agree to disagree and still be friends."

"Oh you do, do you?"

"Why not?"

"What about 'no ulterior motive'?"

He tweaked her nose again. "If my memory serves me, I didn't answer you on that one. Besides, I caught a peek at your groceries, and you, my lady, aren't going to make it to old age if you don't eat better than that."

She could argue with him all day, but he sat motionless. His persistence both aggravated and tantalized her. "I'll make you a deal. I really need to start sorting through Brianna's things, so I'll go to the house for a while and come back later, say around five o'clock."

"If that's as good as it gets."

CHAPTER 14

Chance Eliason was a huge, powerful sun. At a safe distance he warmed her, but venturing too close, she could get burned. Nevertheless, she felt herself being pulled into his aura. She knew the signs. She knew the game. She also knew how tired she was of short-term relationships, but she didn't have the energy to commit to anything more than that. If she could make it out of Rosswood with her heart intact, that was all she asked. "Stay strong for a few more days," she begged herself as she swung into Brianna's driveway.

She hauled the boxes into the house, tipping and almost losing control of them, and left the door ajar a little too long. The kitten slithered inside.

"I forgot about you." Kat picked up the kitten with the intent of tossing him outdoors, but he mewed and nuzzled her hand with his wet nose. "For heaven's sake, are you still hungry? I don't have anything for you besides milk unless you'll eat some beef stew."

Allowing him a sniff of the opened can, she drew him outside and emptied a portion of the stew into the saucer. The kitten plunged in, giving Kat the opportunity to sneak inside and get to work.

In the bedroom she filled a box with Brianna's underwear and T-shirts. She folded a few heavier shirts from the closet and tucked them on top. As hard as it was to handle Brianna's clothes, she blanked her mind to keep her emotions in check. So far the trick was working.

She set the box she'd seen earlier on the closet shelf on the living room rug, not knowing what to expect. In the warmth of the heater, she sat cross-legged with boots off, wiggled the top of the box free, and discovered a handful of snapshots scattered atop a stack of papers.

Kat examined a photo of the two sisters at ages three and eight, sitting with their mother on the old plaid sofa. Their mother's hair was long and flipped up on the ends. Brianna was dressed in a Pooh Bear jumpsuit, and Kat had on a blouse and corduroy pants. All three were smiling genuine smiles. Kat could see it in their sparkling eyes.

She studied the other photos: the girls at five and ten, tongues out, hamming it up; Brianna at ten in her brand new polka dot swimsuit, her hair in pigtails, taken against the backdrop of a rented cabin on the Oregon coast.

Her mood withered at the sight of the last picture: Brianna with Uncle Will. His slicked-back raven hair gleamed in the sunlight. All smiles, he had his arm over her shoulder, squeezing her to his side. But Brianna didn't mirror his enthusiasm; she stood like a stick figure with vacant eyes. The photo was ripped through Will's face, as if Brianna wanted to destroy the nightmare it represented.

Kat stared at her sister's likeness. "I'm sorry no one believed you, Brianna, least of all me." She couldn't stop the tears, and she wept until a faint, persistent mewing captured her attention.

She rescued the kitten from outdoors and scooped him into her arms. She gave the door a swift kick.

She glanced at the photo one more time, which brought up another rush of emotion. Like a cloak of steel, the guilt of the past weighed heavy on her. Too drained to do anything else, she hugged the kitten to her chest and collapsed on the couch.

≈

He peered in the window. He knew it was risky. She looked so sweet and innocent sleeping with the pussycat. He longed to touch her.

He told himself to be patient, not to rush, but how could he remain calm now that she was back in his life, his target. It was a miracle, a gift that wouldn't be denied.

The pressure inside was building, like a fist in the gut spurring him to act. He clawed at his thigh again and again, trying to stop the urge to satisfy his insatiable need.

He had to think things through, make a plan. Last time he'd bungled it, made a mess of it. He didn't want to spoil it this time.

His mind twisted into the past. It was his parents' fault. His father was in and out, and when he was home, he was distant and menacing. But it was his mother's voice that taunted him. "You can never do anything right." Her haunting laugh spilled into him. "Discipline is the key," she'd say to the father. "The boy needs more discipline."

He flashed back to the time when he was eleven years old and his mother caught him pleasuring himself. For punishment she'd forced him to stand naked against the wall in front of everyone in the family, praying until his voice gave out. With these thoughts, he raged.

The urge to act needled him, but he fought against it. Discipline was the key. Timing was everything. But his body forced him to act now.

Lucky for him, the door wasn't latched. Just as he pressed his hand to the wood and pushed it open, beams of light lit up the trees, warning of an approaching car. He slunk around the house into the shadows.

≈

Chance parked in front of Brianna's house and checked his watch. The time was edging past six o'clock. Kat's SUV was in the driveway. She hadn't showed up for dinner and hadn't cancelled. Because of the crank calls, he felt the need to check up on her; at least that was his excuse.

Must run in the family with these women. Even though Brianna and Kat were different in personality, they were cut from the same cloth. They both touched his nurturing side, an instinct that had been buried until Meredith's illness.

Approaching the house, he noticed the partially opened door. Coming closer, he heard only the gentle whirring of the heater fan. "Kat?" When no one answered, he stepped inside and found her asleep on the couch with a kitten curled up on her belly.

He had to smile. Here was this tough, balls-of-fire woman, tearing through life on her own, indifferent to animals, cuddling a kitten. He backed out quietly, dragging the door with him.

"Chance? Is that you?" A groggy-voiced Kat asked him to come in.

"You left it open a crack. I was worried." He shut the door and jiggled the knob to make sure it was securely latched. He neared the couch. "Who's your friend?"

Kat swung her feet off the sofa, and the kitten sprang to the floor and stretched its legs. "A stray, and I don't know why it picked me of all people. You know I'm not an animal person."

"You look like a natural to me."

Kat shooed the kitten outside. "The little bugger showed up this morning, and I thought he'd be gone when I got back from town, but no such luck. I didn't buy any cat food."

"Looks like you'll have to get some."

Kat gave him an oh-brother look and switched on the lamp.

He raised her chin and gave her a breeze of a kiss, which she didn't resist. "Your eyes are swollen and red." He ran his thumb down her cheek to wipe away traces of tears. "Have you been crying?"

She gestured toward the opened box. "I was looking at some pictures of me and Brianna when we were kids. It reminded me of our not-so-pleasant past."

"Would you tell me about it?" He yearned to know everything about the woman, even the pain.

"What time is it anyway?"

"After six."

"I was supposed to be at your house an hour ago. I'm so sorry. I was exhausted. I've ruined our dinner, haven't I?"

He laid his hands on her shoulders. "Don't you worry about dinner. I brought it with me."

He went out to get the Crock Pot. On his way back in, the kitten darted in after him. Kat grabbed the stray to put it out.

"Let him stay," Chance said. "He might like some roast beef."

"The little moocher had beef stew."

"That canned garbage?" Chance plugged in the Crock Pot. "Are you sure the kitten's a he?"

"How would I know?"

Chance held the kitten up to have a look. "Female. You'll probably want to have her spayed." He set her on the floor, and she rubbed against his leg.

"It's not staying here that long."

"Take her to Seattle with you when you go."

"Why don't you take her home?"

He rubbed his hands together, his eyes flickering with mischief. "She'll make a mighty fine meal for Zeke."

"Oh, stop it."

"Now that you know the kitten's sex, why don't you give her a name while she's here, instead of calling her 'It'?"

"I don't name animals. You name her."

"She's your kitten."

"She is not."

"Okay, It, it is."

"Don't be silly," Kat said. "I'll call her Tiger."

"That's original."

Kat gave him a playful punch on the arm. "You're exasperating."

In one smooth motion he grabbed her wrist, entwined their arms, and pulled her toward him. "And you, woman . . ." He inhaled the sweet scent of her. "You're one of the sexiest women I've ever met."

She shattered the moment by pulling free and rattling around the kitchen for plates and silverware. Kat wasn't one to be tamed easily. Like Banjo, the white burro that had suffered mistreatment, Kat needed expert handling. Like Banjo, she needed tender care.

Watching Kat and Tiger devour the meal he'd prepared gave him pleasure. "Did you accomplish anything in town this morning besides getting the boxes?"

"I talked to the sheriff."

"And what did our illustrious civil servant have to say?"

"He gave me a different version of Brianna and Tim's relationship. He told me it was Brianna who pestered Tim after they split up, not the other way around."

"He's full of it," Chance said. "As I told you, it was Tim who came storming out to the ranch begging Brianna to take him back."

"Why would the sheriff say otherwise?"

"Because he's Tim's father," Chance said. "More likely than not, that was the story Tim told him. Or, he's protecting his son. Look at the mess the world is in today. Isn't that because people see the same things differently? And we fight over our differences. If we can't have peace in our own backyards, how will we ever accomplish it worldwide?"

"I believe that, but how did this turn into a lecture about world peace?"

"Sorry. I just meant if the sheriff sees the situation his son's way, the opposite way you do, he'll fight you on it."

"I'd rather not fight the sheriff over anything," she said. "Maybe he *is* obligated to take his son's side, but I still don't like his lousy attitude."

"Join the club."

Kat finished her last bite, and Chance asked if she wanted more. "I couldn't, really, but it was heavenly. I don't know when I've had a meal like this."

He tossed another morsel to Tiger, who purred with delight. Kat gathered the plates.

"You sit still," he told her. "I'll do the dishes."

"Listen, you've done enough. I'll put them in the sink and do them later."

Chance meandered to the opened box and picked up the picture of a young girl and an older man. "Is this Brianna with your father?"

Kat, who was busy running water over the silverware, shut off the tap, used her jeans for a towel, and snatched the photo from his hand. "Uncle." She tossed the photo into the box. Tiger dove in to investigate.

"Come here." He sat Kat on the couch. "I saw that look of contempt. Tell me what happened back then." From the way her breathing increased after his suggestion, her resistance was building. "It's all right, Kat, I won't judge it."

"Brianna's is not a pretty past."

"Whose is?" He squeezed her hand. "Tell me what happened to her."

"Brianna didn't tell you?"

"Like I said, when she worked for me, she was happy. I guess she never felt the need to bring it up."

"I can't blame her for that," Kat said. "She was ten years old when it started. Our family life was crazy. Dad drank excessively. That's how our parents died, in a car accident. He was drunk. Our mother was always making excuses for him. They were pretty much occupied with each other, trying to make their marriage work." She shook her head. "No one knew."

"I take it Brianna was sexually abused."

"My mother's brother," she said. "It was so unlikely, too. He was a quiet man, married, never drank a stitch of liquor in his life. He'd come over to visit when our parents weren't home, and stupid me, I'd beg to go out with my friends while he was there. It was a way to get out of babysitting."

She paused with a heavy sigh, leaving Chance to wonder whether or not it was too painful for her to continue. "She tried to tell us, first Mom, then me, but we didn't believe her. Mom flew into a rage and called her a liar. I just blew it off and wouldn't listen. No one dared tell Dad."

"What happened after that? How did it end?"

"Will kept visiting, and with no family support Brianna couldn't stand up to him. She just accepted her fate. She withdrew into her own world, and no one ever noticed. So sad, so terribly sad."

"How long did it go on?"

"About seven years. That's what Brianna told me later, but I wasn't around to know for sure. The worse part was I left her home with the bastard, and then when I turned sixteen, I left home for good just to get away from it all."

"That's called survival, sweetheart," Chance said. "Where did you go when you left home?"

"I hooked up with an eighteen-year-old boy I'd known for about a minute. We hitched to Seattle, lived in fleabag hotels, panhandled on the street. It wasn't one of my finest hours." Tiger jumped up on her lap and kneaded her legs.

"She's showing you affection."

"I don't know why." She stroked the kitten's fur.

"Finish your story," he said.

"I ended up lying about my age and got jobs waitressing and cleaning hotel rooms. I knew how to type a little, so I joined a temp agency and worked in various offices until I landed a receptionist gig with a real estate firm. Maggie, my savior, thought I had potential. She mentored me and encouraged me to take the real estate exam. The rest is history." She laid her head on Chance's shoulder.

"That's one remarkable story of determination," he said. "I'm just sorry you had to go through the misery."

"All that misery makes me what I am today. Isn't that what they say?"

"We're all the product of our pasts."

"What about you? What's your story?"

He kissed the top of her head. "That, my dear, is best left alone. Why don't you come out to the ranch? This house holds too many memories, and for one night you can forget about the past."

She sat up and looked him in the eye. "I'm not ready for a relationship."

"Did I say anything about a relationship? All I'm offering you is my guest room."

As she rose, Tiger tumbled onto the rug. Chance grabbed hold of Kat's hand before she could walk away. "Come to the ranch with me."

"I'd rather stay here."

"Do you want me to stay here with you? I don't think you should be alone."

"I've got Tiger to keep me company."

"What if you get another phone call? Will you promise to call me no matter what time it is?" With an affirmative nod, she indicated she would, but he had his doubts.

Tiger meowed. Kat let her out and stood at the opened door. "I'd like to call it a night," she said matter-of-factly while averting her eyes.

She'd put up the walls, and he knew she regretted telling him her secrets. For a woman like Kat, vulnerability was a weakness. "You keep the leftovers. You might need them for Tiger. I'll get the Crock Pot later."

"Thank you for dinner."

He moved a stray hair from her face. The pain in her soul shined right through her eyes. "Come with me, Kat."

She kept the door open, and Tiger jetted inside. "Good night, Chance."

$$\approx$$

Kat leaned against the doorjamb until the roar of the truck's engine faded away. Why had she revealed so much about herself? And why had she misinterpreted his offer to stay in his guest room?

The man could be tender and caring. But in matters of the heart, Chance was an expert. When she was at her weakest, he tried to tempt her into going to his ranch, to his guest room. Guest room. Hah! He as much as admitted a relationship wasn't on his agenda. No, he didn't want a relationship. He wanted a one-night stand. He didn't say it, but it was as clear to her as newly polished glass.

She went into the bathroom to wash her face and said to her mirrored reflection, "You're doing better, Kat. You're not falling for every Tom, Dick, and Chance. You're going to get through this unscathed. Just stay strong." The warm water felt good trickling over her skin. She patted her face dry.

The instant her cell phone rang, she dropped the towel. She'd forgotten to turn her cell off. Determined to clamp it shut if she heard one heavy breath, she flipped it open and was relieved to hear Maggie's gravelly voice.

"I'm so glad it's you," Kat said.

"I tried to call your sister's number, but all I got was a busy signal."

"It's off the hook."

"And why? Phone problems?"

"I was getting calls on that phone."

"You mean those calls?"

"Yes, and I think the man is here in Rosswood."

"Are you sure?"

"No, but I found out Brianna was getting the same calls before she died. If he's the same pervert, I don't understand the connection."

"Maybe Brianna talked about you to someone she knew and spilled too much personal information," Maggie said. "That could be dangerous. I think you should come home and deal with it from here."

"Nothing bad is going to happen, Maggie. It's just annoying. I'm going to wrap this up in a few days, and if I don't find out who's doing this, I'll turn it over to the police. I promise."

"What do you mean, find out? How are you going to find out? I don't like the sound of that."

"Don't worry. I'm just asking around. I'll be careful, Maggie, I will," Kat said. "So, how is everything going without me?"

"Everything is fine, except your clients are all sad you're not here to hold their hands, especially your favorite client. It's a good thing I talked you into taking your personal cell phone instead of the one you do business on, or the man would be calling you every day."

"Thank God for small favors, but I won't be much longer."

"Are you getting rest?"

"Somewhat."

"I take it the visions are still with you."

"I'm afraid so."

"I want you to take your time and do what you have to do, but I have to say, I'd like you to get out of there as soon as you can and go on a real vacation."

"I'll be home soon."

After the call Kat made a point of shutting off the cell phone. She went looking for Tiger and found her in the living room curled up inside the box lid. The kitten lifted her head and stared sleepy-eyed at Kat before burrowing down again.

Once Kat was in bed, she tossed and turned, couldn't will herself to sleep. The heater was humming in the living room. When she got up to turn it off, she spotted the opened box.

Curious again, she sat and picked through the papers, which turned out to be Brianna's children's stories. One was about a bear, another about a princess. Kat read partway through the bear story, finding it cute and clever.

Buried under the remaining stories was a stack of rejection slips, most of them form letters with an occasional handwritten thank-you. The dates on the stories and letters were old, nothing in the last two years.

But Lenny Faulkes said she sent out manuscripts within the last two years of her death. So did Chance. So where were the latest copies? Even if she'd stored them on her laptop, she had to have kept hard copies for herself, but she didn't have a printer. Lenny might know the answer to that. He seemed to be chummy with Brianna. He seemed to know a great deal about Brianna.

CHAPTER 15

With both phones out of service—Brianna's landline off the hook and Kat's cell phone shut off—and no midnight visions, Kat had a more restful night. For the first time in months, she felt hopeful she was nearing some semblance of closure.

As much as she hated to admit it, talking about her past and venting her tears had lightened her emotional load. She could thank Chance for that, but she wouldn't want him to know he'd played a significant role in her well-being. His ego was big enough already.

Sometime during the night Tiger had joined her on the bed and snuggled into the curve of her body. When Kat made a slight move, the kitten woke and arched her back, stretching and yawning.

Kat scooped her up and put her outside. Clouds had rolled in overnight, and the wind was building. The maple leaves, left on the branches, twirled in the breeze. After showering and dressing in jeans and another of Brianna's work shirts, she brought Tiger in. Kat was beginning to like the company.

She ponytailed her hair and left her face clean and natural. It was a relief not wearing makeup. There was no one in Rosswood she cared to impress. For a fleeting moment she thought of Chance.

She washed dishes and cleaned the Crock Pot. Returning it meant her connection to him would continue, at least for one more day.

Tiger pawed the cupboard door, begging for pieces of the meat Kat was cutting up from last night's supper. Kat tossed her a few morsels. The kitten tackled the scraps with zeal. Kat ate a slice herself, preferring as usual to grab breakfast on the run.

The three boxes were already filled and it hadn't made a dent in Brianna's belongings; Kat totally had miscalculated the enormity of this project. She would need several more boxes, a thrift store to haul them to, since there was none in Rosswood, and a truck. If Benton had a thrift store, that would solve one problem. Chance had a truck, but that would necessitate complicating their friendship. She didn't want to be beholden to him.

An alternative would be to rent a U-haul, hire someone to drive it to Seattle, and deal with Brianna's stuff later. No, she would deal with it now. She wanted absolute closure.

Tiger objected to being placed outdoors again by meowing and squirming in Kat's arms, giving Kat mixed feelings about leaving the kitten again. Before, she'd hoped Tiger would scamper off and find another home, but now she wasn't so sure. With no satisfactory choice, she set the kitten's bowls near the entrance to the house and drove toward town.

Up ahead on Randall Road, she saw the blue jacket flared by the wind and the frizzy hair ready to take flight. She slowed alongside Tilly and rolled down the window. "Can I give you a lift?" Tilly increased her stride, and Kat inched alongside her, causing another vehicle to careen around the SUV. "I won't hurt you. You don't even have to talk. I'll just drop you off wherever you want to go." But she hoped the girl would volunteer something about Brianna.

Tilly stopped walking, and Kat hit the brakes. The girl climbed inside and shrank against the door as far away from Kat as possible.

Kat checked the rearview mirror. No cars were behind her, so she crept along, giving her more time with the girl. "I've been cleaning out Brianna's closet." She glanced at Tilly to get her reaction, but Tilly just stared out the window.

"You know, you're about Brianna's size. If you want any of her clothes, you can come by the house and pick out what you want. You said you were Brianna's friend. I'm sure she would want you to have them." Tilly shifted a little away from the door, but wouldn't answer or look at Kat.

The turn onto Center Street was coming up, and Kat wanted to know more about Tim Holmes. "You said Tim wasn't Brianna's friend." She didn't reply, and as soon as Kat swung onto Center, she squeezed the door handle, forcing Kat to come to an abrupt halt. Tilly sprang from the car and ran across the street to the café.

That went well. Kat hoped for another opportunity with Tilly but for now continued through town to the post office. It had that same stuffy, closed-up smell about it, and Kat wondered why they never opened the door once in a while just to air it out.

Lenny Faulkes had his back to her. By the sound of envelopes hitting the sides of the postal boxes, someone was slipping mail into the slots. Kat was the only customer.

The bulletin board was covered with the same ads she'd seen before, but hers was gone. She walked up to the counter and cleared her throat to get Lenny's attention.

Lenny swung around. "May I help you?" His face was twisted in agony while he fidgeted with an envelope, turning it from one end to the other.

"I came in to take my ad off the bulletin board," she said, "but I see it's already been removed."

"Oh, y-yes," he stammered. "Tim Holmes told me he got Brianna's car, so I took it down. I didn't think you'd want it left up."

"Thanks. I didn't."

His pitiful, hopeless expression made her uncomfortable. He wasn't the jovial, overly-friendly postman she'd met earlier. The door opened behind her, but Kat kept her attention on Lenny. She showed him the paper with the phone number printed on it. "I'm curious. I wondered if you recognized this number."

He fumbled for the glasses that hung from a cord around his neck, but before he could set them in place to take a look, a thickset woman with unkempt cropped hair came out from behind the postal boxes, marched up to the counter, and peered over Lenny's shoulder. "Why are you asking about this number?" she said, her eyes lasering into Kat.

"I've been getting unwanted calls on my cell phone, and that was the number displayed. I'm trying to find out who the prankster is. Probably a teenager with nothing better to do. Probably nothing to it."

"Maybe you should let the sheriff handle it," Clare said. "Right, Lenny?"

Lenny's jaw twitched, but he was alarmingly quiet.

"That's what I'll do if it keeps up," Kat said.

Clare grunted while reaching under the counter for her purse. On her way out she gave Kat a condescending glance.

When the door closed, Lenny's sigh was as loud as the sound of a balloon deflating, and all the molecules in the room felt as if they were moving again. His face looked ten years younger, but he wasn't smiling. He shoved the paper toward Kat. "Uh-uh. Never saw this."

Then all she could smell was the overpowering odor of stale tobacco. She glanced to the left and jerked from the closeness of Doug Jones.

The warmth of his breath grazed her neck as he leaned on the counter with one hand and extended an arm over her shoulder, embracing her in a cocoon, while tossing an envelope at Lenny. "This here was in my box. It doesn't belong to me."

He shifted positions, and Kat stepped out of his web. "Cops won't do you no good, sweetheart. You just give me the word, and I'll be your bodyguard." He breathed deeply into her hair, and she stepped farther away. "You sure do smell good. Is that coconut I smell? I love coconut. Reminds me of palm trees and naked ladies." He touched her hair along the side of her face before strutting out the door.

"He's a nasty, nasty man," Lenny said.

"Does he bother all the women in town?"

"Just the pretty ones," Lenny cooed, his smile returning.

"Listen, Lenny, I found some stories Brianna wrote, but there's no printer at the house. I wondered where she did her printing. Do you know?"

"As a matter of fact, Kaaat, I let her use the one here. Not on government time, of course. She'd come into the post office before closing time, and I'd let her make whatever copies she needed. She brought her own paper. She was very good about that."

"Well, that solves that mystery," Kat said. "I'm sure it was a lot more convenient for her to come here than to travel all the way to Benton."

"I tried to help her as much as I could. Yes, I did. She was such a sweet, sweet girl." His eyes had taken on a dreamy glow, and he was shifting into his maudlin mood—a good time to leave.

"Any mail for me today?"

"None so far, but if you get something, I can deliver it."

"That won't be necessary."

"Really, Kaaat, I don't mind."

"I'll just pick it up here." Kat gladly left Lenny muttering to himself.

On her way down the sidewalk Tim Holmes strode toward her and blocked her path. "If it isn't the lady with all the questions."

He sounded as if he were ready for a fight, more confident than he was before, but Kat was in no mood to deal with another disagreeable man. She tried to move around him, but he sidestepped along with her. "My dad said you've been asking questions about me. Something about phone calls to Brianna? I didn't bother her after we split. She came after me. So, if you have any more questions, ask me, not my dad."

"Fine. I do have one question." She thrust the paper with the mysterious phone number at him. "Does this number belong to you?"

He gave the paper a passing glance and bumped shoulders with her before continuing up the post office steps and disappearing inside. Her upbeat attitude flitted away, replaced by an eagerness to leave Rosswood. She drove to the general store, anxious to get more boxes, so she could finish her job here.

When she entered the store, Hank glanced up from a magazine he was reading. Considering their opposing viewpoints on the development project, she couldn't discern whether or not to make idle conversation. If she had one more incident with a disgruntled man, she couldn't be held accountable for her actions.

She looked him dead in the eye, daring him to make one unpleasant comment, but he simply nodded and smiled. She'd gauged him right. He was the type who had to have his say but didn't seem to hold a grudge.

The chatter of women's voices drifted up from dry goods. A man was whistling near the dairy section.

She found a bag of cat food on the far left aisle near the empty boxes, two of which she hauled to the front of the store. She laid the bag on the counter.

"Got yourself a cat, do you?"

"A temporary boarder."

"How old is he?"

"He's a she, and she can't be more than a year if that."

"There's a vet in Benton if you want to get her spayed."

"I plan to find her a home long before that." She exchanged cash for the cat food.

"You getting all your packing done?"

"I'm working on it. Do you mind if I take more boxes? I'm going to need more than I originally thought."

"Take as many as you can get in that fancy car of yours."

"Thanks, Hank."

After she'd loaded the SUV, she spotted Wilma opening up her shop. Kat rushed to catch up with her.

"Well, howdy, Kat. Let's get out of this blasted wind." She let Kat in first and primped her hair in front of the wall mirror. "How's it going over there? I hear you've been packing up Brianna's stuff. Making any progress?"

"Slowly."

"I also heard you've been asking around about a phone number, that you got some teenager bothering you. I ran into Clare."

"I'm only speculating." Kat showed her the number, certain of all the people in town Wilma was her best shot.

Wilma examined the number, turned the paper over, examined the number again. "It sure seems familiar. I just can't place the darn thing." She stared at it once more. "Damn. It's not coming to me."

"Yours is the most encouraging response I've received so far," Kat said. "Give it some thought, and let me know if you have any idea. Whoever is calling me is probably harmless."

"How can you be so sure?"

"They're just phone calls, nothing more than that."

"Maybe you shouldn't take this so lightly."

"That's what Chance said."

Wilma's eyes lit up, and Kat knew she'd made a terrible blunder. "So, it's Chance now."

The door opened, compelling Kat to step aside and allow in a woman dressed in slacks, sturdy shoes, and a car coat draped over her petite body. Wispy brown hair covered parts of her face.

"June Bug. How're you doing today?"

She peered up at Wilma, her hair shifting, showing the telltale signs of a yellowing bruise. She spiked her hair down again.

"You go on back, honey," Wilma said. "I'll be right there."

June tiptoed to the far end of the shop. She slipped into the restroom, and the door creaked shut.

"You saw that, didn't you."

"You mean the bruise."

"You bet I mean the bruise. That bastard can't keep his temper in check, and she pays the price. Loves those kids, but beats the hell out of his wife." Wilma kept her voice low, but her eyes glowed with rage. "That's Tim Holmes's wife."

"Really. How does he get away with it? His father's the sheriff, isn't he?"

"Tim's the only son, and that boy can do no wrong. Gordon just looks the other way."

"What about a women's shelter? Isn't there one in Benton?"

Wilma flipped the sign on the door to OPEN and turned back to Kat. "If there was a shelter, she wouldn't go. She's got three kids, no family, and she's just too dang afraid of him."

"What about the church?"

"The pastor tried to counsel her once, but she says she loves him. What can you do about that? It's like trying to take salt out of the ocean."

Kat wished something could be done about Tim Holmes, for a number of reasons. "Do you know if he ever hit Brianna?"

Wilma checked to make sure June hadn't come out of the restroom, then whispered to Kat, "I heard rumors he got physical with her, but I don't know firsthand. I never saw any marks on her."

Kat burned inside just thinking about the possibility. The restroom door opened, and Kat said to Wilma in a normal speaking voice, "I hope there are no hard feelings about the meeting Saturday night."

"Honey, if that was the case, I'd be mad at half the town, and it ain't worth it."

"Let me know if you remember anything about the phone number."

"Will do." Wilma wandered into the other room. "Okay, June Bug, let's get your hair trimmed."

Kat drove back to Brianna's, afraid if she stayed in town any longer she might run into Tim Holmes again, afraid if she *did* see him, she couldn't be held responsible for what might come out of her mouth.

CHAPTER 16

Chance had risen early to revise the final chapter of his novel. A few tweaks to the whole manuscript and he could turn it into a memoir, a risky proposition considering the people he'd be exposing. He weighed the ramifications of putting his past on display and how that would affect both his and his daughter's lives and the possibility of having a relationship with Kat. Before publishing the manuscript, he'd judge the best way to proceed.

After making the revisions, he wrote out two checks—one to his daughter, Stella, for college tuition and the other to Francesca, his beautiful Italian mother. Francesca never asked him for anything, but nevertheless a check was in the mail monthly.

Chance owed her everything. He grinned as he recalled the story of how she'd named him Chance. His father had left her when she was three months pregnant. She'd almost miscarried, and it was only by chance that he was born into this world. Later in life when Chance was able, he bought her a home in upstate New York where she'd scratched out a living as a nurse while raising him.

His cell phone rang. Upon flipping it open, he hoped it was Kat. "Hello."

"*Bonjour*, Chance. It has been such a long time, no?"

"Monique."

"It is good to hear you again."

This woman from his past wasn't someone he cared to talk to. His mind churned through excuses to end the call.

"I have a proposition for you."

"Monique, I told you before."

"Oh, we had such a good time, oh, too many years ago," she gushed. "I am in Seattle, darling. Meet me at the Four Seasons. We can catch up on old times, just as we did four years ago. Oh, such catching up we did, do you remember?"

"No, Monique, and you can tell Philip I'm not interested. As I told you then, I'm retired, for good this time."

"You disappointment me, Chance. We work so well together. But you must remember you are still bound by the agreement you made. You were paid dearly."

"That's why you called, isn't it? You're checking up on me to make sure I'll keep quiet." He glanced at his manuscript, knowing full well it would expose the con.

"If you say it, it is so, but I can assure you that you still have a place in the organization. And in my heart. I am faxing you the details of my visit. Do not disappoint me."

"Don't expect to see me. I'm not interested. Goodbye, Monique." He snapped the phone shut. The past. Would it ever stop haunting him?

He switched on the printer. As the machine spit out his latest revisions, he purposely left his fax machine off and opened the window to let out the stench of the conversation. The odors of scattered hay and grazing burros left him feeling surprisingly strengthened and renewed, assured he'd made the right decision to change the direction of his life.

His gaze fell on the picture of his daughter and his ex-wife. Monique was nothing like Meredith. Yet it was a woman exactly like Monique who'd tempted him away from his wife. Meredith was honest and loving, fiery too, like Kat Summers. Although he'd only known Kat a short time, she was the first woman he was attracted to in the same way he'd been attracted to Meredith. If he could break down Kat's defenses, he knew there was a powerful connection between them, an undeniable connection.

He shut off the printer and marched outside where Zeke greeted him, whining and wiggling. Chance paused to give his head a couple of pats and proceeded to the truck. Zeke galloped ahead, anticipating the ride.

Rusty looked up from filling a bucket beside the barn. He meandered across the driveway to meet up with Chance.

"I'm going to Benton," Chance said.

"Anything I can do for ya?"

"No need. I'm just picking up some office supplies. But first I'm going over to Brianna's house. I left my Crock Pot there. Keep hold of Zeke, will you?" Chance slid into the driver's seat, and Rusty stared, chuckling. "What are you looking at?"

"Crock Pot ain't that important." His smile widened. "Sounds an excuse just to see that Summers woman." He grabbed Zeke's collar.

"Haven't you got work to do?" Chance revved up the engine and headed down the driveway. "Damn ranch hand. Eyes like a chameleon. Doesn't miss a thing."

At Brianna's house Chance waited a full minute before exiting the truck, waited for the butterflies to settle. "Damn woman." He planned to ask her to accompany him to Benton, and like a teenager hoping for a first date, worried she might refuse. He viewed his reflection in the rearview mirror, slicked down his hair. "Get a hold of yourself. You're a grown man."

Kat was in the doorway in shirt and jeans, her hair swept into a ponytail, her arms folded. She had a quizzical look on her face.

He strode toward her, hoping she hadn't seen him primping. "I came to pick up the Crock Pot, save you the trip."

He followed her inside where Tiger rubbed against his legs. He scooped the kitten into his arms. "Has Ms. Grown-up Cat been good to you?"

"She's spoiled already." Kat held the Crock Pot out for him to take. "You can have both."

He grinned while exchanging Tiger for the Crock Pot. Tiger meowed to get down and rubbed one cheek then the other over the top of his boots.

"I didn't hear from you last night," he said. "I'm assuming you didn't have any problems."

"I slept better than I have since I got here."

"That's good, Kat. I'm glad," he said, and Kat edged toward the door, giving him no time to dally if he was going to ask her to go with him. "I'm going to Benton. Do you need anything from the big city?"

"I don't think so," she said, "but do you know if they have a thrift shop that takes donations?"

"I'm not sure about that." He lied. He knew exactly where the thrift shop was. "Why don't you ride along with me, and we'll check it out?"

"I don't know. Couldn't you check for me?"

"Aw, come on, Kat. You need a little time away from Rosswood. You need a break. It will do you good."

"Well, all right, but can you wait for me to change and do my hair?"

"You don't have to go to all that trouble. You look stunning just the way you are." He grabbed her arm to prevent her from escaping into the bedroom. "I mean it, Kat. You don't need to do a thing." He came close to embracing her, but he was holding the Crock Pot, and she seemed a little too aloof today. He didn't want to scare her off.

"What about my hair?"

"Leave it be. I like it that way."

She settled her shoulders with a sigh and hunted down her purse. On the way out she hastened Tiger outside.

≈

By the time they were rolling along toward Benton, the noonday sun had heated the truck's cab. Both windows were lowered. Chance's cowboy hat lay on the seat between them. The air felt refreshing, cool on her cheeks, and Kat was glad she'd tied her hair back.

"I went into town this morning and asked around about the phone number, but I didn't get anywhere," Kat blurted without thinking, then realized she'd slipped up. She didn't want him to make a big deal of it.

"What phone number?"

She paused. "Oh, did I say phone number? I meant the phone calls. I was asking about the phone calls."

"Do you want me to check around about that? I could do some digging."

"That won't be necessary. I've got Wilma on it."

Chance laughed. "Then it should only be a matter of time."

"Those calls have to be a prank. Besides, I'm leaving my cell off just in case the jerk gets lucky."

"You shouldn't have to put up with that even if it is a prank. If it keeps up, promise me you'll let me handle it."

"If it gets threatening, I will. If the calls happen again when I get home, I'll handle it there."

The towering pines passed in a blur as Kat withdrew into her private thoughts about Brianna. "I wish I knew what was going on in Brianna's mind. Did I tell you she called me a day before she died? She begged me to visit. She seemed so happy. Isn't there anything else you can remember about her comings and goings? Did she have any other friends I might talk to?"

"I don't know about any friends. So much of her time was taken up by her job at Bertie's and by Tim Holmes, and after that she spent her free time at the ranch." Chance ran a hand through his hair, pushing the wind-blown strands into place.

"She did go to Benton quite regularly to pick up supplies for me," he continued. "She would take her laptop with her. She said she had someone there who printed off her stories for her. I asked her if she wanted to use my printer, but she refused the offer."

"That's odd. Lenny said she mostly used his printer. How often did she go to Benton?"

"At least once a week," he said. "That was Rusty's job, but she insisted on going."

"Did you ask who was helping her?"

"I could have, but I figured it was her business."

Kat slumped in her seat, deep in thought. So much about Brianna's life and death in Rosswood seemed a mystery. At the touch of Chance's hand, she jerked out of her daze. "What?"

"You seem sort of lost today. Are you okay?"

His tender expression spooked her. "Just thinking about Brianna. Why did you care so much about her?"

"Maybe because I spent so much time caring for Meredith when she was sick. Having Brianna around pushed a few buttons I suppose. She needed someone to care for her, too."

Kat shifted around to get a better look at him. "You're an enigma, Eliason."

"Why do you say that?"

"One minute you're hot-tempered and the next you're as soft as a kitten."

He huffed at Kat. "I could say the same about you. I'd say we're a good match."

Kat eyed him warily, thinking how smooth an operator he was. For the rest of the trip she sat back and counted the passing vehicles.

Chance rounded the final curve and slowed into the town of Benton. To Kat it didn't seem much bigger than Rosswood, though the main street was longer with more side streets jutting off in both directions. They passed a church, a tavern, a drugstore, a grocery, a few specialty shops, and a café. Up ahead on the left in plain sight was Katie's Used Goods. Chance inched past the shop, as if he hadn't seen the sign.

"Slow down and pull over," Kat demanded, and he aimed the truck into a parking spot just beyond Katie's. He'd known all along Benton had a thrift store. It would have been obvious to anyone passing through. She tossed him one of her scathing looks. "Go do your business, and I'll meet you back here."

"How about lunch?"

She left him wondering and stepped into the store. A rack of clothes lined one wall, tables of household items took up most of the floor space, and at the back of the store were used appliances. Kat sneezed from the dust.

A lanky woman with short, wavy hair carried a feather duster under her arm and approached Kat. "May I help you?"

"I hope so." Kat coughed and stifled another sneeze. "Allergies."

"Sorry about the dust."

"I wondered if you take donations. I have clothes, small household items, and dishes. I also have a compact washer/dryer, the kind you hook up to a sink."

"Sure, but why don't you consider having an estate sale?"

"I don't want to bother with it. I may be able to give some items away, but I really want to be rid of it all, and in a hurry."

The woman took a business card from her pant pocket and handed it to Kat. "My drop-off hours are on there. Just give me a buzz before you come so I can be ready for you."

"Thanks. I will." Kat walked out into the sunshine, feeling relieved at having a plan and hungry after all, less contentious, too, and ready to take Chance up on his offer for lunch.

Chance wasn't in the truck or anywhere else she could see. He could have disappeared into any one of a number of shops. Peering across the street, she spotted a bald man in plaid shirt and dark slacks entering an office nearby: Nate Wheeler.

On an impulse Kat charged across the street, just missing a passing car, and into the office of Wheeler and Associates. A desk with computer, fax machine, and printer took up half the space. The office was so bare, devoid of any warmth, it looked like the trappings of a fake company, but she knew his main office was elsewhere.

Wheeler came out from behind a partition, stopped and hitched a hip on the edge of his desk. "And what can I do for you?"

The suggestive way he'd phrased the question riled Kat. She didn't know why she was going to ask him. It was just a hunch. "Did my sister ever come in here to use your printer?"

"Maybe she did and maybe she didn't. Why do you want to know?"

"Just give me a straight answer."

"Well, let's see." He stroked his beard. "I seem to recall her coming in here a number of times. Sure, that's right. We had a deal going."

"What kind of a deal?"

"A sweet deal, if I remember right. One favor for another."

Kat felt the heat explode up her spine. She didn't know if he was baiting her, but she despised his attitude.

"Listen, honey, this is how the deal went down," he said. "Your sister came in here one day raising hell about the Rosswood project. When I finally settled her down, I took her into the back room, and we had a nice civilized chat about land use and my company. She calmed down, and we came to a mutual agreement. She told me about her stories, and how she had to use the printer at the post office after hours, so I offered to let her use my printer anytime she wanted to, day or night. The rest was her idea. If I remember correctly, we sealed the deal that afternoon, right back there." He nodded toward the partition.

By now Kat was shaking she was so mad. "You're an asshole."

He stood and aimed a finger into her collarbone. "If you start calling me names, lady, be prepared for the consequences."

She marched out of his office and heard the door slammed behind her. Chance was waiting for her at the truck. Without a look in his direction, she climbed into the passenger seat and folded her arms.

Chance slid in beside her. "I guess lunch is out of the question. Do you want to tell me what happened?"

"Just drive." A good part of the way back to Rosswood, Kat boiled inside. She could have written Wheeler off as a liar, but she knew what Brianna was capable of. Still, he could have been lying, but the arrogance of the man got to her.

Chance seemed to know she needed time to think things through. He never once said a word and only glanced at her from time to time.

Halfway home, Kat rested her hands in her lap. "I thought Brianna had changed. At least, I'd hoped she'd changed."

"She was trying."

"After what she went through with our uncle, she went wild, Chance. She never thought of herself as anything but a sex object. She was obsessed. She didn't feel worthy, ever. I tried to get help for her. She rushed into that marriage with J.W., thinking that would solve everything. All it did was bring her more grief. The year she came to live with me she went to support group meetings for victims of sexual abuse. When she wanted to move to Rosswood, I thought, great, an innocent little town. How much trouble could she get into there? Little did I know, she could find trouble anywhere and make a mess of things."

"Don't blame yourself, Kat."

"I'm not."

"Sounds like you are to me."

She got quiet again.

"Listen," Chance said. "I take it Brianna and Wheeler were having some sort of affair, and if that's the case, he's as much to blame as she is, maybe more."

"Didn't you have a clue when she was seeing him every week?"

"I'm sorry, Kat, I honestly didn't. She never told me about him. She seemed happy. Her mood never changed."

"She never could say no, Chance, never."

Chance squeezed Kat's hand. "Come here." She moved his cowboy hat and let him put an arm around her. He pressed her close. "Come home with me, Kat, and I'll make you lunch, put you to bed."

She started to move away, but he held her tight. "You men are all alike."

"No, we're not," he said. "I'll put you to bed in the guest room, alone. You're weary from your confrontation with Wheeler and all this thinking about Brianna. You haven't caught up on your sleep. One night's rest isn't going to do it."

She let herself relax into him and laid her head against his shoulder. She closed her eyes, and for a while imagined what it would be like to let go into the comfort of this man's arms, let go of the annoyances, let go of the haunting visions of Brianna, let go of the memories this place had stirred up. But she couldn't let her guard down and let this man, whose strength was already washing over her like warm liquid light, knock down her carefully constructed walls. She opened her eyes and pushed away from him. Before he could turn off the highway onto his private road, Kat directed him to keep driving to Brianna's house.

"Why, Kat? You're hungry and tired. You need to rest."

"I can rest at Brianna's house, and besides I have work to do if I'm going to pack her things and get out of this town." As good as it felt in this moment, Kat feared getting used to leaning on Chance.

CHAPTER 17

Chance didn't argue with Kat or try to change her mind. He turned down Maple Lane and parked in front of Brianna's house, just as Kat had asked him to do. She sensed his disappointment, but she had no time to smooth things over. Tilly, who'd been sitting cross-legged in the middle of the lawn when they pulled up, darted behind the maple tree.

Kat looked into Chance's sad eyes. "I need to talk to her. I have to go."

He held onto her arm. "I'll be in touch."

"I'm not ready for any involvement."

"Don't be so quick to decide."

She hesitated, opened her mouth to argue why she couldn't commit to anything, then left him and cautiously walked up the driveway so as not to scare the girl. The truck door closed and the engine's sound grew fainter. Kat looked toward the maple tree and waited.

Tilly edged within a few feet of the house, her gaze on a wiry rose bush. "I come for the clothes." Her head sunk lower.

Kat knew it took all of the girl's courage to utter that simple request. Kat's heart reached out to her. "Please come in, and we'll sort them out. You can show me what you want." She unlocked the door.

Tiger flew around the corner of the garage and slipped inside. Tilly smiled at the sight of the kitten. Kat beckoned the girl in, and the girl knelt near the couch to pet the cat.

Kat brought out a box of Brianna's clothes and held up the first item: a sunny yellow flannel shirt. "This looks like it might fit."

Tilly snatched it from Kat and hugged it to her chest. Her eyes welled with tears.

"I know," Kat said. "It's sad to think Brianna's gone. It's sad for me, too."

Tilly frowned. "Tim's not sad. Tim's mad."

"What do you mean?"

"Tim pushed Brianna. Tim pushed Brianna into a wall."

"Did you actually see him do that?"

"Tim pushed Brianna."

"Where did you see this?"

"Behind Bertie's. He yelled and yelled at Brianna. He pushed her into a wall." Tilly grasped the back of her own head and rocked back and forth. "Stop hitting me. It hurts."

"He hit Brianna?"

"It hurts. It hurts. Then I ran away." Tilly buried her face in the flannel shirt.

Kat pictured Tim Holmes, a wife beater according to Wilma, striking Brianna, or at the very least shoving her into a brick wall, and every cell in Kat's body ached for revenge. If Tilly hadn't been there, she would have bolted out of the house and tracked him down. For her own safety as well as his, it was probably just as well she had to stay put. She went back to the project at hand, but she wasn't about to forget about Tim Holmes.

Tilly took every piece of clothing offered her, even a pair of jeans with holes in the knees. Kat also gave her Brianna's shoes and boots. When they were finished, the closet was bare, except for a couple of warm shirts and a nightgown Kat wanted to keep for herself.

The whole time they were occupied with sorting through the clothes,

Tiger was rubbing up against Tilly. She picked up the kitten and cradled it in her arms.

Kat watched the interaction with interest and formulated an idea. She wasn't sure she was ready to give Tiger up; the darn kitten was growing on her. But she had to be realistic about it. At home in Seattle she'd have no time to care for a pet. "Maybe before I leave town, you can take her home with you, if it's okay with your grandmother," Kat said, and Tilly actually smiled a reply. "That's what we'll do then."

Kat filled two boxes with clothes. "When I go out later, I'll drop these off at your house. Will you ask your grandmother if she can use anything from Brianna's kitchen? There are dishes and silverware and other odds and ends. She can have anything she wants. And if you think of anything else about Brianna, will you tell me?"

Tilly nodded, reluctantly handed Tiger to Kat, and edged toward the door. She gave the kitten a last glance and ran off down the driveway, hugging Brianna's shirt.

Kat gave Tiger the last of the milk and realized there was nothing in the house she cared to eat. Before stopping at Hank's for fresh supplies, she'd track down Tim Holmes and let him know just what she thought of him. She hadn't forgotten what Tilly had said, not by a long shot.

While hauling out the box of Brianna's clothes, Kat had a twinge of remorse, yet holding on to her sister's things would only prolong the grief and dredge up memories, painful and otherwise. Kat wanted everything gone.

She placed Tiger and her dish on the doorstep and drove down the street to the corner house that bordered Randall Road, which had to be one of the earliest homes built in Rosswood. It was in desperate need of a new roof, a paint job, and in all probability various other repairs.

Sweeping the front porch was Tilly's grandmother, an old-fashioned country woman, slightly overweight in a dowdy flowered dress, her thin graying hair eased into a bun. She was nothing like the hip grandmothers Kat knew who took Pilates and water aerobics classes to keep their weight down, had their hair dyed, and dressed in the latest styles from Macy's. She stopped to look at Kat.

Kat carried a box to the bottom step. The smell of simmering meat drifted out from inside. "I'm Kat Summers, Brianna's sister. I brought these clothes for Tilly. Did she tell you I was coming?"

The old woman eyed Kat with suspicion. "She told me, and you can set that box right here." She pointed to a spot next to her.

With a look of anticipation Tilly burst outside, wearing one of Brianna's shirts over her tattered blouse.

Her grandmother said, "You help her, now, hear?" And after the boxes were on the porch, she said to Tilly, "Did you thank the nice lady?"

Tilly sunk into herself, a murmured thank-you easing out of her mouth.

The grandmother shifted the broom to one hand and squeezed her fist. "Dang arthritis. Gets bad in the cold." She shuffled to the door. "I can take them dishes off your hands if you want. Anything else you might have, I'd be obliged."

"You're welcome to everything in the house," Kat said. "After I box it up, I'll bring it over. Do you have any use for a portable washer/dryer combination?"

"What might that be?"

Kat described the appliance and explained how it hooked up to the sink.

"Hmm . . . We could make use of it, huh, Tilly?"

Tilly eked out a smile, and Kat had the feeling this was like Christmas to both of them. "I'll find someone to haul it over before I leave town."

"We'd be right grateful to you." She opened the screen door and paused a moment. "I could brew us up some tea if you want to come in a spell."

"Oh, no, but thank you," Kat said. "I have something important to do in town. Can you tell me which street I turn on to get to the auto repair shop?"

"Turn left up Second Street. Your car need fixing?"

"I need to talk to the owner."

The old woman snorted. "You mean that fool with the motorcycle. That gosh darn thing nearly gave me a heart attack the night your sister died."

"Really. Did he visit her that night?"

"Heard that motorcycle of his buzzing up the street after midnight. Woke me out of a sleep. Gosh darn thing. There oughtta be a law against them."

"Do you know what time he left her house?"

"Don't really know. Couldn't tell exactly when he was coming or going. Must of fell back to sleep. Did hear it twice that night. It's kind of foggy. Memory's not so good no more."

"Interesting." Kat backed away from the porch, anxious to get to Tim Holmes.

Tilly charged after her. "Grandma says Tiger can stay."

Kat looked to the old woman for an approving nod, but she'd already gone inside. "Before I leave town, I'll talk to your grandmother to make sure. If she tells me it's okay, the kitten's yours."

Tilly gave Kat a stiff hug and ran into the house. Even in death Brianna was doing a good deed. She made all this possible. Despite all her problems she was a good-hearted soul.

Now to Tim Holmes, the man who'd knocked Brianna around and who apparently had visited her the night she'd committed suicide, allegedly committed suicide. Kat was beginning to have her doubts.

She kept her foot lightly on the gas pedal, restraining her anger and her urge to speed to her destination. All she wanted to do was let Tim Holmes know how she felt about his ugly treatment of her sister, let him know she knew. If it weren't against the law, she would do more than tell him off.

When she turned up Second Street, the gas pumps and the two-bay auto shop came into view. One bay was empty. The other housed an older Buick, jacked up on a ramp. Worn-out tires were stacked high alongside the building. She pulled up to the pumps and got out to fill the tank.

A young man in overalls with dirty blond hair and a clean-shaven face hurried out from under the Buick. The name on his uniform was Pete. "I can help you with that, ma'am." He took the gas nozzle from her. "You new around here?"

He was probably the one person in Rosswood who didn't know Kat's business. "I'm staying a short time." She peered into the shop's office adjoining one of the bays. "Is the owner around?"

"He left for lunch quite a while ago. But I can help if you have a car problem."

"It's not about my car. My business is with Mr. Holmes. Do you know when he'll be back?"

Pete shrugged. "Can never be sure." After twisting the gas cap, he wiped a hand on his overalls and took Kat's money. "You want me to tell him you were here?"

"No, never mind." She headed back to town, parked in front of Hank's, and crossed the street to Bertie's, hoping to find Holmes. Making a scene in public was not her first choice, but she was mad enough not to care. Or she could drag him outside to have a private talk in the alley, just as he'd supposedly done with Brianna.

In Kat's state of mind the smell of grease and beer nearly gagged her. Only half the tables at Bertie's were occupied and the pool tables were quiet, as was the jukebox. The only person at the bar was the sheriff.

No sign of his son.

She'd already alienated the sheriff once. Tim Holmes had warned her not to ask his father questions about him, but to hell with Tim Holmes. She lit on an adjoining stool. Before she could say a word to the sheriff, he nodded to Bertie, gave Kat a menacing look, and ambled off.

Bertie cleared away his coffee cup. "By the look on your face, you're annoyed, irritated, or totally confused."

"All three."

"The sheriff didn't look that agreeable when he saw you."

"Have you seen his son? I thought he might've come in here."

"Not in a while," Bertie said. "He was briefly in here earlier, but I don't know where that ol' tomcat is hanging his hat these days."

Kat reared back, wide-eyed. "Is this Bertie gossiping? You told me you didn't do such a thing."

"That's not gossip. That's a fact. Everyone in town's seen him with one gal or another." She poured coffee for Kat. "It's on the house. Can I get you something else?"

Kat ordered a turkey sandwich to go. "Then you saw him and Brianna together."

"That's another fact," Bertie said. "You want to know more facts? Saw them with my own eyes. They liked to huddle up in one of the booths. I never did like seeing her with the likes of him, but it was none of my business. She had a lot of mood swings when she was with him. That's for sure."

"Do you remember if he ever hurt her physically?"

Bertie looked around, then leaned toward Kat. "There was one day she went outside on her break. When she came back, she high-tailed it to the bathroom, upset about something. I followed her to see what was wrong, see if I could do anything for her. She was rubbing the back of her head. Then she splashed water on her face. When she turned around, she had a red welt the size of a quarter on her upper cheek, pretty close to her eye. I asked her who did it, but she just shook her head and barged past me. I figured it was Tim, but I wasn't sure. I hadn't seen them together for a while."

Bertie's help, Sue Ann, had been hovering near Bertie, waiting to give Kat her order. "Tim did it."

Bertie's face hardened. "You shouldn't go butting into business that's not yours."

Sue Ann shrugged with a nonchalant look. "Everyone knows Tim likes to mess women up."

"Sue Ann."

"He can't keep his hands to himself, whether he's loving or hitting. I oughtta know." She strolled into the kitchen, the doors swinging in unison.

"Don't mind her," Bertie said. "She exaggerates to high heaven."

"If I didn't know any better, I'd think you were defending Tim."

"Just like to stick to the facts."

"That's the best way to be."

Bertie wiped the counter next to Kat. "Why on earth do you want to dredge up the past about your sister? I imagine it can only be painful for you."

"I guess I want to fill in the gaps, so I can move on." Kat left out the questions that were growing into suspicions.

"I can understand that," Bertie said. "After my ma died, I found out she was having an affair about nine months before I was born. Could have been my real father. A person needs to know those things."

"That's so true." Kat took the sack and slid off the stool. "Thanks for the information, Bertie."

"Hope you find out what you need to know."

Before she left Rosswood, Kat was determined to discover the truth about Brianna's relationship with Tim Holmes, no matter how painful it turned out to be, no matter where it led.

Instead of going straight home, she drove to a park across from the auto shop, sat in her car, ate her sandwich, and waited for him to return. As the sun paled in the western sky, only Pete milled around the shop. She waited an hour with still no sign of Holmes. She lost patience and figured she'd hunt him down tomorrow even if she had to show up at his house and confront him in front of his poor wife.

On her way through town, she stopped at Hank's to buy a carton of milk. Coming out of the store was a petite woman, her dark brown hair squarely shagged. She wore a low-cut black sheath with a black cashmere cardigan draped over her shoulders. Her flats were tiny, like ballerina slippers. This woman was dressed for a summer's day in Phoenix, not an autumn day in Rosswood. Kat felt chilled just looking at her.

On passing, she gave Kat a brief, harsh stare and got into a late-model dark blue sedan. If Kat seemed out of place in this town, this woman would never fit in in a million years.

CHAPTER 18

*Z*eke's persistent barking alerted Chance to the arrival of an unfamiliar visitor. As he approached the kitchen window, the barking stopped. With Zeke in check Rusty stood by a dark blue sedan, talking to a woman in a black dress: Monique Bouvier.

At the sight of her, the knot in Chance's stomach tightened. His jaw clenched in anger. Wasn't it just like Monique to come to him if he wouldn't come to her? He should have known she wouldn't take no for an answer.

He wished the woman ringing the doorbell was Kat. The coconut scent of her hair still lingered on his collar.

Shaking that thought, he remembered the manuscript sitting in full view on his desk, the novel that, most definitely, was not for Monique's eyes. He rushed to shove the papers into the bottom desk drawer.

When he reluctantly answered the door, Monique's eyes lit up with pleasure. She smiled as if she'd been expected all along.

The curves of her body, which he knew by memory, were accentuated by the sexy lines of her dress. It gave him pause. He reminded himself to keep his distance, even when she threw her arms around his neck and kissed both cheeks, her highly perfumed body wiping out Kat's subtle scent.

Held back by Rusty, Zeke wiggled and yipped. Hunched over the dog, Rusty grinned, seemed to be enjoying the scene on the porch. Chance peeled away Monique's arms and brought her into the house, thus blocking Rusty's view with a closed door.

"What are you doing here and how did you find me?" he asked, though he knew quite well what her answer would be.

"How silly a question that is. You know we keep tabs on you." She tossed her sweater on a dining room chair, slid an arm around his waist, and looked up at him. "Surely you have not forgotten we keep tabs on all our associates, past and present."

"I'm quite aware of that." He stepped out of her grip. "I know how the organization works, Monique, but you don't make personal visits to a place like this unless you want something from me. And I have nothing to give, not to you or the organization."

"Oh, but you are wrong," she said. "You have a promise to keep to the firm."

He thought of his manuscript as he read the edge in her tone, verging on a threat. He was thankful he'd buried it from her sight.

"And, I hope before this night is over, a promise to me as well. I have waited too long to be with you."

His muscles ached with tension. "First of all, the organization has nothing to worry about. I have a new life here. They know that. And I'm not anxious to change it in any way."

"Oh, it is not me, Chance. I would never accuse you, but there are those who believe otherwise. They sent me to make sure you are satisfied here, that you will not cause problems in the future."

"What do they think I'll do? It's been five years."

She circled around him and peered into the kitchen. "I have traveled all day, Chance. Can we get comfortable? Do you have wine?" When he didn't respond, she spotted a bottle of Merlot on the counter that had recently been opened and set it on the table. She found wineglasses in a nearby cupboard and poured them each a glass.

She was determined to stay, so he agreed to hear her out. She waited for him to sit, then pushed her chair near his, slipped off her shoes, and rested her feet on his lap. "Do you remember our first meeting, darling?"

He volunteered nothing, not a yes or a no, only toyed with the stem of his glass, so she brought up their first encounter. Whenever they were together, she loved hashing over old times: After his first successful assignment for the organization, they'd sent him to London for rest and relaxation. A colleague, Monique, showed up at his hotel suite to sweeten the deal.

He remained stoic, revealing no emotion or recognition, as if the memory of their initial meeting had been lost in a fog. She continued to recount the times they'd worked together in various parts of the world, including the United States. Still, no glimmer of fond remembrance in his eyes, no wistful smile.

She poured herself another glass of wine, and his remained untouched. "You are so quiet, Chance. What are your thoughts?"

Nothing he cared to share with her. He stared at his glass and wished Kat were here in place of Monique, yet prayed at this particular moment Kat wouldn't surprise him with a visit. "I think this conversation is over. Shouldn't you be on the road back to Seattle?"

She glanced toward the window. The sun had set, and the light in the room was dimming. "It is too late. May I stay here till morning?"

"That wouldn't be a good idea." He lowered her feet to the floor.

"You know I cannot drive in the dark. And I have not said all I need to say."

"Save your breath," he said. "I know what you're going to say to me."

She placed her hand on his knee. "It is imperative, Chance. I must remind you of Gerald Morningstar. Do you remember him?"

"Don't bother me with the details."

"Then you remember he was a, what do you say, whistleblower. Last year he turned on the organization. He had been out five years, the same as you. They get antsy after too long because of him."

Chance stood and shoved in his chair. "I know about Morningstar, and I know what they are capable of, so save your words, Monique."

"I came here on my own as a friend." Her eyes softened. "I wished to see you, yes, to warn you of what they are talking of now. I do not want you to get hurt like Gerald."

"There's nothing they can do to me."

"Oh, but you are wrong. If you say or do anything."

"What makes them think I plan to cross them?"

She paused, glanced at her wineglass, and eyed him steadily. "Just let me be your friend and warn you of what they are thinking, that you might bring misery to them as Gerald has done. You left so suddenly. They worry you will do the same. They want you back in the organization, Chance."

"That will never happen." He poured out his wine in the kitchen sink, the liquid slithering down the drain, leaving tiny red splatters.

It would be pitch dark before Monique made it to the mountains, and she did suffer from night blindness, at least that was what he recalled. He was resigned to having an overnight guest, albeit an unwelcome one. He'd lost his appetite, and instead of cooking dinner, he made her a ham and cheese sandwich and showed her the guest bedroom.

While he was outside fetching her overnight bag, Zeke bounded up to him, wagging his tail. Because Monique was allergic to dogs, he asked Rusty to look after Zeke.

"It ain't none of my business, boss, but I thought you'd takin' a liking to that Summers woman. Who's this lady?"

Chance scrubbed Zeke's coat. "It isn't any of your business. I'll see you tomorrow." He gave the dog's rump a swift pat. "Go with Rusty, boy." He watched Rusty meander toward the barn shaking his head with Zeke in pursuit. He returned to the house.

Monique had come back to the kitchen to get more wine. "Will you not drink with me, Chance?"

"There's a TV in your room if you get lonely." Though it was still early, he retreated to his bedroom, hoping to keep a safe distance between them.

CHAPTER 19

On returning home, Kat had sorted through cupboards, throwing out stale food—old pancake mix, cereals, flour. She'd tossed out the canned goods as well. No telling how long they'd been stored.

She'd worked with only her socks on, and by late evening her feet were chilled from the bare floors. She went in search of her slippers.

Her mind skipped to Tim Holmes and what he may have done to Brianna. The ire rose in her again. She wouldn't let the matter slide.

Rounding the bedroom doorway, she accidentally kicked a slipper under the bed. She switched on the lamp to have a better look and realized she'd also disturbed the scatter rug. On the wooden floor was a reddish brown blotch that looked like smeared blood.

When Kat knelt and touched the stain, a horrendous stab of shock and terror lit into her, her imagination reeling with bits and pieces of a macabre scene: hands on a woman's neck, a terrifying struggle. She lifted her hand. The images instantly disappeared.

Was Brianna murdered here? That thought was too horrible to consider, too foolish even. They'd discovered her body in the garage. Kat shooed the notion away and dragged the rug over the stain.

She looked up and could have sworn the curtains fluttered. But the window was closed all the way. Her mind was definitely playing tricks on her.

She reached under the bed and felt around for the slipper. Her hand butted against a hard object. She pulled out a box, filled with more of Brianna's stories.

Kat picked up a manuscript, expecting to be calmed and entertained by a charming children's story about a duck or a dog or a little girl. The title was innocent enough: Jack Meets Jill. By the second page delight changed to disbelief. Brianna had taken a child's nursery rhyme and turned it into a dark erotic fantasy.

Kat skipped to the back page and found a copy of a contract from a porn magazine, signed by Brianna, along with a copy of a check in her name, dated six months before she died. The pay was exceptional.

She must have needed the money. No wonder she never showed these stories to Chance.

To discover how far back in time Brianna had written these particular stories, Kat began to rifle through the box in search of more signed contracts, but the blast of a motorcycle engine interrupted her. She shot into the living room and flipped on the porch light. In the driveway Tim Holmes's Harley sputtered to a stop.

Kat prickled with anger and panic. She didn't want to be alone in the house with him, so she met him outside by his motorcycle. "What are you doing here?"

He tucked his helmet into the crook of his arm. "Pete said you were looking for me, and then later he saw you parked across the street watching the shop. Said you'd been there at least an hour. I figured it must be important, so what did you want to talk to me about?"

"I wanted you to clear something up about your relationship with my sister."

"I already told you."

"Just hear me out." How would she ask him if he beat up Brianna without inciting him? If it were true, Kat wanted to tear him apart, but now that they were alone in the dark, she didn't feel quite so brave. "Look, I'm pretty tired. Why don't we talk tomorrow at your shop?"

"I came all the way out here. Just tell me what you want to know. I don't have all night."

This dark, dead-end street wasn't the place for a confrontation with Tim Holmes. "I'd really rather talk to you tomorrow at your shop." She turned to go inside, but he grabbed her arm.

"I'm here, okay?" His voice was steady, but searing.

The feel of his rough hand fueled her anger even more. She yanked her arm free. "Is this how you treated Brianna? I heard you knocked her around."

"I never did that."

"That's not what Tilly said. She told me she saw you shove Brianna into the wall behind Bertie's."

"Tilly? That girl's nuts. I never touched Brianna that way."

Against her better judgment, Kat said, "If you beat your wife, what would stop you from manhandling my sister?"

"Yeah, and who's the bitch who told you that?"

"I saw your wife, and it's not hard to put two and two together."

He filled his lungs and between clenched teeth blew out a long, ragged breath, as if he were trying to maintain control. His hands closed into fists.

Now that it was out in the open, Kat couldn't hold back. "Did you know Brianna was writing for porn magazines?"

"Porn magazines." He seemed surprised but not enough for Kat.

"Did you put her up to it?"

"You know what, lady? You're just asking for it." He stepped toward her, then stopped himself. Muttering a parade of obscenities, he put on his helmet and mounted his bike. He backed down the driveway and lurched the bike forward, burning rubber.

Kat's wobbly legs almost gave out on her. Where had the courage come from to confront a man like Tim Holmes? Or was it stupidity?

She longed for a hot bath, but settled for a quick, tepid shower and a cup of steaming chamomile tea. Afterward, she shoved the box under the bed and climbed under the covers with Tiger by her side. The argument with Tim Holmes had drained her. The tea had relaxed her, and she fell into a deep sleep.

≈

He had to see her again. If he strained his eyes, he could barely make out the outline of her body. That wasn't good enough. The curtains blocked his view, and it was way too dark. The grass was prickly on his ankles. Too many spider webs lurked in the shadows. He had to get closer. He had to touch her. He tugged at the window frame, but it wouldn't budge.

The weeds and vines were devouring this old house. He crept around to the front door, looking for a way in. He kept his flashlight pointed low, just enough light to guide his way.

The old road, leading from town through tangled trees, was a stroke of luck for him. No one traveled it anymore because it only led to this broken-down house on a dead-end street.

The woman inside was his release, Brianna's gift. He had to get closer tonight. He had to run his palm across the curve of her hip.

Another stroke of luck. The doorknob jiggled free. She forgot to lock the door. No doubt she forgot on purpose.

He slowed his breathing to quiet his yearning heart. He didn't want to wake her. He wanted to touch her, a taste of what was to come.

He tiptoed ever so softly across the room. The floorboards groaned. He waited, listening for sounds from the bedroom. Nothing.

He snuck to the doorway. There she was, sleeping like a sweet, sweet memory.

His breathing picked up, came in short, choppy bursts. His palms were hot and clammy. He wanted to wait, but he couldn't wait. He had to feel skin against skin.

Maybe this time it would be different. Remembering their last encounter, he dug into the flesh of his palms to dampen the anger. No, he told himself. Not now. Go slow. But he had to touch her.

She was lying on her side, facing away from him, and just as his hand hovered over her leg, she whimpered in her sleep, startling him. As he backed from the room, the door slammed shut. In a shocked haze he fled the house.

～

Kat rolled onto her back, alarmed. She'd heard a thunderous noise, like the door crashing shut, then a rattling sound. She bounded from the bed, heart thumping, and found Tiger in the living room with her back hunched and the door partway open. Kat had a vague feeling she'd forgotten to lock it before she turned in for the night. She couldn't be sure.

A sick feeling replaced the uncertainty. After her encounter with Tim Holmes, she'd been so stressed she hadn't given the door a thought. She was certain she'd closed it. On the other hand she was positive the door banging shut was what woke her. And now it was open again. But everything in the room was in its place. She rummaged through her purse and found nothing missing.

This time Kat made sure the door was securely locked and braced a chair under the doorknob. She scooped Tiger up and went back to bed, but she wouldn't sleep.

For a while she listened for any little disturbance—the house settling, the refrigerator's hum—and fought the urge to close her eyes. But it was no use. Soon she dozed restlessly until the kitten's growl scared her, and she woke in a daze.

At the foot of the bed was a filmy outline of Brianna's body, her face anxious and troubled. A voice, faint but distinct, pleaded, "Help me." In a blink the image slipped into the void.

Kat shivered under the covers. Was she going crazy? First, the vision, now a voice, a voice that cried for help. Help her, how? And if it truly was Brianna's spirit, had she tried to get Kat's attention earlier in the night by slamming the door? Logic told Kat this was all nonsense, but a tugging of her heart told her otherwise.

Questions were piling up, questions that needed answering: Why was there blood on the floor? Who was the perpetrator of the crank calls, and was there a connection? Why had Tim Holmes shown up at the house the night Brianna died? Something about Brianna's death wasn't adding up. Was that why Brianna haunted her?

Kat had to tell someone her concerns, but who could she trust? She ran down the list of characters in this town but ruled out every one of them. Unfounded rumors were too easily spread. Her only choice was Chance Eliason. He was discreet, he was private, and he was the one person who genuinely understood and cared for Brianna.

Kat wrapped a wool shirt over her pajamas and in the middle of the night huddled on the couch with the kitten.

Chance had read until midnight. With Monique in the house, he'd remained hyperaware. He didn't trust her. Once, he'd heard footsteps in the hallway and the bathroom door click shut.

Just as he was drifting into a light doze, a grating noise startled him awake and on his feet. Avoiding the creaks in the floorboards, he slid his door open and walked cautiously to his office.

Monique glanced up from his desk and froze. The bottom drawer was ajar, and it looked as if she were about to rummage inside. The strap of her flimsy nightie slipped off her shoulder, revealing part of her breast. "I needed a pen," she said.

He knew exactly what she needed. He shoved the drawer inward and gripped her upper arm until she winced. No way would he leave her anywhere in his house alone. He dragged her into his bedroom and shoved her onto the bed. "Get in."

"You have to understand, Chance, I am only trying to protect you."

"Get in the bed, Monique. Now."

She scuttled under the covers, and Chance slid in next to her. "Don't get any ideas," he warned. "I'm just keeping an eye on you. In the morning you're gone."

"But, darling."

If he turned his back on her and fell asleep, it might give her the opportunity to sneak out, so he lay facing her. She snuggled up to him, her soft breasts against his bare chest. Her breath was hot and ticklish. It'd been a long while since he'd felt the warmth of a woman in his bed.

Years ago, when he was young and foolish, he wanted this woman so badly, he'd begged her to leave the organization and run away with him. In those days, to her, he was any other man. Now, here in his bed, she meant nothing to him. Yet, she was so close, so alive, her body heady with perfume. Why not give in to temptation and have sex for the sake of satisfying his own needs?

"Let me make love to you," she whispered, as if she'd read his mind.

Her fingers inched up his thigh, giving him a surge of longing, but in his mind's eye all he could see was Kat's face. He stifled a moan and grabbed Monique's wrist before she moved any farther up his leg. He wouldn't give her the satisfaction of knowing she still had that effect on him.

He pushed her onto her back and pinned her down with an arm across her chest. She squirmed to free herself, but she was no match for his strength. "Do you not want me? You know I want you," she said.

His body craved the release of sex, and it would have been so easy to let Monique—this woman whom he'd been close to in every way imaginable—fulfill his desires, but all he could think of was Kat. He asked Monique to face away from him, and she reluctantly turned onto her side. "Go to sleep, Monique. I beg you. Just go to sleep."

CHAPTER 20

As the room brightened with morning light, Kat considered packing up and heading home, but with no sleep to speak of, tattered nerves, and a million questions bombarding her, she needed to stay put. As much as she hated to admit it, she needed Chance Eliason.

Tiger stretched and yawned, jumped off the couch, and wandered into the kitchen to munch on her kibble. When Kat opened the door, she didn't have to call Tiger's name twice before the kitten jetted outside.

While Kat was in the bedroom dressing, she kicked the rug aside. The bloodstain was exactly where she'd discovered it. She hadn't imagined it. In the natural light the stain most definitely looked swirled and messy, as if someone had hastily tried to clean it up.

She glanced at the foot of the bed. Brianna's ghost left a shuddering memory.

She grabbed her purse with the intent of driving to Chance's house, but it was only seven o'clock. She lay on the sofa and dozed until a knocking woke her.

She wasn't expecting anyone, unless Chance had read her mind. Though the way she'd distanced herself from him, it was unlikely he'd come around, uninvited.

She opened the door, half expecting to see Chance, but staring back at her wide-eyed was Lenny Faulkes, dressed in baggy slacks and a pullover sweater. His lower lids hung like sagging drapes. He held up an envelope. "Sorry to intrude, Kaaat, but this came for Brianna."

"Aren't you making your rounds a little early?" She was annoyed he'd even come to the house.

"It's nine o'clock, Kaaat."

She glanced at her watch. She'd napped two hours.

"Oh, now Kaaat, I thought you might want this. I didn't know if you were coming to the post office, and this looks important." He shook the envelope. "Feels like it might be a check. In my business I would know these things. And isn't the return address interesting. Looks like it's from one of those filthy magazines. I wonder what business Brianna had with them."

As if he didn't know. From Kat's discovery the night before, Brianna had received others in the mail. Kat snatched the envelope away. "Thank you for bringing it by, Mr. Faulkes."

"Lenny."

"There's no need for you to make special trips here."

"Oh, I don't mind, Kaaat. It gets me out of the office, if you know what I mean." He glanced past her. "This is a nice old house. I used to stop by once in a while to bring Brianna's mail. I sure miss her. It's nice having you here, though. Makes the place seem alive again. It sure does. And oh, by the way, if you ever need any help with anything, anything at all, I'm available after hours."

"I really don't," she said, "but did you ever come here to help Brianna?"

"Oh no, I never did, although I offered many times." He clucked his tongue. "She always seemed occupied with that Tim Holmes. I never did see what she saw in him. He is such a bad man. I warned her about him. Are you sure I can't help you? I really don't mind. I always wanted to help Brianna. I just loved her, you know."

Kat backed farther into the house. As she began inching the door closed, Tiger squeezed inside. "No, but thanks, again, Mr. Faulkes."

"Lenny. Please, Kaaat, call me Lenny."

She shut the door and peeled back the curtain to watch him leave. He sat in his car and stared at the garage a long while before finally driving away.

She pet Tiger. "What a busybody and maybe just a little bit creepy." Tiger meowed.

Kat opened the envelope. Lenny was wrong. It wasn't a check, just a letter, an interest in Brianna's work. She tossed the letter in the trash.

"Well, I hate to do this to you again, but I have to leave the house. And you, my little friend, have to stay outside." She replenished the kitten's dish and left Tiger on the step, greedily gobbling her food.

Before getting into her car, she looked in the garage, wondering what was so interesting to Lenny Faulkes. She yanked on the rope, knowing full well it wouldn't budge. The metal arm was kinked. It didn't make sense to her that anyone could suffocate from carbon monoxide with a door halfway closed. Add that to the list of unanswered questions.

On the way to Chance's house, she rehearsed what she would say to him. In a very businesslike manner she would ask him to go out to breakfast with her. After all, she wanted to discuss Brianna, not give him any false hopes. He seemed bent on starting some kind of relationship with her, and she couldn't let that happen, could she? Would it hurt if she did?

Lost in thought, she slowed near the turn-off, anxious about initiating anything with Chance, even an innocent meal. At the entrance to his private road was the dark blue sedan, the car she'd seen at Hank's. Her heart sank. On impulse, instead of turning in, she drove past his driveway and veered right at Pine Road, made a quick U-turn, and paused at the stop sign. As the blue car passed by, heading out of town, the woman in the black dress glanced Kat's way.

It was obvious to Kat the woman had spent the night with Chance. What other conclusion could there be? Kat's instincts were right; she knew not to trust him that way. Her cheeks burned. Why did she even care who Chance slept with? She had no hold on the man.

She was exhausted, bizarre things were happening to her, she had mounting questions about Brianna's death, and now this. She needed time to think. Tears came easily.

She turned left toward town. As she approached Chance's road, Rusty was waiting to turn in and waved to her from his truck, but she had no inclination to wave back.

Guided by a force propelling her forward, she bypassed Maple Lane, turned the corner into town, passed several parked cars, and swerved, just missing a pedestrian. Near Bertie's, Doug Jones stopped talking to another man and stared at Kat. Lenny Faulkes hailed her from the post office steps. She ignored his smiling face and continued on.

Up the hill toward the cemetery, she had to brake to make the sharp curve. Sheriff Holmes's cruiser rounded the corner from the opposite direction. As their cars met, he slowed and motioned for her to stop. She wiped away the tears and rolled down her window.

"Headed to the cemetery?"

"I thought I would."

His head bobbed, and he took his time to respond. "Heard you had a little talk with my son last night, accusing him of roughing up your sister."

She gritted her teeth, held her tongue. She wanted to lash out, tell him how she felt about it, but lacked the energy to push back. "We had a discussion."

He jabbed between his bottom front teeth with a toothpick. "You've been on Tim's case ever since you got here, seems to me. I thought you and I had a little talk about that a while back. What are you trying to manufacture here?"

She fought the urge to argue with him. "Nothing, Sheriff. Nothing at all."

"Okay, then. Let's not have this conversation again, you hear?"

She kicked the car into gear and took the curve, glad to end the exchange and be out of his sight. After parking her car, she took a cleansing breath to forget about the sheriff and concentrated on her goal of visiting Brianna's grave.

In Rosswood everything was old, including the local cemetery. Large granite headstones dated back to the late 1800s, the town's mining era. Part of the site was overgrown with weeds, but the newest graves were well cared for, the grass around them neatly mowed.

A modest rectangular headstone in pink granite marked the gravesite with a rose engraved next to the B in Brianna's name. Lying above her name was a real rose, a long-stemmed white rose.

Kat knelt and let the tears flow. Her chat with the sheriff seemed a million years away. "Was that really you last night, Brianna, or just my imagination? Ever since you died, you've been haunting me, pestering me. What do you want from me?"

The wind kicked up, swirled in a whirlwind around her, then settled down again. Though the sun warmed her, she felt the gooseflesh rise.

She touched the tender, velvety petals. The rose was fresh, recently purchased. She knew of no flower shops in Rosswood, but she could be wrong. Perhaps there was one in Benton. "At least someone in this town still cares about you. Maybe it's Chance."

"I wish I could say I'd been so thoughtful."

She started at the sound of his voice. She'd been so focused, the noise of a vehicle's engine hadn't registered. She squinted against the sunlight but couldn't see his face. He grasped her shoulders and helped her to a standing position. She was angry, frustrated, but she couldn't stop the tears. He held her and let her cry. "I wasn't even here when they buried her, Chance. I was closing on a major deal that day. I just laid down the cash and bought her a burial. What kind of a sister am I?"

He rubbed her back with reassuring strokes. "You did the best you could at the time. Maybe closing that deal was just a smokescreen. Maybe you couldn't face seeing her put into the ground."

Kat sobbed until the sobs turned into sniffles. He handed her a handkerchief. She dabbed her eyes and blew her nose. "It's all my fault, you know."

He lifted her chin. "What's all your fault?"

"I let her come here, and for all I know, someone murdered her."

"Murdered her. Whatever gave you that idea? She died from carbon monoxide."

"That's what I wanted to talk to you about," she said. "But how did you find me?"

"Rusty saw you drive past the road about the time Monique left. He said you didn't look happy. I had a feeling why. You weren't home, so I drove through town. When I didn't see your car, I stopped in at the post office. Lenny said he saw you drive up the hill. I wanted to explain."

"About the woman? There's nothing to explain. You have your own life." She twisted out of his hold and tromped down the cement path. The heel of her boot caught in a crack, and she tumbled to her knees. He was there to help her up. "Damn boots." She stepped forward, wobbled, and broke into tears again.

He cradled her shoulder and guided her as she limped the rest of the way to her car. He opened the passenger door. "Get in. I'm taking you home to my house." When she tried to protest, he interrupted her. "After I look at that knee of yours and do some explaining, you can tell me about your murder theory."

"What about your truck?"

"Let me worry about that."

CHAPTER 21

Kat curved into the seat and let Chance take over. The fight in her had just about vanished. Until now she hadn't realized how tense and worn out she was, thinking about her sister's death. The guilt was also a constant burden, a weight she couldn't shake off.

They arrived at his house in her SUV, and Kat didn't even stir when Zeke bounded up to the car barking. At the sight of Chance, he quieted down and wagged his tail.

Chance opened the passenger door and ordered Zeke to stay back. Kat let Chance saddle an arm over her shoulder and escort her into the house with Zeke trailing along. Chance left Zeke outside.

He sat her on the couch and handed her a throw blanket. "Scoot out of your jeans. I want to look at that knee." He unzipped and tugged off her boots. Without balking, she slung the blanket over her lap and winced as she slid denim over skin. With care he lifted her leg and folded the blanket above her knee. "Looks like the beginnings of an angry bruise. There's some scraping, but it's not too bad."

"I'll be all right."

"I know you will, but right now you need a little TLC. Stay right there." He walked down the hallway and turned in at the bathroom.

To Kat, the blast of water in the bathtub was a comforting sound.

He returned, the concern still etched on his face. "I've run a nice warm bath for you, something to soothe. Besides being distraught, you look like you haven't slept a wink."

The image of the woman in the blue sedan popped into Kat's mind, and she couldn't hide the pout. "I could say the same about you, only you had someone to keep you company."

"I'll save that explanation for later. Right now you need to relax."

She shrugged an apathetic response. With the blanket draped around her, she followed him into the bathroom where he left her to soak in a lavender-scented bubble bath. She sank into the water. How she'd missed this simple pleasure.

As heavenly as it was, she couldn't stop wondering if the woman in the black dress had lingered here, enjoying the same treatment as she. When he knocked on the door, she was still thinking about the mystery woman. "What do you want now?"

Without asking, he cracked the door open partway, and she immediately sank farther under the blanket of bubbles. He kept his eyes askance, set a steaming cup of tea on the tub's ledge, and turned to go.

"Is this how you treat all your women?"

He faced her, his eyes boring into hers. "I think we'll have that talk now."

The warmth in the room chilled. She sank even farther into the water, praying the bubbles would last through their conversation.

"You want to know about the woman."

Of course she wanted to know, but she wouldn't say it. She felt foolish because she had no right to ask. This man was driving her crazy.

"Her name is Monique. I've known her for years. We used to work together, but I can't say any more about the work we did." He paused. "Yesterday she showed up unannounced and uninvited."

"Did you sleep with her?" Kat blurted and felt foolish again, like a jealous teen.

He ran a hand over his mouth and chin, pausing a little too long for her liking. "It's not what you're implying."

Somehow she wasn't reassured. She lay back and closed her eyes, too exhausted to think of a slick comeback. The latch clicked shut.

The next time she opened her eyes, the water was lukewarm. No one else was in the room, thank goodness, since all the bubbles had evaporated, leaving her naked body completely exposed.

She emerged from the bathroom in her shirt and underwear, the blanket slung around her middle and the teacup in one hand. She traipsed into the living room in search of her jeans.

Chance was sitting on the couch with his neck cranked back, his jaw slack and his lips parted. When she set the cup on the coffee table, his eyes shot open.

"Thanks for the tea," she said. "I think I slept a little. I'll just get my jeans and dress in the other room."

He caught her arm and drew her down on the couch. "We need to talk."

"I thought we did."

"You know what I mean."

Her blink of a nap hadn't erased the drain of the preceding night, and she wasn't in an argumentative mood, but she sat a comfortable distance away from him. "So, go ahead and talk. I'm listening."

"Are you?"

"I said I am."

He sighed in frustration. "I can't tell you any more about Monique because then I would have to explain my past, and if I did that, I might jeopardize my life and perhaps yours. Do you understand?"

"You're being vague and just a little dramatic."

"You're going to have to trust me."

How could she trust him? "Were you lovers?"

"Before I moved here," he said. "But I'm going to be honest with you. We met in Seattle once and spent a night together for old time's sake. I wasn't involved with anyone back then, and this time she wasn't welcome here."

"You're involved with someone now?" She knew it.

"Just hear me out," he said. "Monique and I slept in the same bed, because after I put her in the guest room, I caught her snooping through my personal effects. I didn't want her out of my sight, but I never touched her in a sexual way. I hardly slept. I had to stay vigilant."

"That sounds like such a crock. A woman like that in your bed and you wouldn't at least want to gratify yourself?"

"There's only one woman I want, Kat, and that's you."

Kat hugged the blanket to her body. Her head spun with the question of trusting Chance, plus her own issue of letting go. "Why didn't you send her away?"

"Because she suffers from night blindness. It was too late."

"How convenient. What about the motel?"

"I made an error in judgment," he said. "I put her in the spare room and figured she'd be gone in the morning, no problem. But she wandered into my study to gather information. She lied to me about the real reason for her visit. I can't explain more than that."

"Right. Secrets and more secrets. Why should I even believe you?"

"I care about you, Kat. You're the first woman in a very long time that I've seriously been attracted to in this way. I'd at least like to explore these feelings with you and see where they lead."

"You don't even know me that well."

"I know you better than you think I do. Remember, I spent a lot of time with your sister."

"She and I are nothing alike."

"You may have gone down different paths," he said, "but there's one thing you have in common. Brianna may have had her problems, but underneath it all she had a heart of gold. I could tell by the tender way she cared for the animals. And under all that bluster of yours, you do, too."

"Sure I do. Look how I treated my own sister."

"Those tears you shed at the cemetery were enough to convince me you cared deeply about her, more than you let on."

She did care about Brianna, but caring about her hadn't changed anything. "Chance, I learned something about her that I could never have imagined her capable of. And it has to be my fault. I never should have let her leave Seattle and her support group." Kat's throat thickened. To maintain control, she took in a breath, but she couldn't stop the tears.

He moved closer and settled his arm over her shoulder. "You're exhausted, Kat. Let me put you to bed."

She sniffed and snorted, trying to gather her composure. She was too worn out to think.

"Come on. Sleep will do you good." He helped her to her feet, and she dragged the blanket around her.

He put her to bed in his room, a room with clean sheets, totally aired out of another woman's scent. With the blanket clinging to her, she slipped under the covers. She didn't fight Chance, but she fought sleep, waiting for him to leave. But he stayed close. Before she faded into sleep, she heard his soft snores.

~

Chance woke first. It was still light outside, but the braying burros alerted him to the time of day. In a minute they'd quiet down since Rusty would be tending to their dinner. He and Kat had slept all afternoon into the early evening. He hoped the animals wouldn't wake her. He wanted to keep her here as long as possible, hoping she would spend the night. He rolled onto his side, facing her, and ran his palm lightly down her arm. He could get used to this.

She stirred, and he retracted his hand. She yawned, then raised her head and cast a disoriented glance around the room. "Where am I?" She looked at Chance, panic in her eyes, then at his clothed body on top of the covers. "Oh." She lay back and sighed. "How long have I been sleeping?"

"It's six now. I'd say a good five hours."

"Oh, no, I'll never sleep tonight."

"I bet you will. You were exhausted, still are."

"I haven't slept well in months."

He propped on his elbow to look at her. Her hair was tangled and messy, but she was never more enticing. He wished he could act on his desire, but it wasn't the right time. "Tell me why you haven't slept well. Has there been something else bothering you, besides Brianna? Looming debts, an old flame?"

She smiled a sleepy smile, rousing the dimples on the sides of her mouth. "Debts, no. Old flames? I have lots of them, but they all burned out a long time ago." Her smile dimmed. "Brianna's death is my principal worry." She scooted up against the headboard and so did he.

"Tell me your concerns."

"I don't know, Chance. I seem to be getting these strange feelings, ideas, really. For me, things just don't add up. I'm starting to question whether Brianna actually took her own life."

"Explain."

"Okay, but you'll probably think I'm crazy," she said. "I know I was told she committed suicide by turning on her car's engine in her garage. Asphyxiation by carbon monoxide poisoning. But the garage door doesn't even close all the way. The metal is buckled. I've pulled it as hard as I can, and it won't budge. It gets stuck halfway. Wouldn't that let too much oxygen in? Did you know that about the garage door?"

"I can't say that I did. Whenever I stopped by, the door was always open. I didn't have a reason to question it. But the sheriff investigated."

"What about all those crazy calls she was getting before she died? Maybe it's connected. And I found dried blood under the rug near her bed. It looked smeared, like someone tried to wipe it up."

"I'll give you the crank calls, but after her death, I never heard anything about blood in her house. Maybe she had an accident or cut herself."

"No, Chance. She was fastidious. She would never have left blood on the floor like that. And Tilly told me she saw Tim Holmes rough Brianna up behind Bertie's, and Tilly's grandmother told me she heard his motorcycle late that night going to Brianna's house."

"Are you thinking Tim Holmes had something to do with it? He's an S.O.B., but I don't think he's capable of murder."

"He beats his wife, and he beat up Brianna."

"I just don't know, Kat. Like I said, her death was investigated."

"You said yourself the sheriff would protect his son."

"Maybe from being accused of harassing phone calls, but not murder. The sheriff said they found her early in the morning. Maybe she was upset after he left."

Kat shifted the pillow into a more comfortable position. "I've been thinking a lot about this, and the bottom line is Brianna had no reason to commit suicide. I know she was troubled at times, but everyone I've talked to here says she was happy before she died. You said so yourself. You said she was the one who broke up the relationship. So why would she kill herself over him?"

"That's a good point," Chance said. "She seemed very happy, especially after she rid herself of him."

"Then what about this? If he kept pestering her to go back to him and she wouldn't, maybe he got so mad he lost control. A man who's as abusive as he is could do anything if provoked far enough."

"True."

"I didn't tell you this, but he came to the house last night because he wanted to know why I was looking for him. I'll tell you what. It wouldn't take much to push him over the edge."

"Kat, you should be careful."

"I can handle it."

"Still, you need to be cautious, especially when you're alone in that house. Why don't you move into my guest room for the rest of your stay here?"

Kat leaned away from Chance. "You sure know how to bring the conversation back to what you want."

"I only want you to be safe."

"Safe in your bed."

"That's not what I meant. I think staying here is the logical thing to do."

"Yeah, well, there's no logic in any of this. Do you know I'm seeing Brianna's ghost now, and hearing her voice?" Kat's own voice wavered.

"Kat . . ."

"I am, Chance. Last night the door slammed and woke me up. There was no one in the house. Later her ghost was at the foot of my bed, and her desperate voice cried out to me." Kat turned away from him.

He hated to see her tortured this way. He linked arms with her and gave her a nudge closer, but she threw off his arm and inched away toward the edge of the bed. The old Kat was returning, aloof and defensive.

She stood with the blanket around her waist. "I'm going back to Brianna's."

"Now?" He didn't want her to leave.

"Tiger's outside."

"Did you leave food for her?"

"Yes, but—"

"She'll survive one night." He rounded the corner of the bed and stationed himself between her and the door. "I wish you'd stay."

"I'm not that tired, and I'll probably be up most of the night anyway," she said matter-of-factly. "You were nice enough to listen to my outrageous theory, but I don't think you're taking me seriously."

"I *am* taking you seriously. It's just that it took me by surprise. I hadn't considered her death to be anything other than what I was told. Give me time to think it through."

"Excuse me, but I have to go. I have work to do. Besides, what would I do here?"

"Hmm . . . I could think of something," he said in jest.

"I'm sure you could. Where are my jeans?" She sidestepped him and headed into the living room.

"Whatever you want to do," he called after her in exasperation, "but aren't you hungry? Can I fix you a meal, take you out?"

With the blanket over her lap, she squeezed into her jeans, careful of her bruised knee. "Do you have any lunchmeat? A sandwich will do."

"If you'll give me thirty minutes, I can make you a hot meal."

She zipped up her boots without answering him and stalked into the kitchen. Chance gave in and made them both a turkey sandwich. While she ate, he brought Zeke inside, dragging him through the doorway and across the linoleum. Zeke slid and scraped his nails, trying to keep from being banished to the garage. He whimpered and pawed the closed door.

Kat asked to have her sandwich wrapped to go, giving Chance the impression she really couldn't stand spending one more minute with him. The woman was both hot and cold, a description, if he remembered right, she'd given him.

She edged toward the door, and he grabbed his keys and left his sandwich uneaten. "Can you at least give me a ride to my truck?"

"Fair enough."

But he didn't think her going home at all was fair.

They'd lain in bed discussing Brianna's death well into the evening. It was already after nine. Outside, the moonlight shimmered through the trees, deepening the shadows.

CHAPTER 22

If it weren't for the SUV's headlights, the cemetery would have gone unnoticed. Tucked away in a hillside of sprawling maples and ancient pines that thickened at the rim, the graveyard was dark and shadowy. The eldest headstones, tall and stalwart, caught the light just right, appearing like phantoms in the night.

Kat edged her car closer to Chance's truck, the lone vehicle parked across the road. She waited for him to unbuckle his seatbelt.

"I don't think you should be alone, Kat. Are you sure you won't reconsider and stay at my house?"

Too many thoughts were roiling, too many questions about her sister's death, her need to close up the house, and now Chance's confession of how he felt about her. His asking had too many implications.

Maybe he was the type who knew exactly what he wanted, but for Kat one week was too soon, too fast to begin a relationship, or an affair, or whatever he was asking of her. As attracted as she was to him, in the past she'd allowed herself to be swept into the bliss of new love with disastrous results. She needed time to think things through. "Not tonight," she murmured.

He exited the car and leaned inside. "I'll follow you to make sure you get home all right."

"That's not necessary."

As she chugged through town—deserted except for a few cars parked outside Bertie's—and turned left onto Maple Lane, his truck followed. Though she'd objected to it earlier, this chivalrous act comforted her.

But her comfort was short-lived. In the driveway her headlights revealed the door to the house was wide open. She tried to recall if she'd forgotten to lock up. Thinking back, she was certain she let Tiger out. She'd told Chance as much. But had she actually locked the door?

By now Chance was tapping on her car's window. She'd been so fixated on the house she hadn't paid attention to the lights looming behind her.

"Didn't you lock up when you left?" He opened the car door for her.

She hurried ahead. On the front step she accidentally flipped over Tiger's dish, scattering the kibble. She switched on the overhead light and gasped at the room's condition. The lamp lay on the floor. A chair was cast on its side.

Chance pushed her back, then disappeared into the bedroom. Coming back into the living area, he said, "No one's here. You can come in now."

She set the lamp on the end table and took stock of the room. Brianna's afghan was heaped on the floor next to a shattered coffee cup. When she bent to right the chair, he instructed her to leave the rest alone for the sheriff to see.

She crossed the room, avoiding a broken chunk of ceramic. The shaft of light, shining into the bedroom, revealed jumbled bedcovers strewn with Kat's clothes. "Who would do this?"

"Is there anything missing?"

She righted the bedroom lamp. On the closet shelf the blanket was shoved to the side and dangled precariously on the edge. The laptop was still in its place as was the box. "Nothing."

"Let's leave things be. In the morning we'll contact the sheriff. For tonight, you're staying with me."

It was too late to find another place to sleep. She had to stay with Chance. Given the situation, she wanted to stay with him, at least stay in his guest room. "All right, but first there's something I need to check out." She dislodged the box from under the bed, thereby disturbing the throw rug and reminding her of the bloodstain. "Chance, I want you to look at this." He knelt beside her, and she raised the rug for him to see. "This is what I was telling you about."

He touched a finger to the swirled stain. He looked at Kat, concerned.

She removed the box and the laptop from the closet shelf and stacked all of Brianna's papers into one box. "I'm not leaving these here." She gathered everything and left the room.

"You shouldn't remove anything," he said, pursuing her.

"I'm not leaving this for anyone else to see."

"What was in the box under the bed?"

"Wait till we're back at your house." She checked in the kitchen. Everything looked normal, nothing moved or broken. Her gaze fell on the bag of kibble. "Tiger. Where is she? I can't leave her."

"Whoever broke in probably scared her off. She'll be back."

"I can't leave her, Chance. What if she comes back, and I'm not here?"

"Put a bowl of food by the garage. Believe me, she'll come around. She's got a good thing going here. We'll stop by early in the morning and check on her." While Kat took care of Tiger's dish, he examined the door. "Doesn't look like anyone broke in. You must have left it unlocked."

"I know I locked it. I always . . ." She thought about the door slamming shut in the middle of the night, too spooked to bring it up again. "I usually do."

"I checked the window in the bedroom. It was cracked open a little. Maybe whoever did this came in that way."

"I'm sure I locked that, too. I mean, I think I did. I just don't know. What about calling the sheriff now?"

"We could, but knowing Holmes, since nothing is missing, he'd tell us to lock the door and call him in the morning."

She gave the room one last look before he locked up. "He's that lax?"

Chance shrugged, then walked to the garage and gave the door a tug. It wouldn't budge past the halfway point.

On the drive to Chance's place, Kat realized she only had the clothes on her back, the clothes she'd worn all day—her jeans, shirt, and boots. She hadn't thought to grab her makeup kit or a change of undies, which, she suddenly recalled, seemed strategically placed in a row on top of her jumbled clothes. She shuddered at the thought of some weirdo handling her intimate apparel. Anger bubbled up, displacing the fear.

Chance's house was warm and cozy, exactly as they'd left it. Zeke barked from inside the garage, and Chance squeezed through the doorway while soothing him with tender words. Kat heard a ball hit the garage wall. Chance walked in from the kitchen area and offered her a glass of ice water.

She set the box on the coffee table and slouched on the sofa. She felt limp from the stress of the situation, but her mind was honed on tossing theories around. "Do you think Tim Holmes did it? He was that mad."

"I don't know, Kat, but obviously, someone's trying to scare you."

"Tim Holmes. He's the one with the temper and the motive. I've been challenging him, and he doesn't like it. Maybe I'm getting too close to the truth. I've made him pretty angry."

"If you're measuring it by whom you've angered, there are other people to consider. What about Nate Wheeler?"

Her body stiffened. "You're right. I pissed him off, too, but . . ." Kat sucked a quick breath in. "Oh, my gosh, what if Brianna was having an affair with Wheeler and she was threatening to tell his wife? Think about it, Chance. He'd have a motive for killing Brianna." She paused. "No, it has to be Tim Holmes. He was with Brianna the night she died."

"Aren't you jumping to conclusions? You don't even know if this murder theory of yours is true. There was an investigation."

Slumping again, Kat reconsidered. "I don't know anything for sure, Chance, except for the fact that I can't believe she'd commit suicide, just like I can't believe what she was writing about." She searched the box and tossed him one of Brianna's manuscripts. "Take a look at this."

After reading a little, he blew out a whistled breath, but continued to read on. Kat skimmed one of the other stories. She squeezed his arm, causing him to look up.

"What is it, Kat?"

"Here, look at this." She pointed to the middle of a page. "See the word 'pussycat'? That's what the pervert on the phone calls me. He did it in Seattle, and he's doing it here. That means whoever's been harassing me must know about these stories. How else would he have known to use that word?"

"What's the story about? Maybe there's a clue to the identity of this guy."

"It's called 'Sister Love,' and it's about a man who fantasizes about two women." She scanned the first two pages and dropped the manuscript as if it were broken glass. "How could she write this garbage?"

Chance collected the pages and skimmed what Kat had read. "Do you get that the man in this story is nuts and goes after both these women? Think about it, Kat. What if the man who harassed Brianna read this story and is now harassing you?"

"But the man acted on his fantasies." Kat suddenly felt sick to her stomach.

"Your murder theory might not be a theory at all. I'll tell you one thing, theory or no theory, you're staying here for the duration."

Any other time she would have protested, but not now. "What about the sheriff? Shouldn't we get him involved?"

Chance checked the calendar on the kitchen wall. "I've got an appointment early tomorrow morning in Benton. But as soon as I get back, we'll call the sheriff and meet him at Brianna's. We can explain your theory to him then, although I don't know if it will do any good."

"When will you be back?"

"By eleven at the latest."

She nodded, knowing full well she wouldn't wait for him. She was perfectly capable of handling the situation herself.

≈

The braying burros woke Kat. Her neck hurt from being kinked sideways and drool had dripped from her mouth onto Chance's shirt. For clues to the identity of the caller, they'd continued reading the stories. Sometime during the night she'd rested against the warmth of his body and had fallen asleep. Now it was light outside.

He stirred when she pushed away from him and slid his arm out from behind her shoulder. He shook the kinks out.

"What time is it? How long have we been sleeping?" She groaned in the process of stretching her legs from a curled-up position.

Zeke whimpered at the kitchen door.

"It's after seven." Chance rose, arched his back. "I've got to clean up and get to Benton. Do you want to come along?"

"I think I'll stay here."

"Why don't you go into the guest room and get some sleep? I'll wake you when I get back."

"I'll just stay here." She stretched out on the sofa and grabbed a scatter pillow for her head.

He placed a blanket over her and brushed a stray hair from her face, his expression warm and affectionate. "I'll be back soon. Rusty is out at the barn if you need anything. He'll keep a watch on the house."

"Hmm . . . mmm," she muttered, closing her eyes. She heard the clip of Zeke's nails across the kitchen floor, a door close, and a shower running. She dozed but heard Chance leave by way of the front door and his truck's engine sputter to life. The rich smell of coffee hung in the air. Sometime while she'd slept, he'd made a pot.

As soon as he was gone, she flung the blanket aside and went into the bathroom to wash up. Her hair looked a fright. Another ponytail day.

Coming out of the bathroom, she had the urge to snoop around, discover more about this mysterious man who, by chance, had come into her life. She peered into his study. As tempting as it was, she'd have to let this opportunity slide. More important now, she needed to contact the sheriff before Chance returned.

CHAPTER 23

Empty, the one-room church seemed hollow, gutted of life. A draft swept through, chilling its only inhabitant: Chance Eliason. He'd called Pastor Fletcher earlier while Kat slept and arranged to meet him in the sanctuary to pick up the petition.

Chance sat in the back row, waiting for him to arrive, and imagined Sunday services sandwiched between two parishioners. He could not. He'd never been a churchgoing man unless he counted the times his mother dragged him by the ears to St. Mary's.

The last time he frequented a church, besides the meetings he attended here, was at Faith Lutheran Church in Boston for Meredith's funeral service, held there at the insistence of her parents. He shuddered at the memory—the funeral itself and the cold shunning of her family. They never cared for Chance. Considering his background, they had a right to their opinion.

He cringed at the man he used to be. If only he had a chance with Kat.

He couldn't shake the feeling she would call on the sheriff without him. The woman was independent, gutsy, and difficult, to say the least. But that was what he liked about her. That, and the feel of her sweet-scented body snuggled against him. His cheeks stung with heat at having those thoughts inside the walls of a church. His mother would heartily disapprove.

Of all the days to have something planned. Heading back to his ranch was what he really wanted to do, but he'd cancelled his appointment once and didn't want to reschedule. Also, he had an obligation to deliver the town's petition. He just hoped to heaven Kat would handle the sheriff with kid gloves. Holmes could be as difficult as Kat.

Pastor Fletcher strode down the middle aisle with papers flapping in his hand. His rubber-soled shoes squished on the hardwood floor. His hair was mussed, and his cardigan sweater was buttoned cockeyed. "I'm sorry to keep you waiting, Chance. I lost track of time."

Chance took the petition from him. "I appreciate your minding this. This is the first opportunity I've had to run it to the courthouse."

"No problem at all. We had a good turnout that afternoon, and as you can see, most everyone signed."

Chance skimmed the pages. "I'll file this and hopefully it'll make a difference."

As he strode from the church, the pastor caught up with him at his truck. He knew what was coming next and decided to waylay the message. "I don't intend to show up on Sunday, so you can save your breath."

"Actually, I was worried about Ms. Summers." The pastor's face reddened. "I know she's still in town because whenever I come here I make a point of driving by just to check. In fact the other night I saw lights across from the house, you know, on that old road leading to town, the one nobody uses. It's so bumpy and overgrown with grass I was surprised."

"What kind of lights?"

"They might have been taillights. I'm not sure. They were moving away from me through the trees. It just seemed strange. I don't know anyone who uses that old road, probably kids. Anyway, she ought to let the congregation help with her grief. Everyone needs comforting."

"That's up to her, don't you think?"

"If she's as fragile as Brianna, God rest her soul, I'm sure we could help her."

"Why don't you let Ms. Summers decide that?"

"I just worry about her, you know? Staying in that house must be deeply depressing."

Chance placed a hand on the pastor's shoulder. "Leave Ms. Summers's welfare to me. You have enough to worry about."

The pastor tsked and wagged his head. "And I'm supposed to be the one doing the comforting."

≋

Chance slowed in front of the Benton County Bank where Nate Wheeler was exiting the building. Chance parked and waited for Wheeler to enter his office. No sense in exchanging polite chitchat. Besides, he wanted to get back to Kat as soon as possible. The pastor's observation—seeing lights in the woods across from Brianna's house— disturbed Chance. At least in his house Kat was safe.

The bank building was as ancient as the town, one of the first buildings constructed. Tall, circular beams of polished oak gave the interior a stately look. It smelled of old wood and old money.

A woman in a navy blue pantsuit and short, stylish hair motioned him into her office. With her help he set up a personal bank account for his daughter and transferred a large sum of money into it. He instructed the woman to send the blank checks directly to Stella.

He left the bank, satisfied he'd made the right decision to allow her the responsibility of budgeting the money he gave her, instead of sending checks drawn from his own account. Stella was like her mother in every respect, and Chance was confident she could handle the responsibility.

Nearing his truck, he spotted Wheeler at the window of his office with a cell phone to his ear. Chance wanted to get back to Rosswood, but he couldn't pass up an opportunity to fish around for information. He had his own suspicions about Wheeler.

Wheeler snapped the phone shut just as Chance entered. "What do you want, Eliason?"

"So, I see you're in town."

"Yeah, so?"

"Were you around last night?"

"What if I was?"

Chance lifted a shoulder. "Hell, I don't know. I thought maybe your conscience was bothering you, and you might have something to confess."

Wheeler grazed Chance's arm as he passed by to open the door. "I have nothing to say to you."

Chance was on his way out but made a point to stop and face Wheeler. "If you had anything to do with trashing Brianna's house, the sheriff will be contacting you, but you could save the county a lot of time and effort if you would just confess and get it over with."

"Get out."

"You read Brianna's stories, didn't you?"

"What stories?"

"Come on, Wheeler, I know Brianna came here to use your printer."

"I never read them."

"She printed them here. Were you blind?"

"I said I didn't read them. Now if you don't mind, I have work to do." He pushed the door toward Chance, but Chance blocked it with his foot.

"What's the matter, Wheeler. Was Brianna going to tell your wife about the two of you?"

Wheeler glared at Chance, his lips pursed in defiance.

"You better think twice about terrorizing Kat Summers."

He nearly shoved Chance out the door.

Chance watched him flip open his cell phone and stride into the back room. Chance bet he was calling his lawyer. If he was guilty of anything—messing up Brianna's house or worse yet, having anything to do with her death—he would certainly need one.

Or perhaps Wheeler had nothing to do with any of that. For Chance, just having an occasion to needle him was satisfying.

One more stop at the courthouse to deliver the petition, then he'd hurry back to Rosswood to help Kat.

CHAPTER 24

Rusty toed his feet into his cowboy boots, slipped on his hat, and took one last drag from his cigarette before snuffing it out and leaving his one-room cabin located on Chance's property. On seeing Rusty, the burros trumpeted their greetings. He was late getting up.

He wandered over to pat the friendly ones gathered by the fence. He loved these four-legged beasts about as much as he loved Brianna. Only she would never know that now. He smoothed the neck of an old gray jenny, who blinked an appreciative eye.

Chance had left a while ago. Through the haze of sleep, Rusty had heard the truck's engine. He noted Kat's SUV stationed in the same spot as it was the night before.

"Brianna's sister is one fine-looking woman, and I can't for the life of me understand why the boss is stringing her along. Had that French lady the other night. You saw her, didn't you? Another looker." He stroked the burro's forehead.

"The boss, he's greedy when it comes to women, if you ask me. Might like the taste of one myself, except I like 'em one at a time." He shook his head low. "Too bad about Brianna."

≈

Kat locked the door to Chance's house, knowing she didn't have a key but hoping to catch up with him later. If not, she could always stay at Brianna's house, as unpleasant as that might be, or get a room at the motel. She'd been in Rosswood over a week now, but she wasn't about to leave town without calming her suspicions.

The air was chillier than an October morning in Seattle, but fresh and crisp, unlike the clogged city air. Brianna's shirt was hardly adequate.

A few burros hugged the fence line with their eyes focused on Rusty, who swaggered up to her. "Howdy." He tipped his hat as he sidled up to her car.

Tired and irritable, she needed to press on to meet Sheriff Holmes, and she wasn't in the mood to chat, if that was what he had in mind. She smiled, but got into the car, hoping he would get the message. She rolled down the window. "Can I help you?"

He peered in at rather close range, the tobacco smell as ripe as the smell of alcohol, reminding her of Doug Jones, the ranch hand from town. "Just wondered if you needed anything, since the boss is gone."

"I'm fine, thank you."

"Noticed your rig here overnight. You stayin' here now?"

"Not for long. There was a minor problem at Brianna's house." She stuck the key in the ignition, hoping to end the conversation.

He curled his fingers over the opened window. His nails were crammed with dirt. "That Brianna. She was a spunky one." He grinned, showing his crooked, yellow-stained teeth. "A looker, like you."

Intrigued at his reference to her sister, Kat relaxed her hand. Maybe he could provide some information. "I hear she spent a lot of time on the ranch."

"Oh, yeah. She loved them animals. We spent lots of time together working the ranch, and she never once moaned or complained about anything. That's the way she was. She was a real hard worker. Wished

I'd had the guts to ask her out."

"You never did?"

"Not rightly. I just fantasized about it once or twice. Knew a gal like her wouldn't give a fella like me a second look."

He paused, perhaps waiting for Kat to say something to the contrary, but she took the silence as a cue to start up the engine. "Well, I really need to go. I have an appointment to attend to."

He shoved his hands into his pockets. "If you ever want to get familiar with the ranch, I'd be pleased to oblige."

She squeezed out a smile, slowly backed the SUV around, and aimed for the highway. A strange conversation. Was he coming on to her, or was he just being polite? It occurred to her that a rejected ranch hand, even if Brianna had let him down easy, could be a suspect. Then again, maybe not.

The sheriff's cruiser was already parked in front of Brianna's house, and he met Kat at the door. A powerfully built man, he stood a head above her.

"Have you been here long?"

"A few," he replied.

She let him inside the house, which was as cold and unwelcoming as a winter's cave. He gave the room a long, steady look before kneeling to examine the broken cup and the crumpled afghan. Kat followed him into the bedroom where with very little effort he tugged open the window. "Hmm . . . Must've come through here," he said.

"I don't think so. When I got home, the door was wide open."

"Could've left by way of the door. You should keep your windows locked anyway." He turned his attention to the clothes heaped on the bed, seemed to zero in on Kat's undies, blatantly laid out in a row. He picked up a pair of pink bikinis and dropped them on the others. "Anything missing?"

Her cheeks heated, and she inwardly cursed Chance for insisting on keeping her clothes where they'd found them. "It was just trashed."

"Hmm . . ." He rubbed the point of his chin.

"Is there anything you can do?"

"Don't know that I can."

"What about fingerprints?"

"Did you touch anything?"

"Maybe."

"That's the problem, see? There's nothing missing here, and you've touched the evidence."

"But there must be something you can do to find out who did this."

He edged past her and strode into the living room.

"Wait a minute." She charged after him.

He turned, nearly knocking into her. "I'll file a report, but there's nothing more I can do. You'll just have to be more careful about locking up."

"The house was locked. I'm sure of it," she said, though in all honesty she was no surer of locking the door than she was of the time she fell asleep last night.

"My advice to you is to finish up your business and head back to Seattle. It seems you've made yourself an enemy. Someone doesn't want you here. If I were you, I'd take the hint." He walked off.

Anger shot through Kat like blistering lava. "Is this what you call police work in this town?"

He wheeled around. His narrowed eyes spoke a thousand words.

"Is this how you investigated my sister's death? When I came here six months ago, I trusted you'd done your job, but now I'm not so sure."

"And what do you mean by that?"

She took a deep breath to calm down. "Look, Sheriff, I don't want to argue with you, but my own instincts tell me Brianna could have been murdered."

"Murdered. You think your instincts are better than all my years of doing this job?" His voice remained level, even though he was clenching and unclenching his fists. "Tell me something. What makes you such an expert in police matters?"

"I just think you may have overlooked a few things."

"Like what?"

She asked him to step into the bedroom where she kicked the rug aside and unearthed the bloodstain. "Like this."

He grumbled under his breath. "Saw it."

Incredulous, she stared at him. "Well, tell me what you think it's from? I'll tell you what I think. To me it looks like blood that was wiped up intentionally."

"This case was investigated and closed six months ago." He stomped out of the bedroom with her following along.

"I've been getting disturbing calls, same as Brianna," she said, "from someone here in Rosswood. That's quite a coincidence, don't you think?"

"Could be."

"If you aren't going to take that seriously, what about the garage door?"

"What about it?"

"You said you found her in her garage, poisoned from carbon monoxide. How could that be when the garage door won't even close? It's stuck halfway open, and there was plenty of fresh air from outside."

He looked at her as if she didn't have a brain. "Did you ever think she might have extended a hose from the tailpipe into the window of her car?"

Kat hadn't thought of that. "What happened to the hose?" But he was already at the door about to step outside. "Sheriff, wait. I'd like to see that hose."

He looked at her, his face pinched tight. "I take offense that you would question my ability to carry on an investigation. And if I remember right, a while back you were perfectly happy with it."

"This has nothing to do with your abilities."

"Sure sounds like it does to me. Now if you'll excuse me, I have more important work to do than to discuss a case that's been closed for half a year."

Undaunted, she followed him to his cruiser. "Did you know your son was seen roughing up Brianna, and he was at her house the night she died? Did you investigate that? In fact, where was he last night?"

Sheriff Holmes, who'd already opened the door to the cruiser, slammed it shut. The air between them was bitter cold. "I don't have to defend my son, no way, no how, but I will say this. Tim was with me last night, so your blown-up theory about him scaring you and messing up Brianna's house won't fly." He pointed an index finger at her. "So, listen up. The investigation into your sister's death was comprehensive, and it was done right. Case closed."

He backed out of the driveway and sped off in the direction of town and left Kat wondering why almost every encounter she'd had with the man turned into a sparring match. Was it a clash of personalities, or did he have something to hide?

The prickly feel of a kitten's claws surprised her. Tiger was purring and using Kat's leg as a scratching post. "Ouch, you little rascal." She cradled the kitten in her arms. "You aren't lost after all."

She replenished the kitten's dishes and watched her gobble up the kibble. "What am I going to do with you? Zeke would make you his own personal play toy. As much as I'd like to keep you, I think it's time to let you go." Kat's heart tugged at the thought of giving her up.

"What's the matter with me? I can't take you to Chance's house, and I can't leave you here. It's the best thing for both of us." Tiger lapped water, then brushed against Kat's legs. "You're making this awfully difficult, but I better get this over with before my softer side gets the best of me."

With Tiger secured in one arm, Kat drove down the street to Tilly's house. When Tilly answered the door and saw the kitten, she burst into a huge smile. She wore one of Brianna's plaid work shirts and a pair of her jeans, both slightly baggy but in better shape than the clothes she'd been wearing. She gently extracted Tiger from Kat's arms, and Tiger purred and rubbed up against Tilly's cheek.

So much for loyalty. "I'm going to run into town and buy some kibble and kitty litter for you. I don't think she should be outside for a while, or she might just wander back to Brianna's house."

As Tilly nodded and brushed cheeks with the kitten, her grandmother opened the door wider, bringing forth the odor of fried eggs.

"I hope it's all right if I leave Tiger with your granddaughter."

"I don't know if we have the means to take care of her."

"You won't have to worry about that," Kat said. "Before I leave town, I'll arrange with Hank to keep you supplied with food and litter. He can send me the bill."

"Well, that's right nice of you, but I don't like to be beholden to no one."

"Please. You'll be doing me a favor by looking after her. I'd have to feed her if she was at my house."

"Well, then, Tilly, you tell the lady thank you."

The shyness snuck back into Tilly's eyes, and she lowered her head while thanking Kat.

"I'll drop off the things from Brianna's house I promised you as soon as I get them packed up." She stepped off the porch. "Oh, by the way, I was wondering if you happened to hear that motorcycle coming down this street last night?"

"Can't say that I did, but I mighta been snoozing in my chair about then. I took me a couple aspirins for my arthritis. That darn thing coulda got by me."

"All right then. I'll be back with the kitty supplies." Watching Tilly snuggling Tiger, Kat shooed away the ridiculous feeling gnawing at her. How could she be attached to a silly little kitten?

She directed her thoughts to her conversations with the sheriff and Tilly's grandmother. There seemed to be no real evidence Tim Holmes had been at Brianna's house the previous night, unless the sheriff was lying.

CHAPTER 25

As usual most of the cars in town were huddled in front of Hank's, Bertie's, or the café. Kat parked on the side of the street she came in on in front of the doctor's office. She was putting away her keys when a rapping sounded on the windshield.

Doc Conklin crowded her view. "I saw you from inside," he explained as she rolled down the window, "and I wondered if I might talk to you."

"I only have a minute."

He stepped back to let her exit the car. He had on a short-sleeved shirt and on his right forearm was a tattoo of an eagle's head and a cross with the words *For God and Country* superimposed. "How about coming into my office. I'd rather not talk out here."

"What's this about?"

"Brianna. There's something I want to tell you, and actually show you, but not out here. This town is a regular gossip mill." He placed a hand on her shoulder and guided her inside.

The reception area looked the same as before, an empty desk in a dreary room. Even the vase with the dried flowers had been removed.

"Doesn't anyone ever get sick around here?"

"Thursdays are usually slow. People around here like to take care of themselves. They take pride in it. I don't know why they even need a doctor here half the time, but I've been here ten years now, and I can't seem to leave. The town grows on you."

"Why did you end up here, if I might ask?"

"I wanted a fresh start."

"A divorce?"

"Something like that."

Kat thought better than to step any further into his personal life, or she would never get out of here. "What did you want to tell me? You said it concerned my sister."

"Why don't we step into my office?"

"Can't you tell me here?"

"I need to show you something. It's in my office." He turned down a narrow hallway, forcing her to trail after him, and ushered her into a tiny square room with no windows or other doors.

On the walls were anatomical charts and a framed diploma with bold black letters indicating he'd received his medical training in Puerto Rico. Curious, she wanted to ask him about his choice of schools, but she cautioned herself to stay out of his private life.

He dug into a desk drawer and handed her a photo of Brianna, showing her with a bruised cheek. Her eyes were lifeless.

Kat felt a jolt in her gut. "What happened to her, and why do you have this picture?"

He rested his palms on his desk. "You see, she came in one day, and I decided to snap the picture in case she ever went to the sheriff to press charges." He took the photo from Kat and pointed to the bruise. "This was evidence of her mistreatment."

"Did she tell you who did this to her?"

"She wouldn't confide that to me. I asked her many, many times, but she wouldn't cooperate. I think she knew if I wasn't a doctor, I'd have broken the coward in two. Oh, I had my suspicions."

"Who did you suspect?"

"I warned her to be careful, but she wouldn't listen to me."

"Did this happen more than once?"

"I hate to admit it, but I'm afraid so. Mainly, bruised arms she could cover up with a shirt. The coward knew what he was doing."

"Why didn't you report this?"

"I wanted to many, many times, but she wouldn't have liked that. We had our differences, your sister and I."

"Why didn't you tell me this the last time I was in here?"

"I'm sorry I didn't," he said. "I thought you might stop in another time. I would have told you then. You see, your coming here brought up memories of your sister, and it brought up a lot of hurt because I lost one of my lovely patients." He looked off into the distance. "Yes, she was a lovely girl."

"It sounds like Brianna made quite an impression on you, as she did with most of the people in this town."

"Indeed she did."

Kat edged toward the door. "I really must go."

"Won't you stay for tea? I'd love the company."

"No, thank you. I have some shopping to do."

"Well, then, I'll look forward to our next visit. Maybe I'll think of something more to share with you. You will come back, won't you?"

She gave him a curt smile and strode from the office. Without many patients to speak of, the doctor seemed like a lonely man. Good or bad, Brianna had made an impression on everyone in this town.

Kat crossed the street to Hank's store. In the back she found a cat box, kitty litter, and a bag of kibble. She hung around the counter while a gentleman with a fisherman's hat finished talking to Hank. She recognized the man as one of the diners in the café. On his way out he tipped his hat to her. The bell on the door jingled.

Hank grabbed the cat box. "Still got that kitten, I see. Looks like you're giving it a home to stay."

Kat explained about giving the kitten to Tilly and arranged with him to keep her supplied with cat food and litter. She wrote a check to cover the expense for the next six months and wrote down her Seattle address. Hank filed it away.

On the ledge behind Hank, she spotted a plastic vase filled with miniature white roses. "Where did you get those flowers?"

"Those?" Hank twisted around and back to Kat. "My wife brought them in. Thought I needed to brighten the place up. They are kind of pretty."

"Where did she get them, may I ask?"

"Probably got them in Benton on her last shopping trip. There's a little flower section in the Thriftway. She wants me to put something like that in here. Says we carry everything else. Says people would buy them. But I told her I got no room for it."

Kat thought of Brianna. "Would you sell them to me?"

"Those aren't for sale. They're just for decoration."

"I'll pay you, vase and all. How about thirty dollars?"

"Thirty dollars. They ain't worth that much."

"Forty? With forty dollars your wife could buy three times that amount."

With a cheery expression he set the vase on the counter. "Sold. Though I don't know why on earth those flowers are worth that much to you."

"I'm going to put them on my sister's grave." She opened her checkbook again.

"In that case you just forget about the money. I'm sure my wife would understand."

Kat filled out the check anyway. "You're saving me from having to go all the way to Benton, spending all that money for gas. You're doing me a favor."

"I think you should just take them. We thought a lot of Brianna."

"No. I insist." Kat folded his hand over the check.

"Much appreciated."

She crossed the street with the cat supplies. The doctor's office was dark inside. At least he wasn't at the window staring at her.

She returned for the roses, and when she was leaving Hank's store, she nearly bumped into Wilma, who held a cup of coffee away from her smock, the liquid sloshing from side to side. "Whoa, girl, do you want us both to wear this?"

"Sorry. I wasn't paying attention."

"Hey, nice flowers. What are you doing, dressing up Brianna's house while you're here? Are you planning to stick around?"

"Can I ask you a question?"

"Sure. Why don't you come into the shop with me? I've got someone under the dryer, and I don't want her head to fry."

A faint odor of permanent wave solution mingled with the odor of hairspray. A lone dryer whirred in the background.

Wilma went into the back room to check on her customer, then returned to Kat. "What is it you wanted to ask me?"

"Have you given any thought to that phone number?"

"To tell you the truth, no. Too damn busy." Wilma snatched a pad and pencil from the desk. "Write it down again. If I stare at it long enough, it might just come to me."

Kat jotted the number on Wilma's notepad. "Another thing. I've noticed fresh flowers on Brianna's grave."

"Is that where you're taking those roses?"

"Yes, and I wondered who else might be doing the same." Knowing Wilma's curious nature and penchant for gossip, Kat didn't want to arouse her suspicions. "I'd just like to thank them."

"Boy, I don't know the answer to that," Wilma said. "Gosh, I know about everything else in this town, but I don't know that. I never get up to the cemetery. Cemeteries give me the willies. I'll get my feelers out there and see what I can find out."

"You don't have to do that, Wilma."

"Let's see . . ." She tapped her chin with her index finger and glanced at the corner of the room.

"It's not that important, really."

"You might ask Lenny. Have you ever noticed the flowers in the post office?"

"Not really."

"Sometimes he brings flowers in. Carnations. Sometimes miniature roses, just like those," Wilma said. "Well, not Lenny, but Clare, I'm sure, although she doesn't strike me as the flower type. It's just that she has more time away from the post office than he does. Of course, sometimes the café brings flowers in. Doc Conklin, too. He probably likes roses. Hell, it could be anyone. Everyone loved Brianna."

"Don't worry about it." Kat glanced toward the back room. "I better run. You don't want to fry your customer."

"That's a fact."

Kat left the shop and crossed the road to her SUV. Everyone loved Brianna was becoming the town's mantra, except for one person, if Kat's theory was right.

A last-minute decision compelled her to stop at the post office. That body odor smell lingered within the confines of the room. No one was at the counter. No flowers were displayed, though the area behind the mailboxes was hidden from view. Lenny's wife, Clare, came out from that direction, her face molded into its usual scowl.

"Is Lenny here?"

"He's out. What can I do for you?" Clare avoided eye-contact and deposited a letter in a bin nearby.

"I wanted to make sure he didn't stop by Brianna's house to deliver mail like he did the other morning because I'm not staying there."

"Lenny stopped by, huh?" Clare's tone showed a curious interest. "Are you leaving town soon?"

"Not yet, but before I do leave, I'll pick up my mail here."

"Suit yourself." Clare started walking away.

"Did I get any mail today?"

Clare grunted a reply and skimmed the table behind her. "Don't see any."

Kat decided to probe a little. "None for Brianna either?"

"I would have said so, wouldn't I?"

"Did you know my sister?"

"Everyone did."

"What did *you* think of her?"

"Don't have an opinion." Clare gathered a stack of letters and wandered out of sight. The clip of envelopes hitting the metal slots started up again.

Wilma was right. Clare was a piece of work, about as personable as a hockey stick. No wonder Lenny chose to deliver the mail personally once in a while, anything to get a break from his disagreeable wife.

On the way up cemetery hill, Kat wondered how two people like Lenny and Clare ever got together in the first place. Kat couldn't imagine a more mismatched pair. She chuckled, thinking about it: Lenny the dreamer, Clare the grouch.

But who was Kat to judge after all the mismatches she'd endured over the years. One Jim Wethersby came to mind, the hotshot lawyer with all the promises, who never delivered any of them. And what about Theodore Smith, that handsome, annoying, upper-class jerk? At least she had the presence of mind to get out of those relationships. With choices like that, she'd rather stay single.

CHAPTER 26

On the road to the cemetery, Kat hadn't passed one car. No vehicles were parked near the graveyard; she had the place to herself. The trees, shading the area, were as still as the headstones. There wasn't a sound anywhere, not even birds chirping.

As soon as she approached Brianna's grave, she stopped short, stunned. Next to the grave, a mound of rich brown soil had recently been dug up. It looked like the beginnings of a new grave.

She set the vase above the headstone. Lying on the granite beside Brianna's name was another freshly-cut white rose. When she touched the petals, a cool breeze whipped up and swirled around her, chilling her. Overcome with a feeling of urgency, she instinctively glanced up.

At the far edge of the cemetery, where the pines thickened into forest, was the silhouette of a man. Or was it a woman? She couldn't tell.

She hastened up the hill toward the figure, but to keep from stumbling over the buckled cement, she had to divide her attention from the path to the woods and back again. In the process her boot heel caught in a crack, and by the time she'd dislodged it, the person had vanished. Or was the person even real?

She searched for an opening in the forest, but the trees were too close together, and there were no trails leading anywhere. Veering to the left, she followed the tree line down a sloping hillside. She saw no one. On the opposite side of the cemetery, an engine struggled for life. She made it to the hill's crest in time to see the tail end of a pickup speeding off in a cloud of dust toward town. The shadows swallowed the details, but she guessed the color was green, or perhaps blue. It could have been black. At least this time she wasn't seeing ghosts.

On returning to Brianna's grave, she kicked the soil into the hole that had been started and stomped the ground flat. In the safety of her SUV, she crept along until she neared the turn toward town. To the left was a narrow dirt road she hadn't noticed before.

The hairs on the back of her neck rose. She felt a instant chill. This place was keeping her on edge. No matter the consequences, she wasn't leaving town until she probed the truth about Brianna's death.

Kat was never so glad to see Chance's old beater parked in front of Bertie's. Anxious to tell him about the gravesite and about her conversation with Sheriff Holmes, she pulled into a spot nearby.

Bertie's was alive with lunch customers and the smell of hamburgers frying. The jukebox pounded out country. A clattering of pool balls sent a roar of laughter into the crowd. Doug Jones came out of the men's room drying his hands on a paper towel and stopped to eyeball Kat. She sought out Chance.

A young couple, then an older man, nodded and smiled at her as she wove past their tables, folks she recognized from the church meeting last week. Most people in town were cordial. Hank, Wilma, and Bertie came to mind, even the pastor and Lenny and Doc Conklin in their own quirky ways. She had rankled the sensibilities of a few, particularly Nate Wheeler and of course the sheriff and his son, who were both sitting in a booth along the far wall. She ignored their stares.

Speak of the devil. Lenny was at the end of the bar, wringing his hands, more than likely wishing Bertie would hurry his order so he could get back to the post office without angering Clare. When Kat sat next to Chance, Lenny quit fidgeting and focused his attention on her.

"You seem a little rattled," Chance said. "Rough morning? I looked everywhere for you. I was afraid something had happened to you."

"Let's get out of here, and don't say you told me so."

"I knew you couldn't wait to see Holmes. Do you want to tell me what happened?"

"I want to get out of here now."

"I thought I'd buy us lunch first."

Obsessed that Lenny was focusing on her, she leaned toward Chance and said in a loud whisper, "We can't talk here."

"Okay. We'll take out." He motioned Bertie over.

Bertie wiped her hands on her apron and picked up two menus. "Do you need these, or do you know what you want?"

"We're going to take a couple of burgers home to my house."

After Bertie headed into the kitchen, Kat scowled at Chance. "What did you say that for?"

"What did I say?"

"You know what you said."

Chance gave her an inquisitive tilt of the head, and Kat repeated his statement to Bertie about them going to his house. "So what if she knows you're spending time with me. What's so bad about that?"

"You saw Bertie's eyebrows. They couldn't have been higher if she'd jammed them up with toothpicks."

"You're too paranoid about this. Nobody in town cares what we do together."

"No, but it's what they might be imagining that bothers me." She swiveled her stool and noticed the Holmes men watching her. "I want to get out of here in the worst way." Her gaze fell on Lenny, and he wiggled his fingers in a pathetic little wave.

Finally, Bertie came through the swinging doors, plunked a sack down in front of them, and bellowed over the music, "How's it going at Brianna's house? Are you getting things done?"

"It won't be long now."

"Sheriff said you had a little problem there. He didn't say what."

"Nothing that I can't handle," Kat said. "Shall we go, Chance?"

He gave Bertie a generous tip. "Keep the change."

"Thanks, Chance. You two enjoy your afternoon."

All the way out the door he gently eased Kat forward with his hand on the small of her back. When the door closed behind them, she brushed his arm away. "What are you doing, marking your territory, letting everyone in this town know you're screwing Kat Summers?"

He laughed. "We both know that's not true."

"And did you see that wink of Bertie's when she told us to enjoy our afternoon? I told you people get the wrong impression."

"There wasn't any wink," he said. "What's got into you, anyway?"

Her shoulders slumped. She knew she was being bitchy. "It's this town. I'm sorry. I'm tired and antsy. I was up at the cemetery, visiting Brianna's grave . . ." She hesitated, deciding not to tell him about the newly dug hole because it would only drive him to be more protective than he already was. She despised being smothered. "I thought I saw someone watching me. I swear this town is making me paranoid."

"Let's go to my house. I want to hear what Holmes had to say."

"First I have to drop something off at Tilly's. Then I have to straighten things at Brianna's and pack my suitcase."

"I'll meet you at Brianna's house."

〜

Tim Holmes shoved his plate aside and guzzled the last of his beer. He'd been intent on watching Chance and Kat until they left Bertie's.

"Didn't take long for the sonovabitch to get some tail."

"To each his own." Sheriff Holmes checked his watch, crumpled a napkin, seemed disinterested in his son's crude observation.

"Yeah, well, I could teach that whore a thing or two."

"You just stay out of it, and mind your own business for a change."

"She's not minding hers. The bitch." His eyes burned with rage.

"You need to stay under the radar, especially now. She's getting suspicious."

"Can't you run her out of town?"

"I've got no grounds."

"Trump something up. I want her gone." He bunched his fists.

"If you hadn't been such a dumb ass and got involved with her sister, she wouldn't be sniffing around right now."

Tim pounded his fist on the table.

"Hey, calm down. You don't have anything to worry about. That case is sealed tight."

Laughter erupted from the area of the pool tables, diverting Tim's attention, but he was persistently flexing his fists.

"Did you hear me, Tim?"

He glowered at his father. "Yeah, I heard you, but I still want her out of here. I might have to put a scare in her, just like before."

Sheriff Holmes leaned in, intent on capturing Tim's attention. "You listen to me, you little shit, and listen good. I'm done digging you out of your messes."

Sue Ann came toward them, and the sheriff sat back. She laid a bill next to his coffee cup. "Want anything else?"

With a wide-mouthed grin Tim's attitude swung around. "No thanks, sweetheart, unless you're serving up a little something of yourself."

The sheriff slapped a twenty on the table. "Keep the change."

Sue Ann snatched up the money and winked at Tim before sashaying to the cash register.

Tim ditched the smile and said to his father, "If you won't help me, I'll do it myself. That bitch won't want to stay here after I'm through with her."

The sheriff sat forward again to make his point. "You do something foolish, and this time you won't answer to your father. You'll answer to the law."

Tim tensed his jaw until it throbbed, then scooted from the booth and stormed outside.

CHAPTER 27

When Kat arrived at Brianna's house, Chance's truck was already parked out front. Without waiting for him to get out of his vehicle, she strode inside and began the task of cleaning up the mess. She was picking up pieces of the ceramic cup when he appeared in the doorway. She kept working.

He walked over, grabbed both arms, and lifted her to a standing position. Tears filled her eyes. "We'll get to the bottom of this, Kat. I promise you."

Her first instinct was to pull away, but then she melted into his arms. "It's not just that. I know it's stupid of me, but when I got here, I wanted to take Tiger into my arms and feel the warmth of her furry little body."

He chuckled. She made a move, but he locked her tight. "I'm not laughing at you. I think it's sweet the way you, a tough, independent woman, are mellowed by a little kitten. You said you didn't even like animals."

"I never said that. Well, maybe I did. I just haven't had any experience with them. Now I know they're a comfort."

"That kitten came to you at a good time, when you needed someone or something to hold on to. But now you have me."

She strained against him enough to break away and gathered up the afghan. He took hold of the opposite end. She folded it toward him, and he caught her in an embrace.

"You're not giving up, are you?" Though she was resisting him, she wanted him to say no.

"You might as well stop fighting it." He brushed his lips over her cheek and alongside her mouth.

A tingling shivered through her. She swallowed hard to stop the onslaught of feelings, but his cologne captured her senses. Her lips met his, resulting in a long, ardent kiss while he slid his hands below her waist and hugged her closer. Her heart ticked wildly.

She shoved her hands in his chest and stumbled backward. "You're dangerous, Chance Eliason." He advanced toward her, a heated look in his eyes, but she extended her arm to him. "It's not going to happen."

"Why not? Your need is as great as mine. I can feel it. You're fighting it, Kat."

"I can't afford to let it go that far." She hurried into the bedroom to sort through the tangle of clothes and bedcovers.

He stood by vigilant, watching her, his hands slung into his pant pockets. He was dressed up in gray slacks and a peach-striped shirt that only magnified his good looks.

She caught herself wondering what his luxurious mop of hair would feel like sliding through her fingers, revealing her deepest desires. The yearning needed to be satisfied, and a part of her wished he would fling the clothes from the bed and make love to her. But one glance in his cautious, perceptive eyes reminded her Chance Eliason was an honorable, sensitive man. He would never force the issue of sex even if he wanted it.

After her clothes were packed and she'd folded the bedding, he took her suitcases outside, and she followed along. "I'll have to come back," she said.

"I'll help you with the rest of it, but not today." He hoisted the suitcases in the back of the truck. "You need to fill me in on your morning with Holmes, and then you need to get some rest."

His telling her what she needed irked her a little, but he was right. She did need a breather from closing up Brianna's house, but not from thinking about her death.

～

Zeke soared off the porch and accompanied Chance's truck the last ten feet until it came to a halt in front of the house. Chance got out and ruffled Zeke's coat. Kat watched them from her vehicle, parked alongside the truck.

Chance grasped Zeke's collar and started to yank him toward the garage with the intention of putting him inside. Whimpering, Zeke resisted and jerked in the direction of the SUV.

Kat exited her car. "Wait, Chance. Don't lock him away. Let me see if I can get used to him."

"Are you sure?"

"No, but I'll try."

"You don't have to. He's a big boy. He can handle the garage for now."

"No, please, let him go."

Chance wasn't so sure. There was a huge difference between a quiet, cuddly kitten and a husky, lick-you-all-over, in-your-face dog.

He edged toward her, still holding on to a fishtailing Zeke. With one quick jerk of his neck, Zeke freed himself and bounded, tongue lolling, toward Kat. She let out a squeal, and woman and dog collided in a mixture of hands and fur. The lunch sack went flying.

Chance charged into the fray and tugged Zeke back by the collar. Kat's eyes were larger than Chance had ever seen them. She looked petrified, but she didn't seek safety in her car or on the porch. "I'm sorry about that," he said.

Kat brushed off her shirt and jeans. "It's okay. He's just overly friendly."

Chance tossed her his keys. "Go on in."

She picked up the sack and crept closer. Allowing a two-foot distance between herself and the dog, she fully extended her arm and tapped his head. He wiggled and yipped.

Chance gradually released his grip and let Zeke go. Zeke ran circles around Kat and leaped in the air once or twice. Her body stiffened, and her face was graced with a teeth-gritting smile, but she stayed glued to the spot.

"Zeke, let's go." Chance slapped his thigh, and Zeke left Kat's side, barreled onto the porch, and waited expectantly at the door.

Chance draped an arm over Kat's shoulder. "I'm proud of you."

"It's your house and your dog. I can't expect you to change your habits for me."

"I don't care. I'm still proud of you, lady. I know how hard that was for you."

On the way up the porch steps, he glanced toward the burros where Rusty was leaning against a fence post, watching them. When he snubbed out a cigarette and disappeared into the barn, Chance thought it odd Rusty simply walked away without a wave or a tip of his hat. Chance shrugged it off and unlocked the door.

Zeke charged into the kitchen and nosed his food dish. He lapped up water.

"I guess I'm old news," Kat said. "That was easier than I thought."

"All he needed was an introduction," Chance replied. "Why don't you sit down, and I'll put on some coffee, or tea if you prefer."

"Coffee is fine."

"I'll make sandwiches and give our hamburgers to Zeke. After the journey they've been on, I don't think they're worth eating now. They're undoubtedly cold, too."

He wiped off the goop and slapped the patties into Zeke's dish. In two seconds they were gone. Zeke thumped his tail on the kitchen floor, expecting another treat. "You big porker. Dinner's later." Chance called him to the door and shooed him outside.

"He can stay," Kat said.

"I'll let him in later. Right now he needs to run off some of that puppy energy."

After the coffee was brewed and poured, he served up veggie sandwiches, including avocado, and settled at the table with Kat. "Finally. Now we can talk about your encounter with Holmes. If I hadn't had the appointment in Benton, I would have gone with you. I wish you'd waited."

"It was as bad as you predicted. Perhaps worse."

"Did he give you a bad time?"

"He was bristly and obstinate. Guess it runs in the family."

"He's not going to look into this, is he?"

"You gave me fair warning," she said, "but I couldn't believe it. He said he couldn't investigate the break-in because we'd already tampered with the evidence. That was it. And after I questioned him about his son's whereabouts on that night, he was completely closed to my theory about Brianna's death."

Chance shook his head.

"What?"

"How in the world did you become a successful realtor with such impeccable people skills?"

"Don't be so sarcastic. He was downright hostile. You should have been there."

"Of course he was hostile. You made a fatal mistake."

"Which was?"

"You should have left Tim out of the discussion. The minute you insinuated he might have been involved, you lost the sheriff's ear. Parents always defend their children."

"I wouldn't know." Her expression turned sulky, and she rose from her chair.

He'd touched a nerve. "Come here." He grabbed her hand and pulled her onto his lap. "I didn't mean to insult your intelligence. It's not easy to get through to a defensive cop, especially one who has an ass for a son. Do you want me to speak to him, see if I can soften him to your theory?"

"No." Her face hadn't lost its pout, but she let him kiss her cheek. "It still bothers me, Chance. Brianna could have been murdered. No, not could have." Thinking about the freshly dug hole, she said, "I know she was murdered. It's a feeling that won't go away."

He ran his hand down her arm and clasped fingers with her. "I found out something interesting from the pastor today when I stopped to pick up the petition. He said he saw what he thought might be car lights on that old dirt road across from Brianna's house."

"When was that?"

"He wasn't sure what night it was, but sometime this week. He said he often drives by to check on you."

"Why's he checking on me?"

"To see if you're still there, is what he said. He was concerned about you."

"Yeah, right. He's just anxious to see me gone."

"Why do you think that?"

"I guess I forgot to tell you he stopped by after the town meeting, after you'd left, and I confronted him about his secret visits with Brianna." Kat gave Chance a rundown of her conversation with the pastor and how he'd become fixated on Brianna until his wife found out.

"There were rumors going around, but nobody knew the details. I certainly didn't."

"I just hope he's not fixating on me now."

"He better not be."

"He was awfully worried I'd stir things up again and tell folks everything I knew. He said nothing sexual happened, but the way he acted, he was probably lying to protect himself. If he lied about that, maybe he's lying about what he saw on that old road."

"What would be the point?"

"I don't know. But the thought of that weird little man hovering near Brianna's house . . ." She slumped against Chance.

"Maybe this will cheer you up," he said. "I had a confrontation with Nate Wheeler in Benton."

"Did that go as well as my confrontation did?"

"About," he said. "I prodded him about the break-in and fished around about his involvement with Brianna, whether he'd read her stories. That sort of thing."

"Did he admit anything?"

"No, and he won't in this lifetime. He was pretty irate when I left."

"We'll never know, will we, Chance?" she whispered.

He'd never sensed her feeling so defeated. He pushed her to her feet. "Let's go for a ride."

"I'm not sure I want to get in the car again."

"Not a car ride," he said. "As soon as I change into my jeans, I'm taking you horseback riding."

―～

Of all the hair-brained ideas, Kat thought, as Chance hoisted her into the saddle of a mare named Hazel. Kat wasn't in the mood for riding a horse, but at least she'd ridden before with one of her male friends, and the horse's barrel between her legs was familiar to her.

Chance mounted a palomino named Jericho. They set off across the pasture at a moderate clip with Zeke barking and keeping pace.

The land on the ranch was flat, leading away from the house, but pine trees dotted the half that sloped upward. They skirted the perimeter. In the pine-scented air, through filtered sunlight, they wound in and around trees.

On their way back to the house, they grazed the back side of Brianna's property. They reigned in the horses at the fence line. Panting, Zeke sat, then edged his forepaws down.

"You were right," Kat said. "This is exactly what I needed."

Chance nodded at Zeke. "That should wear him out. I don't think he'll be bothering you tonight."

When Kat peered at Brianna's house, Zeke's rambunctious nature was the least of her worries. "Do you see that, Chance? It looks like the grass has been tramped down around the house leading to the bedroom window."

He tugged Jericho's reins and positioned the horse sideways to the fence. "Sure looks like it."

"Someone's been watching me." A queasy feeling edged into her and displaced the peacefulness of the ride.

"That's why I want you with me," he said. "It's not safe here. Come on. Let's go back."

They galloped across the pasture with Zeke bounding after them. As soon as they neared the barn, Zeke charged to a water bucket and began gulping as fast as he could.

Rusty met them and helped Kat dismount from the horse. "Looks like you been riding your whole life. I was watching you."

"I've ridden a few times." She moved out of the horse's way and let Rusty take over. She started walking away but was still within earshot.

Chance shifted Jericho's reins to Rusty. "Take care of him, would you?"

"Sure, boss. And, hey, that's a fine woman you got there."

After they'd entered the house, Chance apologized for Rusty's bluntness.

"He thinks I'm your woman." She threw back a laugh. "He's living in a different century."

"I don't know." Chance wound an arm around her waist and squeezed her to his side. "I think he's got the right idea. I Tarzan, you Jane."

She peeled away. "How could I be anything to you? I don't even know you." And she meant it. She'd bared her soul to him, revealed her past as easily as if she'd been on a therapist's couch. "I know nothing about you, other than you have a daughter and a mysterious past."

"Kat, come here." He reached for her hand, but she avoided his touch.

"All right then." He left her sitting in the living room and returned with a large stack of papers, which he dumped in her lap.

"What is this?" Though she already had her suspicions.

"A novel I've been working on. I'm sure you saw it when you snuck into my study the time you used my bathroom."

"I didn't read anything."

"But you saw it."

"Well, yes. So you want me to read it now?"

"If you read it, you'll know all about my past, because it's loosely based on my life."

She held it out to him. "I don't want to infringe on your privacy."

"I want you to know everything, and I think this is the best way."

"Can't you just tell me?"

"I could," he said, "but you'll get more details from the read, and it will give you time to think things through about me and whether or not you'll let me pursue you. If after you read this and you say no, I'll back off. You can ask any questions you want, and I'll tell you as much as I'm allowed."

"Why are you being so forthcoming now? You hardly know me to entrust me with this."

"I want you to trust me if we're ever going to proceed with this relationship."

She eyed him guardedly. "I didn't know we had a relationship."

He planted a soft kiss on her lips. "You can't deny the chemistry between us. That's a start, as far as I'm concerned."

≈

After dinner Kat announced she planned to retreat to the guest room and get started on the manuscript. "I may not come out of the room again. I might just read until I fall asleep."

Chance followed her with her suitcases. The phone rang, and when he came back to her room, she was rummaging for the nightgown she'd packed. He told her he had to go into town for a short while.

"Is anything wrong?"

"Sue Ann, one of Bertie's employees, called and said she had something to tell me, but she didn't want to talk over the phone. She sounded frantic. I couldn't hear her very well over all the noise. Will you be all right here alone?"

"Of course, but what do you think she wants? I didn't realize you knew her that well."

"I don't, but she sounded absolutely panicked. I can't very well leave her like that. I'll just run over and see what the problem is. Maybe Bertie's in trouble."

"I suppose."

"Rusty's usually in his cabin at night, if you have any problems. I'll lock the door on my way out, and I'll put Zeke in the garage so he won't whine at your door. He'll bark if there's a problem."

"You've thought of everything. Now, please go. I'll be fine."

CHAPTER 28

Kat couldn't believe Chance had handed over his novel so easily. It was a symbol of his goodwill, his trust, and to him a symbol of their budding relationship. According to him, after reading the novel, she would either reject or accept him. Either way, she'd have to take a stand. The novel carried great weight.

She snuggled under the very comfy, peach-scented covers and held the manuscript, wondering if she should proceed. If she set it aside, she wouldn't have to get any closer to Chance than she already was. After reading the details of his life, she'd know him in a more intimate way. Was she ready for that?

The room was beginning to darken along with the evening sky. She switched on the bedside lamp, took a deep breath, and turned to page one.

The first chapter told of a young man recently married, who'd graduated from Harvard with an MBA, proficient in Russian and Spanish. While he worked at his first job in a Fortune 500 company, he was tapped by a consulting firm that specialized in government contracts.

So far the man's life seemed normal, nothing that would beg shock or horror. So far so good.

She paused to rest her eyes and felt herself drifting near sleep until the phone rang and prodded her awake. Thinking it was Chance, she padded across the hall and felt for the phone on his desk. No one was on the line. She heard a click.

Refusing to give in to her fears, she started back to her room when the phone rang again. It had to be Chance. She groped for the receiver and put it to her ear. A blast of hushed breaths threw her off base. "Chance, is that you?"

She thought someone whispered her name, but the voice was so soft she couldn't be sure, then whoever was on the line hung up. It took her two tries to set the receiver in place. Had the crank calls begun again? But why here?

While stumbling in the dark for the light switch, she heard, or thought she heard, a thump on the window pane. She spun around and rammed her hip into the corner of the desk. Rubbing the sore spot with one hand, she lifted the blinds and peered out. The night masked whatever truth lay out there—no person, no movement, only starlight and a whisper of a silhouette in the distance. The blinds slid into place. Her imagination was at it again.

She edged from the room and flipped on the hall light. The phone rang again. She refused to answer it. She stood in the hall and let the phone ring itself out.

Zeke remained quiet, a good sign that no prowler was near the house. Nevertheless, she checked the doors to make sure they were locked.

Zeke pawed at the garage door, aware of her movements. She was tempted to let him in for company, if nothing else, but she wouldn't know how to handle him if he became overly playful or, heaven forbid, wanted to sleep on the bed.

Where was Chance? She placed a call to Bertie's and found out he'd already left. It was nearing half past eight.

She left the hall light on and her door ajar and climbed into bed to await his return. She wouldn't sleep now. The house was still. Even Zeke had quieted down. A barn owl hooted close by. Keeping a cautious ear out, she picked up the novel and launched into the next chapter.

The firm that had zeroed in on the main character in Chance's story was unfamiliar to Kat, but Chance could have changed the name. The men who worked there had connections to the various intelligence and security agencies. Lured by promises of women, power, and money, the main character opted in as one of its financial specialists.

Sharp, loud barks erupted from the garage. A car door closed. A rapid knocking sent her dashing from the bed, positive Chance had forgotten his house key. On her way through the living room, she snatched the throw blanket from the couch.

She yanked the door open and was surprised to see the sheriff in civilian clothes—jeans and a leather jacket—standing under the porch light. His gaze lit on her bare feet, then continued upward to her tousled hair. Instinctively, she tightened the blanket around her.

"Is Eliason home?"

"He'll be back any minute. What's this about? It's late."

"I had business elsewhere. I couldn't get here before now." He brushed his hands together for warmth. "Do you mind if I come in and wait?"

She looked past him, hoping Chance would drive up to save her from an awkward situation. "He'll be back soon enough."

"I'll say this to you out here then. Might as well get it off my chest." He paused to gather his thoughts. "Since you came here, there've been an awful lot of accusations tossed around."

His set jaw and piercing eyes told her he might be working up to some anger, so she closed the door a little, narrowing the gap between them.

Zeke's barking hit a feverish pitch as Chance's truck barreled down the drive and swung in next to the sheriff's cruiser. While walking to the porch, he shouted at Zeke to quiet down, and Zeke's bark mellowed to a whine. "What do you want, Holmes?"

"To talk to you."

"Couldn't this wait till morning, or is it some kind of an emergency?"

"I couldn't get to it sooner." He cast Kat a stern glance and said to Chance, "I want to talk to you alone."

Kat didn't need to be told to bow out, but she stayed behind the closed door within listening range.

The sheriff said to Chance, "Got a call from Nate Wheeler's attorney, and it seems Wheeler wants to file a complaint against you for harassment."

Kat couldn't see Sheriff Holmes, but she bet he had a big smirk on his face.

Chance replied, "That's a crock, and you know it. You can tell Wheeler he's got no grounds. Christ, the man has no spine at all, has to hire a lawyer to do his dirty work. He can tell me to my face."

There was a pause, then the sheriff said, "Look, Eliason, I smoothed it over this time, but no more. I'd advise you to stay away from him."

"You could have saved yourself a trip, Sheriff." The doorknob turned, and Kat stepped away to let Chance in. A frown clouded his face. "You heard that, didn't you?"

She nodded.

He wrestled with Zeke to get him outside and within minutes brought him back in, a firm grip on his collar.

"I'm okay with him in here," Kat said.

"Are you sure?"

"Let him go and we'll get this over with."

Released, Zeke made a beeline to Kat. He slapped his tail against her legs while she closed her eyes and patted his head. After charging back to Chance for an approval pat, he went into the kitchen to lap up water.

"That wasn't so bad," she said.

"He's getting to know you."

Zeke wandered into the living room and collapsed in the corner on his large, round doggy pad.

"What happened with Sue Ann?"

"Absolutely nothing." He tossed his hat on the table and ran his fingers through his hair.

"What do you mean nothing?"

"She wasn't there, never showed up. I waited around, had a cup of coffee. According to Bertie's help, she'd been there earlier. He said she made a phone call and left."

"That's odd."

He went to the kitchen sink, picked up a glass. "It doesn't make any sense."

Maybe it did. "There were calls tonight."

"Who from?"

"He hung up the first time. The second time he might have said my name. It rang several more times, but I let it ring. It reminded me of before. Then I thought I heard something outside the window, but it was nothing."

"Why didn't you tell me this when I came in?"

She shuddered a response, and within seconds he had his arm around her. "Kat, I'm so sorry I wasn't . . ." His voice trailed off, and he rolled his eyes toward the ceiling, shaking his head. "Oh, boy."

"Chance, are you thinking what I'm thinking?"

"What better way to frighten you, by getting me out of the house first."

"But why Sue Ann? Surely she's not involved."

He took Kat's hand and led her to her room. "You go on to bed and get some sleep." He kissed her forehead. "If the phone rings, let me answer it. We'll talk about this in the morning, unless you'd like to join me, for protection purposes of course." With a sly grin, he extended an arm in the direction of his room.

Smiling, she waved goodnight and left him behind a closed door. Back in bed under the warm covers, she tossed and turned but couldn't sleep. Picking up the novel where she'd left off, she read about the life of a financial specialist working for a mystery company.

His novel had all the intrigue of a James Bond movie, but the results of the main character's actions were much less noble. Corporations hired men like Chance to seek out leaders, politicians, and heads of state to offer them money in return for making sure the contracts for weaponry and other services were directed the corporation's way. And if they refused, in the case of politicians, money directed to their campaigns would be withdrawn. Bribery and blackmail all in one package. The money offered carried the name "black cash."

Fascinated, Kat read into the wee hours of the morning until she finished the book. Because of a family member's illness, the hero of the story thought deeply about his actions and left the firm. In the end he was running like a fugitive from people who wanted to destroy him.

Kat set the papers aside to digest the implications of such a life. She couldn't imagine the man she knew having once been a part of such an outfit. Or could she?

It was three o'clock in the morning when, weary-eyed, Kat turned out the light. Upon entering the dream world, she found herself running from some unknown force, her breath ragged, her sides hitching in pain. She stopped to catch her breath and was catapulted into a room filled with lights. Various objects—pencils, pillows, plates, and candles—were flying around her. Across the room a woman in faded jeans and a sweater, her hair dark and spiky, had her back to Kat. Kat dodged the objects to get to the woman, who turned around and held her hand out to Kat.

"Brianna." Kat sat up in bed and covered her mouth with a clammy palm, hoping Chance hadn't heard her cry out, hadn't heard her say Brianna's name.

Trembling, she touched the cheek brushed by Brianna's hand. That part of the dream felt real. Kat started shaking. She rummaged in her purse for a Valium and hurried into the bathroom across the hall. When was this going to stop?

As she reached for a paper cup, she nearly jumped out of her skin. Chance stood in the doorway staring at her, for how long she didn't know. He was clad in pajama bottoms with his lightly-tufted chest exposed and his hair mussed from sleep.

"I'm sorry if I woke you."

"I was in my bathroom when I heard you scream." He eyed the hand holding the pill. "Do you really need that?"

"It relaxes me."

He took the pill from her and tossed it in the garbage. He held her close and whispered into her hair, "Come with me, Kat." Without arguing, she allowed him to take her into his room and tuck her into his bed. "I just want to hold you until you fall asleep," he said as he slid in next to her. "Nothing else."

She molded her body to his, and his warmth was all she needed to melt into relaxation. She missed this part of being with a man. He stroked her hair, which further relaxed her.

"I saw Brianna in a dream," she said. "I felt her touch my cheek. I really did. I've seen her, Chance. I see and hear things. I've always had this bizarre ability, but I've tried to suppress it, and I've been able to until now, until Brianna's death. She wants me to know something. I feel it. I just don't know what it is."

"Shh . . . Don't worry over it now," he murmured, as if what she'd said was nothing out of the ordinary. "Just relax and try to sleep."

"Don't you understand what I'm telling you? I'm one of those crazy people. I hear voices. I see dead people."

"I don't doubt what you're saying at all, and there's nothing about you that could scare me away."

"But, Chance . . ."

"Shh . . ." He kept stroking her hair, feathery touches that sent tiny chills up her spine.

She should have drifted to sleep, but all she could think of was how much she wanted him to kiss her and use his tender touch to awaken her body, to awaken the passion she hadn't felt in a long, long time. She rolled over to face him. "I want you to make love to me."

He held her secure in his arms. "There's nothing in the world I would love more than that, but you're weary, darling. You need rest."

"I know what I need, and I need you."

"I don't want to take advantage of you."

"You won't be." She nuzzled his neck, nipped at his earlobe. "I'm the one doing the asking. Please . . ." Seconds turned into minutes. In the darkened room she couldn't see his face, but she felt his heartbeat racing to keep up with hers.

"Are you sure?" He breathed the words into her ear.

She took his hand and rested it below her belly. Her hands slithered down his chest, and she caressed him until he let out a rapid succession of breaths. He brought his lips to hers.

After the first kiss, which deepened into want, every move he made assured her of his choice to be gentle with her, careful, thoughtful, even though his muscles were hard and tense, proving the enormity of his need. He held back, giving her more of his feathery touches and tender whisperings, and kisses all over her body.

"You're driving me insane. You know that, don't you?"

"Darling, I only want to drive you into my arms."

She ran her fingers through his hair as she'd dreamed of doing. The texture was indeed luxuriously sexy. She lost herself in the feel of it until his next stroke took her breath away. If he lingered any longer, she wouldn't be able to put on the brakes.

He seemed to sense the urgency, because in one swift move his arms were around her, and he was gently yet insistently pleasing her. She begged him to stop, begged him to hurry, begged him to stop until she finally let go, and her body peaked and quivered in response to his.

Afterward, he kept her closely cocooned and murmured loving assurances that he would never leave her. A flash of intuition told her that truly he was the man she'd been waiting for her entire life. But she wouldn't reveal those thoughts to him. They were too new, too raw.

Limp from exhaustion, she kissed him goodnight and dozed into a dreamless sleep. An hour later she woke. He slept nearby, his arm butting against hers. She lay still for a while, counting his deep, rhythmic breaths.

Sleep eluded her, and near panic set in. She pressed her hand to her chest and forced her breathing to remain steady to keep from hyperventilating, to keep from waking him. In one moment of unrestrained bliss, she'd let herself buy into the dream of a loving, committed relationship. Thank goodness she'd kept her deepest feelings to herself, kept them from Chance. This way, getting out of this situation would be easier.

She inched from the bed, looked back at him to make sure she hadn't woken him, then tiptoed out of the room. Leaving him like this was difficult but, she told herself, necessary. By doing so, she could leave Rosswood with her fragile heart intact.

CHAPTER 29

Without disturbing Zeke, Kat set her suitcase by the front door and circled back to the living room for the box with the laptop and stories. Zeke looked at her expectantly, but Kat whispered the stay command. The only body part Zeke moved was his tail, thumping the doggy bed.

Rather than rummage through a kitchen drawer for a notepad, she wrote on the back of her business card: I'm sorry. I need time to think.

She snuck one last glance at Zeke before quietly transferring her belongings to the porch. A light breeze fanned manure odors from the barn's direction. The sky was a hazy early-morning blue. The sun was yet to rise over the hilltop, but it was late enough for the café to be open.

She drove past Tilly's house, now dark inside, and thought of Tiger and imagined that silly kitten curled up with the girl. The church parking lot was vacant, except for one vehicle, Pastor Fletcher's Jeep. She pictured him hunched over his desk, preparing for Sunday services.

Compared to the house she'd left behind, Brianna's house was sober and uninviting, and chilly and musty from being locked up. She hauled in her belongings and switched on the space heater.

She tore off a note that had been taped to the door. It read: I stopped by last night to deliver a letter, but you weren't home. Sorry I missed you, Lenny.

She sighed. Either the man didn't listen, or he was as dense as a bag of marbles. She tossed the note in the trash.

Her cell phone hadn't been on in days. When she did switch it on, she prayed it wouldn't ring before she had a chance to connect with Maggie.

Maggie's voice came on the line. "What?"

"That's a nice hello."

"Oh, sorry, dear. Let me get to my coffee." After a moment she said, "How the hell are you? It's like you've been on an island with no phone service. I worry when I can't get you. I sent you something."

"That explains the note left by the postman. Was it important?"

"It's just a thank-you note from one of your clients. I thought it might cheer you up."

"That was thoughtful," Kat said. "I'm sorry I'm calling so early."

"You know I'm always up with the birds. Have you finished there yet?"

"I can finish some of it today, but the heavy cleaning and painting I might have to hire done. I can't stay here."

"What do you mean, in Brianna's house or in Rosswood?"

"Both."

"What's bothering you, Kat? Is it those strange calls or those nightmares?"

"There are other circumstances as well."

"Like what?"

"I can't talk about it right now. It's too . . ." Raw, she wanted to say. Her night with Chance was raw to the bone. She wasn't ready to pick at the details.

"Does it involve a man?" Maggie could always read her. "You listen to me. I'm sorry I ever pushed you into going there. You should come home as soon as possible."

"There's more, Maggie. It's about Brianna's death. I think there was foul play involved."

"What makes you think that?"

"Certain things don't add up."

"Like what?"

"I don't want to say right now."

"Have you gone to the authorities?"

"That's a sticky issue. I think the sheriff's son may be involved, but I can't prove anything. Brianna's house was broken into the other night. There are so many things."

"For God's sake, Kat, you totally slipped that one by me. Were you there when the house was broken into? Are you okay? You sound drunk. Have you been drinking, or is it the pills?"

"I'm not drunk. I haven't slept much."

"You come home," Maggie said. "Today, as a matter of fact. I don't want any excuses from you. For your own safety you need to get away from that place. When you get back, we'll put our heads together, and if there's reason to be concerned about Brianna's death we'll seek counsel. You shouldn't go this alone."

Kat wanted to tell her everything—that she hadn't been alone up until now because of Chance—but she decided to wait. "You're right, Maggie. I'll continue looking into Brianna's death from there. I'll come home as soon as I wrap up some loose ends."

"The sooner the better. That shack isn't worth your sanity. Call me as soon as you get in, no matter how late."

Kat ended the call, took a quick shower in tepid water, and shored her hair up into a ponytail. Over her jeans she slipped on a clean flannel shirt. Mornings in Rosswood were getting chillier.

She surveyed the house and devised how much she'd do before she left town. It hurt to think of Chance. She worried he would come by, so she drove into town and stopped at Hank's to stock up on enough snacks to get through a day: a bag of corn chips, raisins, yogurt, an apple, an orange. Up front she threw in a package of beef jerky. She was the only customer in the store.

Hank rang up the corn chips. "Getting an early start?"

"I'm leaving town soon."

"That's a shame. Folks are going to miss you around here."

"That's a nice thing to say. Maybe I'll be back again." She wrote out a check while he bagged her groceries. "I'm going to need someone to clean Brianna's house and paint the inside. Do you know of anyone who could use a job?"

"I think I could find someone. Maybe Peggy Simmons. She's always looking for odd jobs. A hard worker and dependable, too."

"You have my number in Seattle. Tell her to give me a call. I'll order the paint from you and pay you directly for that."

"That'll work," he said. "You have a safe trip back."

"Thanks again for helping me out."

"No problem at all."

The bell jingled on her way out. She tossed the sack in the SUV, hurried into the café, and made a straight line to the counter facing the kitchen. An aroma of freshly brewed coffee and fried eggs permeated the room.

Bev, the woman who had waited on Kat when she was there before, was wiping up the counter close to Kat. The dark circles under her eyes were almost purple, and she looked as though she'd pulled an all-nighter. She carried the coffeepot to a table of four men.

When Kat came into the café, she hadn't paid attention, but now she homed in on Doug Jones and three of his pool buddies. They were laughing and making comments she couldn't discern.

The waitress hurried back to Kat. "What can I get you?"

"Large coffee to go. Black. And a glass of water, please."

She poured water from a pitcher and set a glass in front of Kat. "It's getting colder these days, cold enough to start snowing again."

"I won't be here to see it," Kat said. "I'm leaving soon, by tomorrow in fact, before I can get caught in any of it."

"Yup, we get a lot of snow in this part of the world. I'll get your coffee."

Just as Bev walked away, Doug strutted up to Kat and slid into the neighboring seat. His day-old beard was dark and stubbly, his eyes bloodshot, his shirt pocket torn. He swiveled the stool to face her and positioned one knee touching her thigh and the other touching her rear. "You aren't gonna take off without a proper sendoff, are you, sweetheart?"

He glanced at his friends, then focused on Kat. "You know, you can do better than that over-the-hill cowboy you've been hanging out with. In fact, if you want to be discreet, I know an old shack in the woods where we can hook up before you go. I won't tell a soul. Just you and me and Mother Nature."

"And you can just cool off." Kat grabbed her glass and flung water in his face.

He leaped to his feet, wiped the drips from his eyes, and brushed the front of his shirt. His buddies howled. He leaned into Kat. "Later, sweetheart. Just you and me and the shack makes three." He strolled back to the table with his chest puffed out and high-fived one of the guys.

They were still laughing while Kat paid the waitress and marched from the café. To collect herself, she sat in her car and guzzled the caffeine, burning her tongue in the process. That jerk was one more reason to get out of this town.

She drove to the post office. All the parking spots were empty, giving her reason to believe she'd be the only customer, but a man in corduroy pants and a long-sleeved shirt was hunched over the counter. As Kat approached, Lenny's eyes took on a dreamy glow.

The man glanced over his shoulder to acknowledge her. "Ms.

Summers."

"Hello, Doctor Conklin."

"I'll finish over there," he told Lenny and smiled at Kat before moving to the table under the bulletin board with what appeared to be an official form of some sort.

Pastor Fletcher walked in, greeted Kat, and wandered to the postal boxes as Kat stepped up to the counter.

"Kaaat, nice to see you so early this morning," Lenny cooed. "You brighten up the room just like Brianna did. I bet you came in for your letter. I tried to deliver it to you. I thought it was important, but you weren't home. You got my note, didn't you?" He pulled a letter from a stack of envelopes and transferred it to Kat. "There you are. The post office always delivers." He chuckled and let out a snort.

"I'm leaving town early in the morning."

"Oh no, so soon?" He stared at her with sad puppy-dog eyes, as if he were about to cry.

She had to repeat his name twice to snap him out of his reverie. "I'd like you to forward my mail and also Brianna's if she happens to get any."

"Oh, yes, well, that reminds me." He shuffled some papers on the table behind him and handed her a manila envelope. "It's from a publisher." He pointed at the return address. "Maybe they want to publish one of Brianna's stories, posthumously." His face reddened. "Oops."

"Don't worry about it."

"I wish you weren't leaving so soon." He fidgeted with a pencil and looked at Kat. "You see, I know you're a real estate agent from what Brianna told me and also from that letter I gave to you. The return address? That was your business address in Seattle, wasn't it? Well, uh, you see . . ." He hesitated.

"What is it?" The sound of fingernails scraping a blackboard crossed Kat's mind. Her patience was wearing thin.

"Well, yes, Kaaat. You see, Clare and I own a cabin in the woods off Pine Road, and we've been trying to sell it, but we haven't had any luck. And I hate to bother you, but you're leaving tomorrow, sooner than I'd hoped you would, and I had this idea. You see, we were hoping, well I was anyway, hoping you might take a look and maybe give us some pointers on how we might move it along. You know, sell it better. I hate to ask you."

"What time?"

"You mean you'll do it?"

"I could take a few minutes. Just give me a time."

"Really?" His eyes were blinking like Christmas lights. Just watching him made Kat's shoulders tense. "Just give me a time."

"Oh, thank you. I know Clare will be happy."

"Lenny, what time?"

"Yes, a time. I can't get away until the post office closes, and Clare, if she agrees, has to have her dinner. Then again, I may come alone. Let's say around six-thirty?"

"Six-thirty would be fine."

"Oh, thank you." He found a used envelope and on the back sketched a map to his cabin. "It'll be so hard to see you go. It's been like having Brianna back. Oh, well, we can say our goodbyes at the cabin."

The pastor, who'd been lingering nearby, waiting his turn, said to her, "I'm sorry to hear you're leaving. I was hoping you'd come by the church, for comfort that is. That's all I ever wanted to give Brianna, just comfort."

"Right." Kat edged outside, glad to get away from both the pastor and Lenny and more than glad to leave this post office for good. She really didn't want to meet Lenny at some cabin in the woods, but he'd been a friend to Brianna. She only hoped later she could easily get away from him.

On her way to her car, the doctor caught up with her. "Ms. Summers,

I couldn't help overhearing you were leaving tomorrow."

"That's right."

"I'm sorry we didn't get to chat again after our last conversation about your sister. I was hoping you might drop by. But now you can't."

"I'm sorry, but I have to return to Seattle."

"It's too bad. I wanted you to stop by for tea. I was hoping we could get better acquainted. Well, I trust you got your answers."

"You mean about Brianna's death."

"Have you been able to settle yourself about it?"

"I'm not sure I have. I think there might be more to it, but right now other circumstances force me to distance myself."

He looked puzzled.

"I know I sound vague, but it's personal," she said. "Are you sure Brianna didn't say anything to you the last time you saw her that might indicate her state of mind and why she did this?"

"Sometimes people do things we can't always understand, and we search for reasons to make sense of it." He latched onto her forearm and stared into her eyes. "Sometimes it's best to leave it be, don't you think that's true?" He gave her arm a slight squeeze. "I do hope the rest of your stay is a pleasant one. I wish you the best of luck."

He ventured past her, walking toward town. She passed him in the car on her way out, thought about waving, but his eyes were focused downward.

CHAPTER 30

"Kat, darling." Chance had been dreaming about her: the sweet taste of her, her auburn hair twined in his fingers, her body soft and supple, her thighs pressing against his, driving him absolutely mad. Craving her again, he reached for her, but she was gone. Her side of the bed was numbing cold, the house cruelly quiet.

He rolled onto his back. Zeke was staring at him, wagging his tail. He licked Chance's arm. "Where is she, boy?"

Chance slipped on his pajama bottoms and checked the guest room. The bed was made, and it appeared as if no one had ever slept in the confines of the room. With Zeke lumbering behind him, he inspected the bathroom. No sign of Kat's presence. He stuck his head in the study. His manuscript was neatly placed on the desk.

Dread flooded in on him at the idea his life's story had soured her. But why had she agreed to make love? For the thrill of it? That wasn't like Kat. Her body had formed to his in the most loving way.

He let Zeke out and found her business card on the kitchen table with the note on the back. She needed time to think. His story was the reason. She must have had second thoughts because of his past.

A shower and breakfast didn't ease the hollow feeling inside. Since he'd left the organization, Kat was the first woman he'd confided in about the secret side of his life, the part he now despised. He felt open and vulnerable, as if a layer of skin had been peeled away.

If Kat needed time to take it all in, he would allow however long it might take. But he wasn't about to give up on her. In the end he would pursue her no matter what. At the moment, though, he would give her the space she needed to think things through, and he would track down Sue Ann to get to the bottom of the events of the previous evening.

Zeke was palling around with Rusty down by the barn, the sun highlighting his golden fur. Chance yelled to his hired hand that he was going into town. Rusty waved in reply. Chance buttoned his shirt sleeves and tossed his jacket into the cab.

When he approached Maple Lane, he was tempted to turn in and drive past Brianna's house. Every ounce of him wanted to check up on Kat. It was his nature to take control, but as difficult as it was, he reminded himself to give her breathing room.

Because it was a Friday at Bertie's, he had to park halfway down the block from the entrance. The Grill was stuffy with the smell of fried food and the packed-in lunch crowd. One lone spot was left at the counter between Doc Conklin and Lenny. He acknowledged them both with a nod.

Sue Ann backed through the swinging doors and handed a sack to Lenny, stole a glance at Chance, and deposited the plate with a roast beef sandwich and chips in front of the doctor, who folded his arms and stared back at her. "What's wrong?" she asked.

"I ordered this to go."

"I don't think so." Sue Ann seemed stressed and irritable. Chance read it in her voice. "Oh, hell, hang on." She snatched the plate and disappeared into the kitchen.

"I'm sure I told her I wanted take-out."

"It's loud in here," Chance said. "She probably didn't hear you."

"I'm sure I told her. I have patients to tend to. I can't sit here all day. She remembered the postman, but not me. I don't know why Bertie puts up with her."

Now the doctor was crabby. Chance let the comments pass.

Lenny placed his money on the counter and said to Chance, "I guess you know Kaaat is leaving town tomorrow."

Chance felt a stab of hurt and disappointment. "I didn't know."

"Oh, I thought you would be the first to know. Hmm . . . Well, she's a jewel, just like Brianna." He slid off his stool. "I should give her a parting gift. Poor thing. She deserves it." He picked up the sack. "Maybe I will."

Lenny wandered toward the exit just as Sue Ann banged through the swinging doors and dumped a sack in front of Doc Conklin. "There."

After the doctor slapped his money on the counter and left, she completely ignored Chance and took off into the crowd like a rabbit afraid of getting trapped. Chance watched her flit around the room taking orders, clearing tables, trying to delay the inevitable. He decided to wait her out.

Bertie, who'd been in the kitchen helping the cook, came out to work the bar and noticed Chance staring into the crowd. "Did Sue Ann take your order yet?"

"When does she take her break?"

"As soon as it calms down around here," Bertie replied. "What's the problem?"

"No problem. I just want to talk to her."

"Did she do something I should know about?"

"No. I need some information about someone she might know. It's nothing to concern yourself with."

"Should be another hour before I can do without her."

"I'll wait," Chance said. "In the meantime I'll have a Reuben."

As the hour ticked by, he fixed his eyes on Sue Ann's movements, which seemed jerky, jittery. Once, she almost lost the plate she was carrying and nearly tipped over a customer's water glass.

Chance paid for his meal and sipped coffee while he waited. A loud roar near the pool tables sent his attention in that direction, and when he looked back, he'd lost sight of Sue Ann. He stood and surveyed the room.

Bertie came out of the kitchen and informed Chance that Sue Ann had just left. "She went out the back, took off outside somewhere."

He burst from the restaurant, scanned up and down the street, and caught her scurrying from the alley past the movie theater. When he reached her and grabbed her to twirl her around, she jerked free and let out a pained yelp. In the sunlight he saw a bruise on her upper arm the size of an orange. "Who did that to you?"

She masked the bruise with her hand. "Nobody."

"Who put you up to calling me last night?" Chance reasoned the man who knocked her around was one and the same.

"No one."

The terror in her eyes made him think otherwise. "Then why did you call? What did you want to talk to me about?"

She shook her head and averted her eyes. For warmth she hugged her bare arms to her chest.

"Sue Ann, is someone abusing you? Because if he is, you need to tell me, so I can get you some help. If not me, then the sheriff or Doc Conklin."

"Just leave it alone, okay?"

"I need to know if someone wanted me away from my house last night so they could harass Ms. Summers. Did you have anything to do with that?"

"God, no. I don't know." She edged around Chance and began walking away, her pace quickening with each step. "Just leave me alone," she shouted before disappearing into Bertie's.

He chose not to press Sue Ann any further, but it didn't matter. He'd already guessed who manhandled her and who possibly put her up to luring him from his house. He hustled back to his truck and drove up the side street to Tim Holmes's auto shop.

Dressed in work overalls, Tim meandered from the auto bay, wiping his hands with a greasy purple rag. On seeing Chance striding toward him with fury in his eyes, Tim jerked to a stop. "Got a problem?"

Chance felt unbridled anger rising. "I think you're the problem."

"What the hell does that mean?" He stuffed the rag in his back pocket.

"You're not going to make this easy, are you?"

Tim turned around but was met with a hand gripping his shoulder. He shoved Chance's hand away. "Hey, what the hell's wrong with you?"

"Why don't you pick on someone your own size?"

"What?"

"I'm talking about Sue Ann. I saw the bruise."

"I don't know what you're talking about."

"I think you do, and I want you to leave her and Kat Summers alone," Chance said while pointing a finger in Tim's face.

Tim's eyes smoldered, and he threw Chance's hand aside. "Even if I did whatever it is you're accusing me of, those bitches probably deserved it."

Bile rose in Chance's throat, heat flooded his arm, and before he could stop himself, he fisted a hand and decked Tim, who staggered backward and fell on his rear. Tim scrambled to his feet, his nose dripping with blood, just as the sheriff's cruiser swung in next to Chance's truck. The sheriff charged into the fray, planting himself between Tim and Chance.

Tim seethed like a wounded bull. "Let me at him."

Sheriff Holmes held Tim back while Chance massaged his fist. Tim wiped his bloody nose with the rag from his back pocket and slowly calmed down.

"What's going on here?"

"He started it," Tim said. "He accused me of all kinds of crap. He's crazy."

"Go back to work. I'll handle this."

Tim scowled at Chance and bellowed, "I want to press charges." Then he stomped into the auto bay to watch.

The sheriff turned to Chance. "We have a real problem here."

"Why don't you control your son?"

"You need to take a step back, Eliason. You're the one getting out of control. I had to smooth it over with Wheeler because you hassled him, and now Tim. An assault on top of that." He opened his palm to Chance. "I want you to relinquish your keys and get in the cruiser."

"You've got to be kidding."

"It's either that, or I'll slap an assault and battery charge on you, and you can have your day in court. Your choice."

Chance squeezed the back of his neck to relieve the mounting tension. He knew he'd crossed the line. He dropped his keys into the sheriff's hand and slid into the back seat of the cruiser.

At the sheriff's office he let Holmes direct him past two vacant desks to the back of the building and into one of two empty jail cells, which in a town the size of Rosswood were rarely used. Chance glanced out the window at a field overgrown with grass and weeds, then sat on a hard cot with his elbows resting on his thighs and his hands clasped together. The door clanked shut, metal on metal.

Chance rose and grabbed onto the metal bars. "You know, Holmes, besides having her house broken into, Kat Summers has been getting unwanted phone calls ever since she's been here. Someone is so frightened of the truth they're trying to scare her off. I'm beginning to believe her theory about Brianna's death, that it was no suicide. What do you think about that?" He didn't get an answer. "Someone should keep an eye on Ms. Summers," Chance yelled as the sheriff left the building.

≈

Sheriff Holmes found Tim at the gas pumps washing a customer's window. The sheriff's shoulders were permanently bunched in pain. Everything he'd done to quell the bleeding from his son's mistakes was crumbling before his eyes. He'd been too lenient with Tim, too soft on him, by overlooking his bullying, his temper, his womanizing. The boy needed discipline.

He waited in the cruiser until Tim finished collecting the money and the car at the pump drove off. He motioned Tim over.

Tim joined him in the front seat. "So, did you slap those charges on the sonovabitch?" His eyes gleamed with satisfaction, and he smelled like a putrid combination of gas and grease, nearly nauseating his father.

"Don't be stupid."

"It was his fault," Tim said. "I didn't do anything."

"Shut up and listen to me. If you don't back off, the Summers woman is going to keep snooping around until she finds out it's true that you were there the night her sister died, and I won't be able to help you. Is that what you want? Now she's got Eliason on the trail, all because you're an idiot. I'm telling you to leave the Summers woman alone."

"But, Dad—"

"Shut up, for once in your life." The sheriff gripped the steering wheel and stared off into space as Tim slumped down. "You're forcing me to take matters into my own hands and see to it that the woman leaves town for good."

"It serves her right," Tim said.

Sheriff Holmes banged the steering wheel with his fist. "Damn it, Tim, just shut the fuck up."

CHAPTER 31

Kat reached into the cupboard for the fluted glass vase and the round casserole dish and cushioned them in a box padded with kitchen towels. This was the last box to go.

She'd worked all afternoon sorting through the rest of Brianna's belongings and packed and transported them to Tilly and her grandmother, a very appreciative pair. Kat also washed and dried the bedding.

A few items Kat couldn't part with and kept in remembrance of her sister: Brianna's gold rings she'd found on the windowsill, the tattered teddy bear Brianna clung to whenever life at home was intolerable, two flannel work shirts, a white mug with Brianna's name emboldened in bright red letters, and the wool hat Tim Holmes had found in the car's backseat.

Kat arched her back, stretching out the soreness, and picked up the apple she'd bought earlier. While she munched the sweet juicy flesh, thoughts of the incredible night she spent with Chance seeped around the edges of her carefully built walls, but she brushed those thoughts aside. Longing for a solid, loving relationship she'd never allow herself to have seemed pointless.

In thirty minutes she had an appointment to meet the Faulkeses at their cabin. The sun was low in the sky, the light fading. She slumped on the couch, tipped her head back, and closed her eyes, promising herself a minute's rest, but more fatigued than she'd realized, she drifted into sleep.

≈

Chance paced the jail cell like a trapped panther. He was tired and hungry, but all he could think about was Kat and how much he wanted to see her before she left town, if that was what she truly intended to do. He hoped her leaving was nothing more than a rumor.

A cold draft swept through from up front. He recognized the sheriff's off-key whistle. "Hey, when are you going to let me out of here? It's been two hours."

Sheriff Holmes appeared with the keys jingling in his hand. He gave Chance a disdainful look but nevertheless unlocked the door and slid it aside, clattering it open. "I don't suppose you've curbed that anger of yours."

"And I don't suppose you've checked on Kat Summers," Chance said, shadowing him to the entrance.

"As far as I can tell, she's in no danger. That murder theory of hers doesn't fly, Eliason. If you ask me, the Summers woman might be as unstable as her sister."

"Watch it, Holmes."

"Oh yeah, I forgot about how it is between you two."

"That's none of your business."

"Remember, I investigated Brianna Whitley's death, and I determined it to be a clear case of suicide."

"And you've never rushed to judgment or made a mistake?"

The sheriff bumped shoulders with Chance on his way to opening the door. "Your truck's outside. The keys are in the ignition. Good afternoon." He ushered Chance out. "Oh, and I'd advise you to keep away from Tim."

Chance groused a reply. His first thought when he wrapped his hands around the steering wheel was of Kat. She wanted space, but that didn't mean he couldn't check up on her to ensure her safety.

≈

He had to see her, even if that meant the possibility of ruining his plans. Kat Summers was leaving town soon. He couldn't let that happen. But he had to be careful. He couldn't afford to bungle this.

The trees afforded him a nice cover. He snuck around to the front of her house, ever so slowly, and peered in the window just to get a peek at her, alert not to be noticed.

Ah . . . She was on the couch, resting, dreaming of him, no doubt. "Soon, we'll be together. Very soon."

But how could she be dreaming of him when she planned to leave town? How could she? The woman was forcing him to act before he was ready. His mother always pushed him. He hated to be pushed.

His wistful thoughts turned wicked and biting. If only Brianna had cooperated, he wouldn't be in this bind, he wouldn't be under this incredible pressure.

He gritted his teeth and pressed his hands against his face. The pain throbbed. It wouldn't stop. The only way to make it go away was to have her in his grip and satisfy his urges. He breathed in short, shallow pants.

He should act now, never mind about later. He couldn't wait another minute to execute his plan. Just as he squeezed the cold metal doorknob, a car's engine roared in the distance and lights flickered through the trees. An intruder.

He lingered until his palms moistened and the lump in his throat thickened, until the thrill of being caught quickened into panic.

He dashed around the house and darted into the woods.

~

Chance slowed to a stop in front of Brianna's house. Kat's SUV was in the driveway, but no lights were on inside. He cut the engine and waited, mulling whether or not to knock. The worst that could happen was a rejection, but the best that could happen was her allowing him to take her in his arms.

Swallowing his apprehension, he stole a peek in the window. She was resting on the couch. He didn't have the heart to disturb her. At least she was home safe.

Despite the fact he'd eaten there earlier, he drove to Bertie's, speculating if Kat woke hungry, she would end up there, too. If not, he'd have an excuse to drive by the house again on his way home.

The Grill was raucous, typical for a Friday evening, with pool balls clashing, voices rising, and the jukebox booming out a tune. He sat at the bar and ordered a beer and a hamburger. He looked around but didn't see any of the usual faces.

Sue Ann, who was taking orders in the main area kept an eye on him, but he never intended to bother her. He rubbed the hand that had dealt the blow to Tim Holmes. Jail time or not, Chance had had the satisfaction of letting the punk know how it felt on the receiving end of a fist.

~

Kat woke, disoriented. She'd heard a loud, grating noise. To hear where it was coming from, she forced herself to get up and listen.

Startled at the scratching sound that came from the back of the house, she crept toward the bedroom to investigate. A shadow of an arm swept the window pane.

Still groggy from sleep, she grabbed the only weapon-like object she could find—Brianna's umbrella—and slipped outside, vowing once and for all to discover the culprit who'd been giving her grief.

The wind kicked up and swirled around her, chilling her legs and flapping her shirt tail. She tightened her grip on the umbrella. While she'd slept, the sun had descended the hills, and the surroundings blended together in shadowy layers.

Hunched with the umbrella in hand, she snuck around the side of the house along the trampled path. When she reached the corner, a large wind gust whistled through the yard, causing a bang from the front of the house.

She wasn't sure how to proceed and began to turn back. But the scraping noise started up again, and she was certain someone was trying to open the bedroom window. Was there more than one intruder?

With the umbrella poised like a spear, she darted around the corner, shouting, "Hold it right there."

Scratching the window was a low-hanging branch. Kat let out an anxious giggle. A mixture of nerves and exhaustion could generate anything.

Even so, just to be safe, she sneaked around front with the umbrella steady in her hand and discovered the wind had slammed the door shut. She jiggled the knob again and again, but no amount of jiggling would force the door open. It had locked from the inside.

"Dammit." Kat marched around back and tugged on the bedroom window. It wouldn't budge.

Her purse and her cell phone were in the house, as was her jacket. She rubbed her arms for warmth. With the wind a factor, the temperature was sinking fast.

She pressed the button that lit up the face of her watch. She was already ten minutes late to her appointment with the Faulkeses. Back around the house, she knelt in front of the SUV's bumper and felt for the magnetic metal box where she kept the spare key.

On the upside, she'd left the directions to the cabin on the passenger's seat. Using a flashlight from the glove box, she figured out her route. She'd take her chances with no driver's license and hope that later Lenny would help her pry the bedroom window open.

No lights were on in the church, nor was the pastor's Jeep in the parking lot. Tilly's house was dimly lit. Kat wondered where everyone gathered on a Friday night, where Chance was in particular. He hadn't tried to contact her. She fought back the empty feeling, the unanticipated disappointment.

She flipped on the heater but hadn't given the SUV a proper time to warm up. It spewed lukewarm air.

Before making the turn onto Pine Road, she glanced to the left toward Chance's driveway in time to see a vehicle's headlights. Her stomach clenched. It may have been his truck, but she'd only caught a glimpse before needing to turn right. According to Lenny's map, the cabin was only a short jog off Pine Road. She pressed on.

In October the dark came quickly to this mountain community. A bitter night was settling in. She jacked up the heat. She wished she'd agreed to meet the Faulkeses earlier in the day or in the morning before she left town.

Because of no driver's license, she lumbered along under the speed limit. The farther she drove, the thicker the trees grew—pines and firs clustered on both sides like a fortress of murky green. With no artificial lighting to guide her, it was darker than in town.

Finally she spotted the For Sale sign Lenny told her to watch for. Its reflective letters flashed in the dark. Just past the sign, she turned onto a dirt road and was snared by the deepening shades of gray.

The SUV snaked over the potholed path, jarring Kat from side to side. Up ahead in the distance lights filtered through the trees. She fought back an unsettling feeling. The thought of turning around crossed her mind, but then a pine grove opened into a clearing, and the cabin materialized.

It was nothing as Kat had imagined. In the moonlight it looked more like a miner's shack than a summer retreat. The wood was weathered, as if it hadn't been painted or stained since it was first built. The windows were tiny squares barely large enough to look through. The porch steps were uneven and saggy in places. The Faulkeses needed more help than she could give them, perhaps the help of a demolition crew.

She noticed no other cars around, but lights flickered inside, rose and fell like flames from a fireplace. When she exited the car, she smelled the wood smoke, confirming her suspicions. Someone was waiting for her.

CHAPTER 32

Without a jacket for warmth, Kat stood on the cabin's porch on a plank that squished beneath her boots, shivering from the forest's deep evening chill. As she raised her fist to knock, an owl hooted so close to the cabin she glanced at a nearby tree, but it was too dark to see any details. When she turned back, the door creaked opened.

The doctor stared back at her. "Come in." He had a warm and friendly smile, but his breathing was fast and choppy. Moisture laced his upper lip, dirt caked the edges of his shoes, and his shirt had perspiration stains under the arms.

Kat looked past him into a room that was sparsely filled with second-hand furnishings: a faded plaid sofa; a worn coffee table facing a roaring fire; a wooden dining table with mismatched chairs. "Why are *you* here?" A cool breeze whipped through the doorway, chilling her back. She hugged her arms to her chest.

"Come in. Come in. I can see that you're cold. You should be wearing a coat. You could catch your death."

She entered but stayed near the door. He slid it shut and stood so near to her she could feel his breath on her hair. She stepped to the side, putting more distance between them.

He motioned toward the fireplace. "I made that for you. Why don't you come and sit by the fire?"

"Where are the Faulkeses?"

"Not to worry. They'll be along shortly. They got hung up on the time and asked me if I would let you in. And I did, didn't I?"

White candles were scattered about on the hearth, the mantelpiece, the table—all burning bright yellow flames. Lying next to the candle on the table was one white rose.

"Didn't I?" he repeated.

"What?"

"You didn't answer me. I said I let you in, didn't I?" His hospitable smile faded, replaced by an irritable glare.

Something wasn't right. "I think maybe I should come back later."

In one quick move he backed against the door, blocking her exit. She had to move farther inside the room just to get away from the proximity of him.

"Why don't you sit by the fire like I asked you to?"

"Why don't you let me leave, and you can tell Lenny I'll come by another time."

He squinted his BB-like eyes, the color deepening.

"In fact, I can stay here and look for myself," she said. "Maybe you should go."

His face darkened into a storm. "That's what you always say to me."

"I beg your pardon?"

"Shut up, Brianna."

She took a step back. "I'm not Brianna. I'm her sister. You know that. Are you all right?"

He stared at her, unresponsive, his face distorted in an odd way that seemed as if he were trying to make sense of what she'd said but wasn't quite putting it together. Something was definitely wrong with the man.

"I think you should move away from the door and let me leave this instant."

"Not this time, Brianna. You're not going away this time."

He obviously wasn't going to let Kat go. She strode to the back of the cabin into a room she thought might be a bathroom, hoping she could lock herself in or find another way out, but she rammed her knee into a metal bed frame. She winced from the pain.

The room had no door to secure against him, so she felt around for a chair, a lamp, a book, anything to use for self-defense. Her eyes acclimated to the dark, and the fire from the other room gave off just enough light for her to realize nothing in this room would help her.

She stationed herself against the wall next to the doorway, listening for his footsteps, and waited for what seemed like hours, the icy feel of the wall seeping into her. She heard nothing but the crackling fire. Her heart throbbed. Her knees weakened.

Slowly, with caution she peeked around the corner, saw nothing but flames from the fireplace. The gooseflesh rose. She smelled the stench of alcohol and drew back. But it was too late. He was on her, grabbing her hair and holding a scalpel-like knife to her throat. She shrieked in horror.

"I wouldn't try to get away this time, Brianna. I asked you to sit by the fire and warm yourself, and that's what I want you to do." He dragged her down on the sofa with him. "In case you're wondering, I've locked the door, and only I know where the key is." He waved the knife two inches from her face.

She swallowed hard and edged away from the blade. Think, she told herself. As frightened as she was, she resolved to talk her way out of this. "What happened to Brianna?" Her voice wavered.

He cocked his head. His eyelid twitched relentlessly. "You're my Brianna, my second chance."

"I'm not Brianna. I'm nothing like Brianna."

"Don't say that. Don't say that," he bellowed. "I read her story. She had a twin just like her."

"That was fiction. Brianna and I are not twins."

"I said you are." Forcing the words through clenched teeth, he tightened a grip on her arm and held the knife at her throat.

"All right, all right. Whatever you say. Tell me what happened to her. They said she died in her car from carbon monoxide poisoning."

"That's not true. They only put her there. I watched them carry her out to the garage. They took her away from me."

"Who are *they*?"

"They, they, do I have to explain everything?" he spewed with contempt.

"Then tell me what really happened."

His brows narrowed, his eyelid twitched, and he leaned into her. His breath smelled like a mingling of bourbon and mint. "They tried to trick me. Brianna didn't kill herself. She loved me too much to kill herself."

He rose and paced in front of the hearth. "She had to be punished, just like the girl in her story. She asked for it. I tried to give her what she wanted, but she wouldn't stop fighting me. She wouldn't stop fighting. She wouldn't stop. I tried to quiet her, but she kept screaming and screaming. I squeezed her neck, just to warn her, and told her to stop making so much noise. She wouldn't obey me. She needed discipline."

He knelt facing Kat and held the knife to her throat. "You won't scream, will you?"

Kat stared down at the blade, inched back a little. Her forehead was punctuated with moisture.

He sat next to her again and sighed. "I want it to be perfect this time. I despise anything messy. That's what made me mad about Brianna. She lived her life messy." He bared his teeth at Kat. "She took up with every man in town, like a tramp. I took care of her. When she needed me, I looked after her. She came to me every time she needed a shoulder to cry on, and what did I get in return? Nothing but the rise of old buried hurts. Don't you see? She teased me just like every other woman."

He took a deep breath. "Everything was fine until she came to town. I'd made a life for myself until just watching her uncovered all the old feelings. She bewitched me."

He glanced toward the mantelpiece. "That candle burned out. I can't have that. Everything has to be perfect." As if entranced, he set the knife on the coffee table and picked up a book of matches, giving Kat the opportunity she needed.

The minute he rose to light the candle, she grabbed the knife. He spun around, and she lunged forward. The blade grazed his upper arm before he knocked it out of her hand. She charged toward the door and shook the doorknob with all her might.

He grabbed the scruff of her neck and growled a laugh. The blood leached into his shirt from the superficial wound. "You can't leave me now, Brianna. I have to show you how much I love you."

She was no match for the strength that came from his madness, and he dragged her back to the sofa. "Sit down and behave, or I'll have to tie you up. We wouldn't want that. Now, where was I?" He combed the hearth and garnered the knife. The blood from his wound was crusting to his shirt. He snuggled close to her. The heat poured off his body.

"What about the Faulkeses?"

"Hah! I tricked you, Brianna. That's how smart I am compared to you. They couldn't come at all, so I did. Lucky for me. I even stopped by your house and looked in your window. Did you know one night I was inside your house watching you sleep? Oh, how I wanted to touch you."

Kat recalled the night the door had slammed. It was true. He'd been in her room. So close. So terribly close to her.

"Are you warm, Brianna?"

Kat said nothing.

"I asked you if you were warm." His tone stung.

She nodded while keeping track of the knife.

"Good. We're going to resume where we left off, Brianna. Do you remember the bedroom?"

No way would Kat agree to do anything sexual he might ask of her. She'd die first. She had to keep him talking until she figured out her next move. "Tell me about your life growing up." She worked at keeping her voice level. "Were your parents around?"

"I want you to lie down, Brianna."

She skimmed the room for an object heavy enough to deal a lasting blow. An ashtray was on the dining table, but it was too far away and too small. The metal fire poker was closest. "Was your mother a good person?"

He fidgeted with his pant leg and began rocking. "I don't want to talk about her."

"Why not?"

"I just don't. Don't talk about her. She was evil." He grabbed hold of the top of Kat's shirt and held the knife to her throat. "Don't ever mention her again."

"Okay, okay." Clearly, Kat had touched a deep wound.

He stood over her and commanded her to lie down. "Do it now, Brianna. I have a second chance to make it right."

He was between Kat and the fire poker, and no way could she get to it without going through him first. She'd have to wait for the right time. But she wasn't about to lie down for him. "Why don't we talk some more?"

"Talk? That's all you ever wanted to do, Brianna. I had to take charge, don't you remember?"

As much as she feared for her own life, her thoughts were of her sister and what she must have gone through. "What did you and Brianna talk about?"

With a resigned groan he plopped on the sofa and huddled next to

Kat, his arm and leg butting against hers. He kept a firm grip on the knife handle and kept the blade hovering near her neck. "No more talking, unless I say so."

With the knife poised, he unfastened the top buttons of her shirt, slid the material over her shoulder, and slipped her bra strap down. Starting at her tattoo, he kissed her skin up to her jawline. His breath was hot and putrid, his lips greasy. "Tell me you love me, Brianna."

She felt the nausea rise. "If I tell you I love you, will you let me go?" A nick of the blade, and she twitched. Her stomach clenched.

"Say it."

"I love you," she said in a robotic tone.

"I'm going to kiss you now."

⁓

Chance looked at his watch. An hour had ticked by, and it was time to go home. Kat hadn't showed up. She had all day to think, and still she hadn't tried to find him. Not a good sign. Dejected, he paid Bertie for his meal and wound through the crowded restaurant. As he was going out, Wilma was coming in. He tipped his hat to her.

"Hey, cowboy, where did that good-looking gal of yours run off to?"

"Who're you talking about?"

"Everyone knows you and Kat Summers have been hanging out together. You two are on everybody's tongue."

"As far as I know, she's at Brianna's house."

"She hasn't come into the shop lately. I was thinking about driving over there, but maybe you could relay a message for me the next time you see her."

"What is it?"

"A while back she asked me about a phone number."

"Phone number? What phone number?"

"She didn't tell you she was getting those crank calls on her cell phone? She had the guy's number, and she was trying to figure out who it belonged to."

Chance thought back to his and Kat's trip to Benton and recalled her mentioning a phone number, but then saying she meant the phone calls. She'd kept that from him.

"At the time I couldn't recall," Wilma was saying, "but I finally figured out where I'd seen that number. I remember I was walking up the steps to the post office and found a cell phone lying on the ground. It had a number printed on paper and taped to the back, but I didn't recognize the number. When I gave it to Lenny, his face went as white as a cotton ball, and he tucked it away fast. He didn't say anything to Clare either because she came in right after me."

"Good God, could he be the one?"

"I thought about accusing him, but Clare came in, and I didn't think I should. Maybe the phone isn't his."

"I'll tell Kat, and she can decide how to handle it."

"That sounds about right," Wilma said. "You know, I can't believe Lenny would do such a thing, really, but with a wife like Clare, who knows?"

"Excuse me," Chance said, "but I have to go."

"When you see her, tell her to stop by the shop before she leaves this place."

With an excuse to talk to Kat, he sped through town past Tilly's to Brianna's house, which was now shrouded in darkness. Kat's SUV wasn't in the driveway. Had she left town already? Perhaps she was at his house. He could only hope. But when he arrived home, his house was also shadowed, and her vehicle was nowhere in sight.

He left the engine running and darted inside to check the messages on his answering machine. One was from Stella, asking him to return her call. Another was from Monique, apologizing and hoping they could meet again. If the woman was nothing else, she was persistent. None of the messages were from Kat. Could she have left without saying goodbye? As he hurried outside to turn off the truck's engine, a sinking feeling settled in his chest.

A pair of headlights blasted him, and Rusty's truck pulled up beside him. Zeke tumbled out of the truck bed, and he yapped and wiggled around Chance.

"I took Zeke for a ride," Rusty said. "Hope you don't mind."

At the moment Zeke's welfare was the least of Chance's concerns. He roughed up Zeke's coat. "Have you by any chance seen Kat Summers's SUV around town?"

"Saw her about half an hour ago turning down Pine Road. I remember 'cause I was thinking at the time no one goes that way this time of night. It's all but darkness down that road."

All but darkness and Lenny's cabin. Chance felt a grip in his gut. If Lenny was the one harassing Brianna and now Kat with those weird calls, it followed that he might be taking this to a new level, and if he had something to do with Brianna's death, he might be luring Kat to his cabin. Lenny the postman. It seemed unlikely, but Chance wanted to be on the safe side. "Take care of Zeke, will you? And call Sheriff Holmes. Tell him to meet me at the Faulkeses' cabin. Tell him it's an emergency."

"What kind of emergency? You want me to go with you?"

"No. I need you to stay here, and call me on my cell phone if Kat shows up. Keep calling until you get hold of the sheriff."

≈

His wet, slimy lips mashed against hers. She wanted to vomit. Between caresses and kisses she'd tried getting him to talk, but she was tired and drained of energy. She'd run out of questions to ask him and was close to giving up.

"This is better, see? You aren't fighting me this time." He kissed her once more and his breathing became ragged and shallow. "Why don't you lie down now?"

Revulsion, like none she'd ever experienced, engulfed her. Her throat was parched, and it took every ounce of determination to fend him off. "I don't think we should hurry." She forced her voice to change from desperation to sweetness. "Don't you want this evening to last? I do. Let's talk for a while longer, then I'll kiss you again and tell you how much I love you. I promise."

His eyes softened. "That's all I ever wanted from you, Brianna." He kissed her shoulder but kept the knife ready to slice at the least bit of resistance.

Outside, a vehicle's engine revved to a stop. He jerked in that direction, relaxed the arm holding the knife. Buoyed by the sound of a door closing, Kat attempted to flee from him, but he caught her by her shirt and placed her in a choke hold.

"You told someone you were here." The muscles in his arms stiffened. She tried shaking her head no.

"You must have told." He tightened his grip, and Kat gasped for air.

Someone hammered the door and rattled the doorknob. "Kat, are you in there?"

"Chance."

"Shut up, Brianna."

In a burst of energy Kat stomped on her captor's foot and elbowed his stomach. He hunched over, allowing her to break free and run to the door. She tugged the doorknob. "Chance, help me!"

There followed a bang against the door. It held firm.

Her captor regained his footing, and from the shadows of the fire-place pulled a handgun from a brown leather bag she hadn't noticed before. "I didn't want to have to do this," he said, pointing the gun at Kat, "but you give me no choice. I'm not letting you go this time. No matter how this plays out, if I go, you're going with me. I've already started your grave. Give me your hand."

"Give it up, Doc." The sheriff's voice rang out.

The doctor lengthened both arms, the pistol aiming at her head. "See now, it's too late. They know I'm here." He shouted toward the door, "Back off. I have a gun."

The pounding stopped.

"Let her go," Chance yelled.

Suddenly, out of nowhere, a frigid breeze swirled through the cabin, snuffing out the candle flames.

Keeping the gun at arm's length, the doctor with wild, probing eyes turned a complete circle, then focused on Kat. "You did it."

Kat, who was as stunned as he was, shook her head vigorously and backed up close to the door.

One by one, each candle dislodged from its holder and floated around the room.

"You're doing this. Make it stop!"

The ashtray hovered above the tabletop. Every object that wasn't nailed down—pencils, pillows, plates, candles—soared around the room, as it had played out in Kat's dream.

Kat crouched against the wall out of the way.

Gripping the gun, the doctor twirled around and around and ducked and dodged as the objects shot toward him. Eyes glazed with terror, he staggered to a stop and shook the gun at Kat, screaming, "Make it stop. Make it stop, or I'll shoot."

Everything clattered to the floor. The ashtray shattered. The fire poker crashed to the stone hearth, creating a deafening sound.

Startled, he swung around, lost his balance, and just as the door was kicked open, stumbled over his brown bag and plunged face-first into the sharp corner of the mantel. He fell onto the hearth and gashed his head on the fire poker.

The temperature of the room warmed to normal.

CHAPTER 33

Sheriff Holmes had been the first to charge through the doorway just as the doctor tripped into the mantelpiece and fell to the floor.

Chance was right behind the sheriff and pulled Kat into his arms, her body trembling uncontrollably. "Are you all right?"

"Just scared."

"I'm taking you to the hospital in Benton just to be on the safe side."

"I'm all right. I'm not hurt."

Pointing his weapon downward, the sheriff nudged the doctor's leg. Satisfied, he holstered his gun, knelt by the body, and felt for a pulse. He shook his head. He rose, viewed the debris around the room, and looked at Kat, mystified. "What happened here?"

"You wouldn't believe me if I told you."

"It looks like a war zone."

"He killed Brianna. He told me as much. He kept calling me by her name. He was insane."

"I knew there was something about the guy I didn't like. He was peculiar and standoffish." The sheriff nodded at Chance. "Why don't you take her home? I'll get her statement in the morning. I'll take over from here."

Chance tried to guide Kat to the door, but she wouldn't move. She said to the sheriff, "Brianna didn't die from carbon monoxide. He didn't put her body in her car that night. Why did you lie?"

Holmes thought a moment, glanced from Chance to Kat. "Did you ever think you needed to protect one of your own? Turns out he didn't need it. Now, go on home both of you."

"No! Not until you tell me what happened that night."

"Kat," Chance said, "let it go. Right now you need to get out of here."

She shook free from him. "I want to know, Sheriff. Tell me what happened."

"All right. If you must know, I'll tell you." Holmes stepped away from the body. "Seems that evening Tim and Brianna had a whopper of an argument in town. There were witnesses. Later, he went out to her house to talk to her and found her dead. That's when he called me. But before I got there, he'd knocked over a glass on her nightstand. In trying to clean it up, he cut himself and his blood was all over the floor." Holmes paused. "The blood. The witnesses. You put two and two together. It didn't look good. He swore he didn't do it, but I had my doubts. Now, if you'll excuse me, I have work to do."

"You'll have to explain your actions to the county authorities, Holmes." Chance removed his jacket and slid it over Kat's shoulders. "Come on, Kat." He escorted her outside. "Are you sure you don't need to go to the hospital to get checked out?"

"I'm fine, really. Just shook up."

"You're coming home with me, and I won't take no for an answer."

"I'm all right, really. I just want to go back to Brianna's."

"You shouldn't go back there. You shouldn't be alone."

"I locked myself out of the house. My purse and my cell phone are in there, so are my clothes. Will you help me?"

"Of course I will, but only if you'll stay in my house tonight, in the guest room, of course. I won't push you."

Kat was too weary to argue.

"I'll drive your car and get my truck later."

"No. Just follow me to Brianna's. I'm okay, really."

"Kat, you shouldn't drive after what you've been through."

She got in the driver's seat of the SUV, giving Chance no choice but to do as she'd asked. She turned on the engine and inched along over the pitted road with his headlights blaring behind her like bobbing white discs.

In Brianna's driveway Chance pointed out to Kat that she'd driven slower than normal in an effort to bolster his case for her to stay with him. To offset his concern she used the excuse of not having her license.

Using his tire iron, he jimmied the door open. While she switched on the light and the space heater, he stood by and waited for her to come with him.

"How did you know I was at Lenny's cabin?"

"I ran into Wilma in town, found out the mystery phone number belonged to Lenny, and knew he had to be your caller. Rusty told me he saw your SUV driving down Pine Road. I feared the worse, that he'd set a trap for you. I told Rusty to call the sheriff. But I never figured it was the doctor, not until Holmes arrived."

"How did he know?"

"He didn't, until he swung by Lenny's house on his way to the cabin. Lenny told him he'd asked Doc Conklin to tell you he couldn't make it to your appointment. Holmes didn't think there was a problem but decided to meet me out here just to make sure."

"It was a good thing he did."

"It must have been terrifying for you." He reached out to embrace her, but she recoiled from the contact. "Did he touch you?"

"He didn't rape me, if that's what you're getting at. He only touched me, but I want to drench myself in the shower, just to get rid of the sickening feel of him."

"You can be alone in my bedroom and use my private bath with the Jacuzzi tub. You can relax in there all night if you need to."

She looked into his caring eyes and knew she was going to hurt him.

"I need time to myself, Chance, and not in your house."

"Why, Kat?"

It would be so easy to give in to him, but she wouldn't let herself.

"Just for a while. Go back to your house, and I'll tie up loose ends here, get myself together."

"I don't want to leave you here in this house."

"Please, Chance, allow me this. I'm in no danger now."

"I guess you're right. After the sheriff's visit to Lenny, I don't think he'll be calling you anytime soon, but you never know."

"I'll keep my cell phone off just in case. I'll deal with him later. Why don't you go? I'll be along shortly."

Before leaving, he turned to look at her. "I'll wait up for you."

Kat stood at the window and watched him drive away. She felt miserable and alone and wished his arms were around her. Why couldn't she just let go and allow Chance into her life? Was it because she didn't want to lose herself in the process, or were the walls so rigid and thick she couldn't find a way to let anyone in? For now she'd do what she'd decided to do on the way back from the cabin.

She loaded her suitcases and Brianna's laptop and stories into her SUV, then came back for the box meant for Tilly, the bedding and other odds and ends. All that was left in the house was the furniture. Maybe she'd arrange with Hank's help to rent the house furnished. She could do this from home. The main thing was to get out of Rosswood now.

She called the sheriff's office and left a message, explaining that she was leaving for Seattle tonight, and if he needed a statement from her, he could call her or her attorney on Monday. She left her cell phone number and her attorney's number as well. She said she preferred not to press charges against Lenny as long as he agreed to stop pestering her. She just wanted to put this whole business behind her and get on with her life.

After the call she found an old grocery receipt and wrote a note to Chance. In it she thanked him for his help and apologized for leaving without saying goodbye. She said it was better this way. Her eyes welled up at the thought of him.

She switched off the lamp, but her attention was guided toward the bedroom where a silver blue light hovered in the doorway. A hint of Brianna's face shimmered inside. Kat stood transfixed. A sensation, like warm water, trickled through her, and she had the distinct feeling Brianna was now at peace. As soon as that thought came to her, the image vanished.

Kat thanked her sister. She knew for certain Brianna's spirit had somehow played a role in keeping her safe.

Before she left, Kat wedged the note in the door for Chance. She had no doubt he'd come looking for her.

She was in no mood to talk, so she quietly delivered the box to Tilly's porch with a note that said goodbye and told Tilly to take good care of Tiger. On the way out of town, she drove past Chance's private drive, giving it a tearful glance.

As she progressed farther and farther from Rosswood in the black of night, with the wind battering her car, the exhaustion she'd kept at bay began to swallow up every ounce of concentration she had left. She blinked fiercely, fighting the urge to fall asleep.

When a yellow neon sign appeared up ahead, announcing The Sleeping Inn, she swerved into the parking lot. The rustic inn was nothing but one long row of adjoining rooms. A tan sedan and a black pickup were the only vehicles wedged in the narrow parking spots.

For the first time in hours, Kat felt a surge of hunger, but no restaurants accompanied the motel, nor had she seen any eating establishment along the way. It was as if The Sleeping Inn had been carved out of the forest.

She traipsed into the office and tapped the desk bell. The dingy room smelled old and musty. A balding man in a T-shirt and jeans came out of a back room and raised his eyebrows when he saw Kat.

"I'd like a room for the night."

He glanced out at her car. "Double or single."

"Single."

"Hmm . . . You look like you could use a night's rest."

She shrugged an indifferent response and signed for the room. Nearby was a coffeepot with what looked like black sludge, the remnants of day-old brew. She passed on the coffee and fed a junk food machine a handful of quarters, but had to hammer the sides to get a package of peanut butter crackers to drop down.

On her way out the proprietor reminded her checkout time was at eleven o'clock and in a monotone wished her a pleasant evening. She doubted his sincerity.

Her room was closest to the office, three doors down from where the black pickup was parked. She hauled everything inside. No sense inviting trouble.

The room was small with a tiny bedside table wedged between two twin beds. There was no TV or telephone. The only uplifting color came from the yellow sunflower in the picture on the wall. The thinning bedspreads were beige.

She threw back the covers to inspect the sheets and then examined the square box of a bathroom with its meager sink and shower. At least everything was clean.

She lay on the bed and listened to the silence. The more deeply she breathed, the more her muscles relaxed and released the built-up tension. With more and more intake of oxygen, her body began to shiver. Yet the temperature in the room was comfortably warm. She couldn't stop shaking. The queasiness in her stomach was unbearable.

She rushed to get up, secured the door with the chain lock, and shoved the top of a chair under the doorknob. Then she ran to the bathroom and retched over the sink in wave after wave of dry heaves. When the retching ceased, she locked the bathroom door.

She shed her clothes and stepped into a hot, steamy shower. In the cleansing spray, she convulsed in tears, releasing all the pent-up terror that had been clenched inside during her frightening ordeal. The water streamed over her head, drenching her whole being, washing away the horror.

Wiping the mirror of accumulated mist revealed a face drained of life—pallid skin, deep moons under the eyes. If Maggie saw her now, she'd most assuredly send her to a spa for a month of rehab. That might not be a bad idea.

She towel-dried her hair, put on her nightgown, and forced the peanut butter crackers down a very raw throat. She drank a glass of water and climbed into bed.

What she dearly needed was sleep, but she remained wide awake. A truck roared by, casting shadows across the textured ceiling.

She thought of Chance and how grateful she was he hadn't witnessed her breakdown. Holding on to him would have been soothing and the smart thing to do. She knew that. But the past had proven that holding on to anyone only diminished her own strength.

Thus far in her life she hadn't needed a man, and she didn't need one now. Even at that thought, her throat constricted, and she curled up and wept, this time for Chance, because he was the first man who'd ever come this close to her heart. Why couldn't she let go and allow him in?

She fell asleep and woke once in the middle of the night both chilled and drenched in sweat. The doctor's horrifying face had infested her dreams. She took in several lung-filled breaths to ratchet down her hammering heart to its normal rhythm. To sleep again, she pictured Chance's loving eyes and imagined his protective arms around her.

She woke around nine in the morning. After dressing and loading the car, she delivered the key to the office and was off to Seattle by ten.

≈

Chance paced the floor. The night before, when he went looking for Kat, he'd discovered the note. It ripped when he tried to pull it from the door, but he got the gist of the message. She'd left for Seattle.

He was angry and hurt. Angry, because she was in no shape to be driving that distance in the dark of night after what she'd been through. Hurt, because he cared for her and hoped the feeling was mutual, especially after the loving experience they'd shared.

He couldn't let the woman who'd awakened his soul march out of his life. He wouldn't. Why on earth had he given her his novel to read without any explanation?

He flicked the edges of Kat's business card, then picked up the phone and called her cell phone number. It didn't connect. He tried the cell phone number on the card, but the result was the same. Undaunted, he tried the office number of Loggins Realty, and a man named Jim Gavin came on the line. "I'm looking for Kat Summers," Chance explained. "I've tried her cell phone but she doesn't answer. I was wondering if you could give me her address and home number if she has one."

"I'm sorry, but I can't give out any personal information about Ms. Summers. If you'll leave your number, I'll have her get back to you. However, she has been on vacation of late. Is there anything I can help you with?"

"No, thanks. I'll try another time." Chance hung up, frustrated.

He let Zeke in and started toward his study in hopes of finding information about Kat on the Internet, but he stopped short of the hallway. "The post office." Zeke whined in response. "We'll kill two birds with one stone. Perfect. Let's go for a ride." Chance waved Zeke forward, and the dog took off for the door.

Last night's wind had blown in another cold front, and Chance zipped up his jacket against the chill. He opened the tailgate, and Zeke jumped into the truck bed. Along the private road the truck staggered over potholes as Chance pressed on the gas. When he swerved onto the highway, Zeke pitched to the side.

At the post office Chance cautioned Zeke to stay put and hurried inside. He had to wait for Angus, one of the town's elders, to finish licking a stamp and hand an envelope to Lenny. Two other people were milling around the postal boxes.

Despite the customers, Lenny seemed preoccupied, fidgety, even dropping Angus's letter. He barely looked at Chance.

"I know about the calls," Chance said as Angus meandered out the door.

Lenny sucked in a breath. "Shh . . . Please, don't say anything if Clare walks in. I never meant any harm."

"Has the sheriff talked to you about it?"

"Yes. Now, I have work to do." His eyes flashed from one envelope to another.

"Didn't he tell your wife?"

Lenny glared at Chance. "He says it depends on what Ms. Summers says. I'll have to ask you to move along. I don't want to talk about this here."

"Do you realize what you put Kat through? I ought to tear you apart." Chance set his hat on the counter. "Why did you do it? I'm not leaving until you give me a straight answer."

Lenny spouted a disgruntled sigh and motioned for Chance to step to the end of the counter out of earshot. "I just . . . I just . . . I don't know," he whispered. "I lost my head. Brianna was so pretty. I couldn't help it. I called her once, and I got so nervous I couldn't say anything. I just kept calling. It got easier and easier. Things got out of control." As he talked, he wrung his hands, swallowed hard, and his expression grew pitiful.

"Come on, Lenny." Chance kept his voice lowered. "I know what you were doing when you made those calls. Isn't that what you did as a teenager with those girly magazines?"

Lenny's face burned redder than his hair. "Shh . . . And please don't tell Clare. She can't know."

"Then you'll have to promise me you will never, and I mean never, bother Ms. Summers again."

Lenny nodded so fast his teeth rattled. "I promise."

"Maybe we can strike a deal. You must have Ms. Summers's home address. She left a forwarding address, didn't she?"

"Oh, yes, but that's confidential. I can't divulge that information. It would be against the law."

Chance leaned within an inch of Lenny's nose and tugged on his bowtie. "We wouldn't want Clare, or anyone else in here, to find out what you were doing while you were on the phone, would we?"

Lenny's pupils dilated. He backed away from Chance, thumbed through a folder, and scribbled on a strip of envelope. He handed it over.

"Not one call to Ms. Summers, or you'll answer to me. You're just lucky I'm in a good mood today."

Lenny whimpered a positive reply and withered into a puddle of despair.

Satisfied, Chance left the post office. Zeke paced the truck bed and greeted him with a few sharp barks. Chance held up the paper and grinned. "We struck gold, boy. Let's go home and execute our plan."

CHAPTER 34

Gray, low-hanging clouds threatened rain in the Seattle area. The moisture in the air cut right through Kat. She shed her boots in the mud room and padded across the cold kitchen floor. Her house, shut tight for almost two weeks, was clammier than Brianna's. She snapped on the heat. The upgraded forced-air furnace would warm her in no time.

Later in the evening she'd sit in front of a toasty fire to melt away any lingering tension, although after the release she'd experienced the previous night, she felt somewhat unburdened. Her only fear was the details of her ordeal might sneak into her dreams.

All the way over the mountain pass, her thoughts drifted to Chance and to her rising guilt over fleeing Rosswood the way she had, leaving a note for a goodbye. Being in her house now, surrounded by her own things, helped steady her, but the emptiness burrowed deep. Stubbornly, she'd left the only man having an inkling of a chance to break down the barriers. In all likelihood her brusque departure had sealed that door forever.

After she unpacked and tossed her clothes in the washing machine, she went to the local market, stocked up on groceries, and fixed herself a balanced meal, vowing to eat better than she had the last two weeks. Her form-fitting jeans had loosened around the waist.

While she ate and waited for her clothes to dry, the phone in the kitchen rang, jogging her memory that she hadn't contacted Maggie.

"Were you ever going to call me? I was worried sick about you," the cranky voice on the line sputtered.

"Maggie, I'm so sorry. I've been in my own crazy world, and I wasn't thinking."

"I'm glad to hear your voice is all. You had me conjuring up all kinds of horrible scenarios."

"You wouldn't be that far off."

"What in the world happened to you?"

"Do you think you could come by anytime soon?"

Two hours later Kat built a roaring fire, which hurled her into the cabin scene in front of the fireplace with her captor's knife fixed at her neck. She shook the image free, wondering how long it would take for the flashbacks to fade from memory.

She prepared a plate of finger foods—cheese and crackers, olives, onion dip, chips—and added cut-up veggies to impress Maggie she was eating better. She placed the dish, along with a bottle of red wine, on the coffee table and hastened to the bedroom to change clothes.

Her bed had always been a comfort with its cozy designer coverings in passionate pink and magenta, but since Brianna's death and the fitful nights, she'd gravitated to the couch. She missed her bedroom and hoped to find solace there again.

After living in jeans and flannel shirts, she gladly changed into a pair of black slacks and a gold sweater. The same went for her high-heeled boots. She relegated them to the closet and slipped on a pair of flats. She felt almost human.

One glance in the mirror gave her pause. Even makeup, recently applied, and a few splashes of her favorite springtime perfume couldn't hide the devastating imprint from the last two days—dark crescents under her eyes and an aura of uneasiness about her. If she acted as if everything were normal, Maggie would see right through her.

Whatever Maggie's reaction, when the doorbell rang Kat's heart skipped with excitement and the anticipation of seeing her best friend. She tossed a log on the fire and answered the door. A draft of misty air followed Maggie inside.

Maggie entered in her classic suit and hat, giving Kat the once over. "You clean up nice, but I can see you're a mess."

"So much for makeup."

Maggie grasped Kat's arm and looked into her eyes. "I want you to tell me everything, and then tell me how I can help."

Kat gave her a hug. "Hello to you, too. Can we sit first and chat about what's been happening at work since I've been away?"

"Forget work." Maggie sat on the couch across from Kat and poured each of them a glass of wine. "I'll just have a sip." She set her jacket and hat on the seat cushion next to her and fluffed up her hair. "You've been through something awful. I felt it in my bones all day yesterday, like arthritis in cold weather."

"You're too perceptive."

"That's what comes when you're close to someone. I called you so many times I could barely get any work done. So, tell me."

As the fire crackled and spit, Kat settled back in her chair with her wineglass, trying to keep her hand steady, and gave Maggie a full account of her surreal experience—from the moment the doctor opened the cabin door to his brutal demise—including what Kat believed was Brianna's extraordinary part in the experience. "It was horrible, Maggie."

"My God, Kat. I never imagined anything that freaking outrageous, that crazy man and all those objects flying around. If I didn't know you better, I'd think you were hallucinating. But I can see you're not doing well. You're pale and jittery. Why aren't you in a hospital getting checked out?"

"I don't need to."

Maggie rose from the couch. "Come on, get your jacket. I'm taking you to emergency."

"No, Maggie, sit down. I'm doing fine. Just a few flashbacks, but I'm sure those will go away."

"Fine, my ass." Maggie sat again and with probing eyes looked at Kat. "You're probably suffering from PTSD. If you won't go to the hospital, I'd advise you to call Dr. Rosen Monday morning. Why don't you come with me, so I can take care of you? I'll see to it that you get in to see him. My God."

"Will you calm down? I'm going to be okay. All I need is rest."

"Like hell."

"Maggie, please."

"All right, all right. So, what happened after the doctor's death? Did you call the authorities? I can't believe they let you leave Rosswood without getting checked out."

"I insisted on coming home."

"That sounds like you, always taking care of yourself."

"I could have had help."

Kat told Maggie about Chance's suspicions and his calling the sheriff, about Chance following her home and wanting to look after her. She tried to sound detached when talking about Chance, but she couldn't help her voice from shaking a little when speaking his name.

"What a freaking nightmare. I can't believe what you've been through." Maggie leaned back with her wineglass. "And that lunatic made all those freaking calls to you."

"As a matter of fact, it was the postman who did that. A strange little man. He adored Brianna, and I guess he transferred those feelings to me."

"What a town." Maggie wagged her head. "So, who's this 'Chance'? I don't believe you mentioned him to me, unless he was one of those reasons you wanted to come home."

Even over the fire's warmth, Kat felt her skin flush. "He's just a man I met there and became friends with," she tossed lightly at Maggie, trying not to arouse too much curiosity.

"That's rather vague. Can you be more specific? How much of a friend was he? How friendly did you get?"

"Friendly, friendly." Kat's face flushed again.

"You mean you had sex."

"Just once and it was a mistake. It was after I'd been getting those weird calls and after there was a break-in at Brianna's house. I wasn't home at the time, but Chance was kind enough to let me stay in his house."

"And you had sex."

"Yes, now can we move beyond that topic?"

"Not on your life. I know you, Kat, and you don't party around, and you don't hook up with anyone unless you have feelings for them, am I right?"

"But every relationship I've ever had I've screwed up."

"You mean you walk away just when things get complicated. You never give them a chance."

"Bingo."

"Why do you think that is?"

"I don't know. Maybe I'm destined to be alone."

"Maybe it's because you left home at such a young age and never had a fulfilling relationship with your father."

Kat tipped her head back and laughed. "Okay, Mrs. Freud."

"You laugh, but it just might be true. So, why don't you call this guy and make nice?"

"I didn't exactly tell him to his face I was leaving town. He's probably mad as hell."

"Oh, boy, that's so like you. But if he cares about you, he'll get over it." Maggie checked her watch. "I have to go. I have phone calls to make. I have a client that needed help yesterday." She put on her jacket and hat. "Why don't you pack some things and come home with me, dear? I don't feel right about leaving you alone."

"I'd really rather sleep in my own bed. I've been looking forward to it." She set her glass next to Maggie's.

"What if Brianna keeps haunting you?"

"I don't think she will. I feel she's at peace now."

"She should be. She got her own brand of justice. I still can't believe that." Maggie walked to the foyer. "Promise me you'll call anytime, and I don't care if it's two in the morning. I'll check on you tomorrow."

"Thanks for being my ear, but we never discussed work or when I should return. Maybe in a couple of days."

"Work can wait. You're still on vacation as far as I'm concerned. I want you to promise to call Rosen Monday morning."

"I will."

"After that we'll see about sending you to a week-long spa for a real vacation. In fact, I already have one in mind," Maggie said, causing Kat to chuckle. "What's so funny?"

"Somehow I knew you would suggest that."

"Great minds think alike, hey kid?" She drew Kat into a warm hug. "And don't give up on men. You could use a little TLC. Think about calling that fellow. Anyone that caring has potential. Great name, by the way. Could be prophetic, as in Kat takes a Chance. Hah!"

"Goodbye, Maggie."

"Bye, my dear." She tweaked Kat's cheek and fled into the nippy evening.

Kat let the fire burn out on its own while she put away the food that neither of them had touched. She checked the locks on both doors, twice, and turned off the lights in the house.

She took the nightlight from the bathroom and plugged it into a bedroom socket. She dressed for bed and retired early. To keep the doctor's face from surfacing, she focused her mind on Chance, his bellowing burros, his beautiful yet modest home, and Zeke, the boisterous pup. Her thoughts circled back to Chance. It was as if he were murmuring in her ear, "Stay strong, Kat. Stay strong."

≈

With morning light blanketing her room, Kat was pleasantly surprised. She hadn't woken from cold sweats, ghoulish dreams, or unsettling visions.

Sweeping the bedroom curtains back revealed a rather gloomy, overcast day, but the ground was dry. It hadn't rained overnight—a good day for a refreshing walk.

She dressed in a clean pair of jeans and a turtleneck, and laced up her walking shoes. She slicked her hair into a ponytail and splashed water over her face. Chance had remarked positively on her natural look, but she wondered how he'd feel if he saw her today, her face exhibiting the revealing signs of battle fatigue. But sadly he wouldn't be seeing her.

For breakfast she sipped orange juice and ate a bite of banana and handful of almonds, considered it a better meal than corn chips and wine.

On passing the fireplace and glimpsing the metal poker, she froze, and the image of the doctor's dead body sent a flurry of shudders up her spine. She grabbed her jacket from the coatrack and went outside to clear away the impressions.

Autumn was in full force in the yellows, oranges, and browns of the surrounding maples. Her neighbor, Mr. Singleton, was busy raking leaves, a chore she also had to do. She waved to him. As usual he acknowledged her with a nod and went back to work. He respected her privacy and rarely pried into her affairs, but if she needed help, he was always available.

The neighborhood was a mix of homes for singles, families, and retirees, with an occasional student rental thrown in. A large Catholic cathedral as old as the city took up half a block. Soon its parishioners would be filing in for Sunday services.

Kat ventured as far as the empty playfield several blocks from her home. A man passed through with his Labrador retriever bounding ahead. The scene reminded her of Chance.

She turned around to go back. All along the way were hints of Halloween to come—a scary pumpkin face sitting on a porch, a cutout of a ghost hanging in a window. A cinnamon scent drifted out from an open door. At the idea of handing out sweets to the neighborhood goblins and witches, her spirits rose. When her slate blue house came into view, she was ready to make a pot of hot apple cider.

Sitting on her steps was a young woman, wrapped in a black car coat over blue jeans with a red wool scarf around her neck. Kat didn't recognize the blond punk hairdo, but the face seemed familiar. What gave her identity away were her penetrating aqua eyes. On seeing Kat, she bounced to her feet and smiled. "Are you Kat Summers? I'm Stella."

"Chance's daughter."

She extended her hand for Kat to shake. "I'm here on behalf of my dad."

"Why don't we go inside where we can talk?" Kat unlocked the door for them and allowed Stella to enter first.

Stella walked into the living room, taking everything in. "Nice house. I like the greens and reds. It reminds me of Christmas. I love old houses like this and all the natural wood."

Kat hung her jacket on the coatrack. "I've been updating it as much as I can. May I take your coat? Would you like something to drink? Tea? Water?"

"No, thanks. I can't stay long."

"Please have a seat then." Kat indicated the chair by the fireplace since Stella was closest to it, and she took the couch. "Chance mentioned you were a student at the university."

"I'm a sophomore this year."

"What are you majoring in?"

"Art history and political science."

"That's quite a combination."

"My mom was an art major, and my dad encouraged me to take political science classes because he said it would prepare me better for getting into law school."

"Is that what you want to do?"

"For now it is. I might change my mind later."

"It's always a good idea to keep your options open."

"Dad said you were a hotshot real estate mogul."

Kat chuckled at the notion. "I'd hardly use the words mogul or hotshot to describe what I do, but he got the real estate part right. Why did your dad send you over here?"

"He didn't. It was my idea."

"Your idea?"

"Yeah. When I talked to him yesterday," Stella said, "he was like super depressed about you leaving Rosswood. He told me all about you, and I'd never heard him this excited about anyone in a long time. Ever since he moved to the ranch, he's kept pretty much to himself, and he was sort of like a womanizer before."

She continued, her eyes animated. "The reason I know that is because he let me read his novel. I know it's really about his former life, before Rosswood. We had this long father/daughter discussion about it because he wanted me to know before the book got published."

She was now on the edge of her seat, taking in a deep breath. "So, anyway, he said he let you read it, and you left Rosswood because of it."

"Is that what he thinks?"

"He thinks you don't like him because of what he used to do," she said. "I had a hard time with it myself at first, because now my dad isn't anything like the man in the book. You should have seen him take care of my mom when she was sick, and they weren't even married then. He took care of me after she died. And even though he traveled a lot before, he always called me and sent me presents and visited when he could. Oh, I almost forgot. He set up a charitable foundation in my mom's honor to help people with cancer, and he is involved in other charities. He really is a good man."

"So, you came all the way over here to plead his case."

"I offered," Stella said. "My dorm is only about ten blocks from here, and I told Dad I was going to come over to see you today. He's really a nice man despite what he wrote in that book. I wish you would give him another chance to explain like he did with me. I read the book, and I still love him." She drew in a long, needed breath.

Kat had to grin at this resourceful young lady for sticking up for her father. "Stella, I can assure you that his book had no bearing on my decision to leave Rosswood. I left for personal reasons."

Stella's expectant expression paled into sadness. "Do you already have a boyfriend?"

"No, it's nothing like that."

"You don't like my dad?"

"You'd make a great lawyer."

"I'm sorry. I'm butting in where I don't belong."

"No, no, it's all right," Kat said. "The reason is I haven't had a relationship in a long time and . . ." How could she state this? "I just got scared.

I didn't mean to hurt your father."

Stella's face brightened. "Then you do like him. Would you call him and explain that to him? He'd really like to hear from you. He's so sad. I can just picture him moping around the house. I hate to see him that way."

The girl's empathy-filled eyes touched Kat. What else could she do? "Okay, I promise I'll call him. That's the least I can do for all your efforts on his behalf. It was pretty brave of you to come."

Grinning, Stella popped out of her chair and gave Kat a quick hug. "Oh, thank you, thank you, Ms. Summers. He'll be so happy. I'm so happy."

"You can call me Kat."

"I'd better go now. Do you want his phone number? I can give it to you."

"Not to worry. I have his number."

"Thanks again, Kat. I hope I see you again. It would be so cool."

"Wait here a second." Kat found one of her business cards in a desk drawer and wrote her home phone number on the back. She transferred it to Stella. "That's my home number. No matter what happens between me and your dad, you're welcome to stop by anytime you're in the neighborhood, or you can call me. Maybe we could go out to lunch."

"That would be awesome. I'd like that." She was halfway down the sidewalk when she turned around. "Dad said something bad happened to you in Rosswood, but he didn't tell me what it was. I hope you're okay."

"I'm fine, Stella. Not to worry."

"I'm glad." Stella waved to Kat and disappeared down the street.

With the help of Maggie and Stella, fate was having its way and pushing Kat to contact Chance. First, she had to think through what she would say to him, if indeed she intended to go through with the call.

CHAPTER 35

*Z*eke scrambled to his feet, and Chance nearly tripped over him, getting to the phone. "Stella, I've been waiting half the day for your call."

"I know, Dad."

"What took you so long? I thought you were going to call me right after you saw Kat. You did see her, didn't you?" His grip tightened around the receiver.

"Dad, I had an errand to run on my way back to the dorm. Do you want to know what she said, or do you want to argue over the time it took me to call you?"

Stella could always match his moods, and he took a breath to release the tension. Zeke's wagging tail swatted his leg, and he motioned for the dog to lie down.

"You saw her then. What did she say? Was she all right?"

"Yeah, I saw her, and she was really nice. She has the neatest house."

"Did you give her my number and tell her to call me?"

"She already had your number, and she said she left because she got scared. It wasn't because of the book."

"She wasn't put off by my background?"

"I guess not. I think she still likes you. At least she didn't say she didn't like you."

"But is she going to call?"

"She said she would."

"All right, honey. I'd better get off the phone just in case."

"Oh, Dad, wait. She gave me her home phone number and said I could call her anytime. Do you want it?"

Thinking the angels were smiling down on him, he wrote the number on the back of Kat's business card underneath her address. "I love you, sweetie. Thanks for helping your old dad."

"I love you, too, Dad. You know this is weird, don't you?"

"I suppose it is."

"I hope it works out for you because I really liked her."

"How did she look, Stella? Does she seem okay?"

"She's really pretty. She seemed okay to me, just a little tired looking."

"Okay, honey, I'll take it from here. I'll call you again soon."

"Bye, Dad."

When Chance turned around, Zeke rose with expectant eyes. He gave Zeke a pat. "Kat said she'd call me, boy. What do you think of that?" Zeke barked twice.

Chance fixed a sandwich for himself and tossed a piece of cheese to Zeke, who caught it in midair. While eating, Chance stared at the phone as if it were a bomb ready to detonate. He hadn't had this itchy feeling since he'd courted Meredith.

Waiting was never his strong suit. He liked taking action, and that was exactly what he intended to do. He slipped Kat's business card into his shirt pocket and jogged into the bedroom to pack an overnight bag.

As he was situating the bag in the passenger's seat of his truck, Zeke ran off to greet Rusty, who was striding up from the barn. "You heading out somewhere, boss?"

"I'm going to Seattle, and I'm not sure when I'll be back. Maybe in a day or two. Would you look after Zeke?"

"Hey, ain't that where that Summers woman lives?"

"I'll call if I get delayed." Chance smoothed back Zeke's coat. "You be good for Rusty." He rounded the bumper and slid into the driver's seat.

"That woman beats out any of them others you've had around here, specially that French lady. If I was you, I sure wouldn't let that Summers woman get away."

For once Chance planned to heed Rusty's advice. When he was well over the pass on the western side of the mountains, he pulled off the freeway and punched in Kat's home number. The line was busy. That meant she was home.

≈

Kat waited out five rings before she hung up. It had taken her all afternoon to work up the courage to call Chance, and he wasn't even answering. She could try his cell phone. But maybe it was better this way. She wouldn't have to explain something as confusing as her life was at the moment.

As the day progressed, the clouds darkened, and the rain changed from sprinkles to showers. The weather didn't matter to her. She was comfy inside. If she could stop thinking about Friday night at the cabin, she might enjoy another blaze in the fireplace. The trouble was that the horrible images wouldn't go away.

She poured a cup of hot apple cider and opened her briefcase on the table. Work would occupy her time now. It always had.

But her thoughts wandered to Chance and why she hadn't been able to contact him. It seemed fate was teasing her, testing her to see how committed she was to connecting with him.

Why did she want to anyway? Because he was a loving, caring, powerful man, and easy on the eyes, no doubt about that. But he was also impatient, stubborn, maddening at times, an overbearing brute. So why bother?

The doorbell rang. She clamped her briefcase shut and looked out the living room window. At the curb was Chance's weather-beaten truck.

Overbearing or not, he was here just the way she remembered him the first time they met on that stretch of road outside Rosswood, wearing jeans, boots, cowboy hat—the most exquisite-looking rancher she'd ever seen. A mix of excitement, anger, apprehension, and every other emotion he could summon up in her roared through her veins. She threw open the door. "What are you doing here?"

"Does this mean you won't let me in after I've driven over three hours to see you?"

True to form, she opened her mouth to spew an irritable, you-weren't-really-invited retort, typical of the edgy banter they'd perfected, but stopped in time before making that mistake. Her pattering heart bore the truth. She widened the space between them, allowing him to enter. "Honestly, Chance, I'm glad you're here."

He took off his hat and hung his rain-spattered jacket on a coat hook. He scanned the living room as his daughter had. "Stella told me your house was nice. I should have known it would reflect your good taste."

"Are you trying to make points?"

"If it helps."

"Can I get you anything to drink?"

"Can we talk first?" He laid his hat on the coffee table and made himself comfortable in the chair across from her. "How are you, Kat?"

"I'm doing as well as can be expected under the circumstances, a few flashbacks now and then."

"You look tired. Are you sleeping?"

"Surprisingly, I am. At least I did last night. I suppose I owe you an apology for leaving without an explanation."

"I can't say I wasn't a bit angry, but I was more concerned for your safety, driving that late at night after what you'd been through."

"I ended up staying at The Sleeping Inn."

"If that was all the farther you got, why didn't you call and stay at my house? I would have respected your privacy. I knew you needed rest and time to process what happened to you."

"I couldn't make you understand why I needed to be by myself, and I'm not sure I can now."

"All I wanted to do was make things easier for you, to offer my comfort and support. You were in a state of shock. I could see that."

She heaved a sigh. "I'm sorry. I really am, but I've always taken care of myself, always. I'm not used to leaning on anyone. It was an automatic response on my part. I did what I always do. I guess I was in shock. Maybe I still am."

An uncomfortable silence rose between them until finally Kat said, "You have a wonderful daughter, Chance. She's tenacious, like you."

"I am tenacious, but only when it comes to something I want very badly."

"Some would call that pushy."

"Is that what you call it, the fact that I'd like to have a relationship with you?"

"No, but sending your daughter over here to find out if I liked you was kind of cute."

He grinned. "Is that how she put it?"

"She was adorable, Chance, putting in a good word for you. She even told me it was her idea."

"But you didn't call me."

"I did call you, but you weren't home. Obviously, you were on your way here. I thought I might try again later."

"I couldn't wait for the call, Kat. I had to see you."

"Now, that's pushy. How did you know I'd even want to see you?"

Her words came out a little too harsh, even though she didn't mean it that way. She lowered her gaze and absentmindedly began stacking magazines on the coffee table.

Chance sat forward, his eyes keenly focused on her. He stood and picked up his hat. "Perhaps I should go."

Astonishingly, his voice was superimposed with Brianna's voice trickling into her consciousness telling her, "Enough bantering. Enough holding back. Let go, Kat. Accept the gift."

Kat felt the push/pull of her emotions—a struggle to be sure. It was so hard for her to relinquish total independence. Yet, Chance's loving nature was what she needed in her life. Deep down she'd always wanted a man she could love and trust, a man like Chance. He'd proven himself in so many ways. Though he might be overly protective, he was kind and gentle, always thinking of her welfare.

She felt the shift inside, the walls crumbling, her deepest, most tender feelings wanting to surface. Her heart opened up to him, and she couldn't bear the sorrowful look in his eyes. "Don't," she blurted. "I don't want you to go. I want you to stay. It's just so hard for me to ask for what I need, and I need you, Chance." She paused. "No, I take that back. I want you. But I don't want to ruin this."

He threw his hat on the table and lifted her into his arms. She rested her head on his chest and felt his heart racing with each breath and his body quivering with emotion. "I want to hold you as long as you want me," he murmured.

Hugging his waist, she looked up and let out a deep, trembling breath. "This feels so right, Chance. But you have to promise me."

"Anything."

"If we start something, you have to hold on and never let me go. I know I'll get scared and try to run from it. I'm so afraid of that. You'll have to fight for us."

He kissed her forehead. "I'm tenacious, remember?"

"For once, I'm glad you are."

He rubbed his palm up and down her back. "With everything that's happened, you probably need to rest. Just tell me what you want me to do. Perhaps I should go."

She cupped his face in her hands and kissed him. "What I really want is to cuddle with you and feel safe in your arms all night long. Maybe you can frighten away the nightmares."

"I'll do whatever it takes, darling."

~

Later, after they'd made love and were snuggled in Kat's bed, Chance asked her if there was anything that bothered her about his past.

"Knowing the man you are now," she said, "I'm having a hard time believing you were involved in anything that deceitful."

"It's not a life I'm proud of, contributing to the misery of the world. I'll always carry that guilt."

"You're making up for it now."

He ran his hand down her arm and clasped her fingers in his. "I hope I can make it up to you, so you'll be able to trust me."

Kat thought for a moment. "I need to know one more thing. Is your life still in danger, like the man in your novel? Are you running from anything?"

He hesitated by pressing her body closer and kissing her neck. He started to kiss her lips.

She drew back. "Chance? Answer me."

"All right. I'll be honest with you. They're always hounding me to come back and work for them. That's why Monique paid me that visit. She's still employed there." He nuzzled Kat's ear. "But let's not worry about that now."

"Why shouldn't we worry about it? What if they come after you? What if *she* comes back?"

"Sweetheart, I don't care what Monique or the organization wants. I consider myself free to do anything, like, oh, I don't know, marry you someday?"

He wrapped her in an embrace so warm, so secure and satisfying Kat let his answer, concerning the danger he might be in, as vague as it was, drift into the ethers. "Marry me? Depends on how tenacious you are."

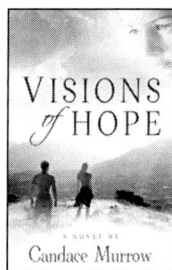